DANGER MIGHT HAVE A FAMILIAR FACE . . .

Priscilla interrupted Neville once more, a sure sign of the depths of her distress. "If you are about to suggest that you can overcome such tendencies because you are a man, then I suggest you save your breath."

"I would never say that to you."

"But you would think it."

"Don't put words in my mouth that I had no intention of saying." He did not want her to guess how close she was to the truth, but he owed her the duty of being honest with her. Or, at least, somewhat honest. "Pris, our situations are different because *I* am not the children's mother."

"That I am anxious for their well-being makes me *more* determined to discover the identity of this murderer."

"A fact that will become well known if you persist in being so hardheaded and shortsighted."

He sighed as she walked past him and out of the room. He had insulted her as he never had before. Mayhap he was a fool not to be completely honest with her, but how could he possibly explain that he did not want her becoming involved with this investigation because he feared it would make *her* the next target . . .

Zebra romances by Jo Ann Ferguson

His Unexpected Bride
A Kiss For Papa
A Guardian's Angel
His Lady Midnight
A Highland Folly
A Kiss for Mama
Faithfully Yours
A Christmas Bride
Lady Captain
Sweet Temptations
The Captain's Pearl
Anything for You
An Unexpected Husband
Her Only Hero
Mistletoe Kittens
An Offer of Marriage
Lord Radcliffe's Season
No Price Too High
The Jewel Palace
O'Neal's Daughter
The Convenient Arrangement
Just Her Type
Destiny's Kiss
Raven Quest
A Model Marriage
Rhyme and Reason
Spellbound Hearts
The Counterfeit Count
A Winter Kiss
A Phantom Affair
Miss Charity's Kiss
Valentine Love
The Wolfe Wager
An Undomesticated Wife
A Mother's Joy
The Smithfield Bargain
The Fortune Hunter

Priscilla Flanders mysteries:
A Rather Necessary End

Haven Trilogy:
Twice Blessed
Moonlight on Water
After the Storm

Shadow of the Bastille Trilogy:
A Daughter's Destiny
A Brother's Honor
A Sister's Quest

And writing as Rebecca North
A June Betrothal

GRAVE INTENTIONS

Jo Ann Ferguson

ZEBRA BOOKS
KENSINGTON PUBLISHING CORP.

http://www.kensingtonbooks.com

ZEBRA BOOKS are published by

Kensington Publishing Corp.
850 Third Avenue
New York, NY 10022

All Kensington titles, imprints and distributed lines are available at special quantity discounts for bulk purchases for sales promotion, premiums, fund-raising, educational or institutional use.

Special book excerpts or customized printings can also be created to fit specific needs. For details, write or phone the office of the Kensington Special Sales Manager: Kensington Publishing Corp., 850 Third Avenue, New York, NY 10022. Attn. Special Sales Department. Phone: 1-800-221-2647.

First Printing: January 2003
10 9 8 7 6 5 4 3 2 1

Printed in the United States of America

For Teresa Brown,
for her hospitality and friendship.
Rock on, Rock Mom!

Prologue

"Got what I want?"

The ragged man grumbled under his breath. He set his shovel next to the open grave and pointed at the wooden box on the ground. It was shrouded by clouds rushing past the moon. "Ain't opened it yet."

"Then do so." The man on the dark horse had his face hidden. It made no difference because the ragged man knew by the irritation in his voice that he was scowling.

"Give the men time." Another voice came from the shadows, a cultured voice that did not belong to the streets. "You are early."

"They have had time enough," retorted the man on the horse. "Much more time, and the watch will be here."

"I pay them well to stay away." A low laugh came from the shadows.

The man on the horse muttered something under his breath. The words were lost as the two men by the grave pressed levers under the top of the casket. As it rose, nails screeched like a tortured cat. They threw the bars on the ground and pulled the top off, tossing it aside.

The ragged man murmured a prayer as he stuck his hand into the casket. Beside him, his silent companion wrung his hands, glancing in every direction, including skyward. No telling what direction damnation might come from when they were disturbing the sleep of the consecrated dead.

Pulling his fingers out of the casket, the ragged man went to the man on the horse. The ragged man held out his hand. Something glittered as it passed from one palm to the other. The glitter vanished beneath a cloak of fine wool.

The rider pointed to the casket. ''Get rid of that. You know what to do.'' He rode out of the churchyard.

Before the clatter of his hooves was smothered by the night, the ragged man was motioning for his companion to pull the corpse from the casket. They tossed it into the back of a dilapidated wagon. It landed on another decaying body.

From the shadows, the voice said, ''Begone with your hideous cargo, my good men. Your work is done here tonight.''

The ragged man whined, ''But there's another shallow grave right over—''

''Begone!''

The two men hurried to the wagon and pulled it out of the churchyard. They paused on the street to throw a blanket as frayed as their cloaks over their stolen wares which they would soon trade for a few guineas.

From the shadows, the fourth man emerged. He looked down at the empty grave, then glanced up at the cross atop the high steeple. He laughed loud and hard.

It was just too easy.

Chapter One

''Do you want to tell her, or should I?'' Mrs. Moore looked up at the butler, who was trying to avoid her eyes. The housekeeper crossed her arms in front of her and planted herself in the middle of the laundry room doorway when Gilbert tried to make his escape.

He regarded her with his usual cool expression, but she was not fooled. He was as distressed as she at the appalling news that had just been repeated in the kitchen by a lad from the butcher's shop. While the cook had peppered the boy with questions, Mrs. Moore had asked Gilbert to join her in this room, where they could speak without being heard by one of the maids or footmen.

''Lady Priscilla needs to know, but not immediately.'' He adjusted the front of his pristine coat that was an identical gray to Mrs. Moore's gown.

''Bad news cannot wait.'' She had worked for the Flanders family almost as long as he had, for she had been hired only a week after him when Lady Priscilla first married more than seventeen years ago. Now the lady's husband was dead and mourned, and she had returned to London with her three children for the final weeks of the Season.

"Quite to the contrary," the butler argued. "Bad news gets easier to swallow after some time has passed."

"But you did not answer my question, Gilbert. Will you tell Lady Priscilla, or should I?"

"Tell me what?" asked Priscilla Flanders as she set a basket on the floor of the laundry room, which looked out, as did the kitchen, onto the small garden behind the house and the stables and coach house on its far side. The view reminded her of her home in Stonehall-on-Sea, save that beyond the stables was narrow Caroline Mews instead of the sea.

She wiped strands of hair out of her face and took a deep breath that was flavored with scents of damp and soap. Kneading her lower back out of sight of the others, she wondered how she could possibly have forgotten how grueling it was to move back to London. She had spent the past year while she and the children were in mourning for her late husband, the Reverend Dr. Lazarus Flanders, at their home in Stonehall-on-Sea along the south coast. Mayhap she had let the hard work slip from her mind because so many months had passed since she left London. Yet it was worth the trouble to bring smiles to her children's faces, which had been too serious since their father's death.

"Lady Priscilla," Mrs. Moore began, then glanced at Gilbert.

"Yes?" She did not want to be vexed with the housekeeper and the butler, but there was still much to do before they retired for the evening.

Gilbert squared his shoulders and cleared his throat. Not once in over a decade and a half had she seen him wear any expression more cheerful than a frown. She had to own she often gave him cause for disapproval, for he had made it clear she should do as other widows did. She should find a wealthy husband and remarry.

"We have heard it has happened again," the butler said.

"Again? What has happened again?" She could think of dozens of answers, many to do with her mischievous son, who was eager to explore Bedford Square—and possibly indulge in some mischief—before they had been there more than a day. Not that it had changed, from what she could see, but Isaac would be eager to poke his nose and fingers into every possible inch of the square in hopes of finding something interesting . . . to a nine-year-old boy.

"Another death on the square," Gilbert replied.

"Another?"

As soon as they had arrived in Bedford Square the day before, Priscilla received a call from Mrs. Lennon. The elderly woman who lived in the house to the right of Priscilla's had been eager to let Priscilla know of the recent happenings on the square. Two servants in houses on the other side had died suddenly in the past few weeks. Priscilla listened because she had enjoyed other conversations with Mrs. Lennon while living here with Lazarus and their three children before he sickened and died.

As soon as Mrs. Lennon departed, Priscilla dismissed the old woman's gossip from her mind. There had been too many other matters to consider: unpacking and airing out the house, which had been closed for over a year; tending to her older daughter, Daphne, and Isaac, who were excited to be back in London; offering solace to her younger daughter, Leah, who was already pining for friends left behind in Stonehall-on-Sea; and trying to deal with the memories that filled each room.

"Yes, my lady," Mrs. Moore said, freeing Priscilla from

her uncomfortable thoughts. "Jarvis, Mr. Lampman's coachee, was found dead in front of Lord Burtrum's house not more than three hours ago."

"Lord Burtrum?"

Gilbert replied in the tone that suggested he was eager to supply any answers she needed, "Lord Burtrum and his family now reside in the house that was Lord Milstone's."

"Dear me." Priscilla sat on the bench beside the cloths that had draped the furniture throughout the house. Several fell to the floor, and she gathered them up, tossing them atop the rest. "Mr. Lampman must be distraught. I believe he has had the same coachman for forty years."

"He is not the only one upset."

At Mrs. Moore's grim tones, Priscilla looked at her thin housekeeper. "Did you know the coachee well, Mrs. Moore?"

"No, my lady, but I did know the butler at Sir Stephen's quite well."

"And," Gilbert said, clearly not wishing to be kept out of the conversation despite his terse answers, "the tweener at Lady Traverson's was the daughter of my cousin's wife's son."

"Mrs. Lennon spoke of those tragedies when she called yesterday. I shall have to extend my sympathies to Sir Stephen as well as to your family, Gilbert."

"You don't understand the half of it, my lady." Mrs. Moore shook her head and rubbed her bony hands together. "The coachee was on in years, my lady, but the butler was far less elderly and the tweener just a young girl, probably of an age close to Miss Daphne's."

Priscilla came to her feet as she glanced from her almost overwrought housekeeper to her stolid butler. Noticing the tic over his left brow that always announced he was distressed, she frowned.

"Are you suggesting," she asked, "that these deaths are in some way suspicious?"

"Three people do not die in such quick succession without some cause, my lady." Gilbert rocked from one foot to the other, a definite sign he was as distraught as Mrs. Moore.

"If they were ill—"

"As fine health as anyone could wish for."

Priscilla was unsure how to answer. There were many ways a person might die, especially in London, where the air could become loathsome when all the chimney pots were spewing forth and the fog was close to the ground.

"There must be a reasonable explanation," she said.

"And, begging your pardon, my lady, what would that be?" The housekeeper swayed, her face as gray as her gown. "I cannot think of a single one."

"Do sit." Priscilla guided Mrs. Moore to the bench. "Gilbert, I believe there is a bottle of wine open in the kitchen. Please bring it."

"I shall be fine," the housekeeper said as the butler rushed out of the room. She picked up the end of one of the cloths and began wafting it in front of her face. " 'Tis very unsettling to think that someone might be preying on servants on this square."

"Please refrain from jumping to conclusions."

"Three deaths—"

"May be no more than a tragic coincidence." Priscilla took the glass Gilbert held out and passed it to her housekeeper. "If it will offer you some comfort, I shall pay Mr. Lampman a call to express my sympathy straightaway. He might be able to shed some light on this matter which will soothe your concerns."

"Thank you, my lady," said Mrs. Moore and the butler at the same time and with such fervor that Priscilla was astonished. It was not like her servants to be this unsettled, even in the midst of such sad tidings.

''While I am gone, Mrs. Moore, please see to the unpacking in the girls' room and remind Isaac that the bottle containing the bugs he was gathering when I last saw him should remain outside.'' Priscilla went out of the laundry room quickly, but heard the two whispering behind her. No doubt distressing each other more with their suggestions of stalkers and conspiracies and horrors about to be inflicted on Bedford Square.

At that thought, she hurried back to the laundry. She peeked in. ''I trust I do not need to tell you that none of the children should be told of this.''

Mrs. Moore gulped. ''His lordship was in the kitchen when the news was brought. How could I ask him to leave?''

Priscilla sighed. This would not be the time to remind Mrs. Moore—yet again—that Isaac might be the fifth Earl of Emberson, a title he inherited with her father's death, but in this household he should continue to be treated exactly as he had been when he was Master Isaac. Her son was not above using his peerage to get his way whenever possible, and she was resolved that he would not grow up to be a self-centered lord like some she had met in London.

''Gilbert, under those circumstances, will you send a footman to find Isaac and return him to the house posthaste? I shall not be long, and there is plenty to keep the children occupied while I am calling on Mr. Lampman.''

When the butler followed her up the stairs, Priscilla was not surprised when he asked her if she wanted the other footman to go with her on her call. Mr. Lampman's house was only a short walk around the gardens in the middle of the square, a journey she had made many times alone.

''Do not fret, Gilbert,'' she said. ''I shall be fine.''

''Those who are dead may have thought the same.''

Bother! She did not need such grim spirits in the house when she was struggling with the hundreds of memories that filled each room and corridor. Even after more than a year, it seemed wrong to be here without her husband and to know that he would not be returning.

As she paused in the entry foyer, she pasted a smile on her lips. The foyer's plastered walls were in need of a new coat of yellow paint, and the niche set next to the door was empty. The statue that belonged there still must be in the attic. Crossing the tiled floor, she picked up her bonnet from a bench by the curving staircase with its elegant wrought-iron balusters. Her father had purchased this house for her and her family when Lazarus left the small church in Stone-hall-on-Sea to serve at St. Julian's only a few blocks away. In spite of the opinions of others, she believed this square to be the loveliest in London.

"Gilbert, I shall be fine." As she opened the door, she asked, "Will you send a message to Brooks's in St. James's and to Number Forty-eight, Berkeley Square?"

"To Sir Neville Hathaway?" He wrinkled his nose. "Do you really need to send for *him*?"

"Can you imagine a better person to help me get to the bottom of this trouble than a man who seems to have the skill of finding trouble all by himself?"

Gilbert did not answer, and his face closed up to hide all his emotions. He looked up the stairs when something crashed. Now, she decided, while he was torn between checking on what had happened and trying to persuade her not to send for Neville, was a good time to leave.

Priscilla tied her bonnet under her chin and went down four steps to the street. The warm breeze sprinkled raindrops on her. A single gray cloud hung over the square. On all sides, the sun shone brightly. She hoped that cloud was not symbolic of what was happening on Bedford Square.

"Don't be ridiculous," she scolded herself. She was letting the servants' uneasiness taint her good sense. Once she spoke with Mr. Lampman, she would share what she learned with Mrs. Moore and Gilbert, who would make sure the rest of the household heard it.

Walking around the central garden, she went to the white house in the middle of the row of brown ones. She climbed the steps, which were identical to the ones in front of her house. Knocking, she waited for an answer.

The door opened only a crack. She was not sure who stood in the shadows beyond it until she heard a young man—Mr. Lampman's footman, she assumed—ask, "May I help you?"

"Would you tell Mr. Lampman that Lady Priscilla Flanders wishes to speak with him to express her sorrow at his loss?"

The door inched back another finger's breadth. The footman said, "Mr. Lampman is not at home to guests today."

"I know this is a grievous time for him, but will you ask if he would receive me?"

"I am sorry if I did not explain it clearly, my lady." The door moved another inch farther open. "Mr. Lampman is not within. He has left for his home in the country."

She nodded. "I see. Thank you." She started to turn, then said, "I would appreciate your expressing to the household the sorrow my household and I feel."

If he spoke again as the door shut, she did not hear it.

Arching her brows at the surprising exchange, because Mr. Lampman's servants were usually the epitome of graciousness, Priscilla went down to the walkway. She paused when she looked at the steps of Lord Burtrum's house. The rumor was the coachman was found dead on them. Mayhap the Burtrums would have something to share to ease her household's anxiety.

This door opened even before she could raise her hand to knock, warning that her promenade around the square had not gone unnoticed. A slender man in a livery so vibrantly red that it would dim a soldier's coat motioned for her to enter.

The hallway was a mirror image of hers, but the walls were covered with a delicately painted silk that suggested she stood in an Asian forest with great trees rising up along the stairs. In the niche, a beautifully carved statue of a nymph cavorted with only a slender length of cloth draped about her. Lord Burtrum obviously had excellent taste in art and decoration if this entry hall was an example of the rest of the house.

The footman nodded when she told him her name and expressed her desire to speak with Lord Burtrum.

"I am sorry, my lady. He is not at home today."

Was everyone on the square away this afternoon? She did not ask that question. Rather, she inquired, "Is there anyone else I may speak with?"

"The earl's son is within, my lady."

"May I speak with him?"

Again he nodded.

Following him up the curving staircase, Priscilla admired the paintings on the wall. Some were landscapes. Others depicted horses or a group of dogs. There were no portraits, which seemed a bit odd, but it might be that Lord Burtrum kept his ancestors in private rooms.

She waited while the footman went to the door of the back parlor to announce her. Hearing a petulant voice, she warned herself not to judge too harshly anyone within these walls today. They must be as upset as her staff. She doubted she would have been at her best if she had discovered a dead man on her front steps.

The footman emerged, his shoulders hunched as if he had received a physical beating rather than a verbal one. He mumbled something while he hurried past her, and she assumed it meant she should go into the room.

Priscilla tried not to gape at the rich collection of paintings and art within the room, but it was impossible. She was not a connoisseur of such things, yet she had enough knowledge to appreciate the fine craftsmanship of the sculptures set on either side of the hearth and the gold candlesticks on the mantel. The latter had curlicues along the sides which were unlike any she had ever seen. She could not guess if they were *au courant* or antiques.

"Lady Priscilla Flanders?" asked a deep voice.

She put on her best smile as she held out her hand to a tall, bulky man. His hair was a few shades darker than her own blond strands. His well-made navy coat and green-striped waistcoat closed over pantaloons nearly the same color as his hair. When he took her hand and bowed over it, she noted his blunt fingers had well-trimmed nails.

Abruptly aware of her own disheveled state, which she should have remedied before she called, she knew she must pretend to be oblivious to the wisps of hair curling around her cheeks and the dusty spots on the front of her light purple dress. What she was wearing had been fine to call upon an old friend under these circumstances. However, these work clothes were inappropriate while making the acquaintance of a new neighbor.

"Will you sit down, Lady Priscilla?" Almost as an afterthought, he said, "I am Cecil Burtrum."

He did not give himself a courtesy title, which an earl's heir might rightly have. Mayhap he expected her to know it, or the family's title might not have lesser ones for the earl's children.

She would have to ask Neville when he arrived. He always

knew these sorts of things about the *ton*. Neville might mock the ways of the Polite World, but he made a point of being familiar with every facet. She was not quite sure why.

Sitting on a chair covered with light green satin, Priscilla said, "I appreciate your receiving me like this."

"Are you calling on all your neighbors now that you have returned to the square?" He made himself comfortable in a wider chair that was more befitting his size. Motioning to the bottle beside him, he asked, "Would you like a glass of wine, Lady Priscilla? It is a fine vintage, and I trust you will not look too closely at its origins." He laughed as if at a private jest, although buying wine from smugglers was nothing unusual among the *ton*.

"No, thank you. And, no, I am not on a round of calls this afternoon. I went to express my sympathies to Mr. Lampman."

"Sympathies?" he asked, his broad forehead furrowing. "Are you sure you don't want some wine, Lady Priscilla? This is the best bottle I have had in many a month."

"No, thank you. Sympathies for Mr. Lampman at the death of his coachman." She tried to hide her shock that Mr. Burtrum seemed honestly uncertain about what she spoke. Hoping she was not overstepping herself, she added, "The man who died on your front steps earlier today."

"Ah, yes, the coachman." He picked up a box from the table and popped it open. Tipping it over, he scowled when only a few dark flakes of snuff fell into his hand.

"I understand he was the third servant to die on this side of the square in recent weeks."

"So I understand as well." He opened a drawer in the table and poked around within it.

Was the man as heartless as he sounded? She had not thought anyone could be, but every word he spoke seemed to confirm that he cared less about the deaths than his own pleasures of wine and snuff.

"My household is distressed," she said, "by the three deaths."

Instead of answering her, he jumped to his feet. The curse he snarled startled her, for she had not expected a gentleman to speak so in the presence of a lady he had just met. He stamped to another table and pawed through the items on top of it.

"How could they have done it again? I have told them that they must never fail to keep this snuffbox full again. Servants! If they had half the wit of my foxhounds, they might be of some use. As it is, they—"

"Your servants might be distressed over the day's happenings."

He frowned at her from across the room. "Happenings?"

"The death of Mr. Lampman's coachee."

"Ah, yes . . . that." He ran his fingers along a shelf.

Priscilla came to her feet. If she gave voice to her thoughts that the one in this household with less wit than a dog was the one having this absurd conversation with her, she was certain to anger him more.

"This seems to be an inconvenient hour for you," she said in the prim tone she used on her children when they did not heed what she was saying. "If you will excuse me, I shall call at a more fitting time."

"Yes, yes." He reached for the bellpull, and she thought he was calling a servant to escort her to the door. When a footman arrived to answer the bell, he demanded, "Why is my snuffbox empty? You know I expect so little from this staff. The very least you could do is order my snuff when the supply grows low."

Priscilla backed out of the room as he continued to berate the footman, who stood in silence, a pose that suggested such harangues were not unusual. Going down the stairs, she realized she had found out nothing to ease her household's worries. She must discover something to assuage their fears, but she doubted she would learn it there.

Chapter Two

No one opened the door when Priscilla arrived back at her own house. She tried the knob. It was locked. Startled, she knocked. She got no answer. Then she heard a shriek. Raising both fists, she hammered on the door.

No answer.

Then another cry came, barely muffled by the door.

Gathering up her skirts, she raced along the street. A lady walking her dog stared as they both moved out of Priscilla's way. She turned the corner and did not slow until she reached Caroline Mews, behind the row of houses. She ran down the narrow street, sidestepping the horse droppings. She counted the backs of the houses until she got to hers, almost exactly halfway along this side of the square. Slipping through the coach house and ignoring the curious glances the horses gave her, she yanked open the door to the garden.

Flowers bloomed in almost every color, and roses were climbing the brick walls that separated her garden from her neighbors'. She paid none of them any mind. Some of the plants were crushed beneath her flying feet. A stitch beneath her left ribs warned her to halt. She pressed her hand to her side as she opened the kitchen door.

Her relief that it was not locked vanished when she heard another cry. As she started for the stairs leading up to the front of the house, she heard the cook call her name.

"Not now, Mrs. Dunham," she answered over her shoulder as she climbed the steps. She would apologize later to the cook for her rude behavior or calm the woman or whatever was necessary. For now she must find out who was screeching and why the front door was locked.

Bursting out of the stairwell, Priscilla saw Gilbert and the pair of footmen at the bottom of the stairs in the entry. They were looking up. Pausing by their sides, she stared at the ceiling.

She was not sure whether to be angry or relieved when she saw her son hanging from the upper gallery as he tried to capture bugs crawling along the ceiling. He shouted his frustration when he failed to get one.

Wanting to demand he stop this dangerous sport at once and ask why he was so loud, she knew she must not startle him and cause him to tumble from his precarious hold on the upper railing. She pushed past the men, who seemed mesmerized, and started up the steps. Isaac, focused on his task, seemed to take no notice of her. Surely he must hear her footfalls. How many other people had come up the stairs since he started chasing those bugs?

"Good afternoon, Pris," she heard as she rounded the top of the stairs.

The fear dropped from her shoulders when she saw her son's ankles were being held very securely by Neville, who was squatting behind the railing. She shook her head and smiled.

Sir Neville Hathaway looked every inch a gentleman from the top of his black hair to the bottom of his boots that shone just as brightly in the sunshine spilling through the front window over the door below. His tan coat was draped over the railing, and his dark green waistcoat seemed even a deeper shade against his white shirt. One dusty footprint on his left sleeve matched the exact size and shape of her youngest's shoes. She saw another footprint on Neville's dark brown breeches just above his right knee.

"Are you having fun?" she asked.

"Isaac was upset. After all the time he took to gather his collection . . ." He yelped when Isaac's shoe struck his other knee as the boy stretched to retrieve another bug. "Take care, my boy."

Priscilla walked along the railing and saw her two daughters ease back behind the doors in the front parlor. She had not wondered if they were involved in this to-do. She knew they had been, because Neville enjoyed getting all her children participating in whatever madness he was, like the Pied Piper, inviting them to join.

However, she knew he would never allow them to do anything that might put them in danger. She could trust him to watch over them, even when one of them was upside down over the staircase railing.

"Neville, I think it would be *de rigueur* to ask a child's mother before inverting him over the stairs in such a hazardous pose." She rested her hand on the polished rail and waited for her heart to stop thudding. Never would she let Neville discover how his antics unnerved her. If she did, he undoubtedly would devise more pranks. "It would be polite to do so."

He lifted Isaac over the railing and set the boy between them. His light brown hair was tousled, and a button, as happened too often, was missing from one knee of his dusty breeches. He wore a guilty expression that she knew was aimed at obtaining her forgiveness. She had seen it too many times—both on his and on his sisters' faces—to be moved by it.

"I thought you understood, Isaac, that the insects you had gathered were to remain outside," she said quietly.

"I did."

She had to own she appreciated how her son readily acknowledged his misdeeds. Such honesty was to be admired, but now was not the time.

"Did you recapture all of them?" She looked at the bottle beneath his palm, which was covering the top.

"Not all."

"Then I suggest you beg Gilbert's indulgence in helping you do so. With a broom and a ladder. Once they have all been retrieved, you need to take them out-of-doors. Then you will help Gilbert with any tasks he might give you the rest of the afternoon."

"Mama—"

She raised one finger and gave him the scowl that subdued him as it had recalcitrant members of her husband's church. The only person who seemed unaffected by it was Neville.

"Yes, Mama." Isaac's smile returned when he added, "Thanks, Uncle Neville, for helping."

"I would say anytime," he replied, "but your mother would become quite testy with me. Go along now and do what she asked you to do." Pushing back the dark hair that fell forward into his eyes, he chuckled as Isaac scurried down the steps. "You look winded, Pris. Could you have been fleet of foot in your eagerness to see me?"

"To save my son would be closer to the truth, although I had no idea I would be saving him from one of your addled ideas." She did not avert her eyes, but met his gaze steadily.

He gave her the grin that reputedly had sent young misses

swooning with delight and their mothers with despair, for even his wealth and title could not compensate for his past. Neville had a dark handsomeness that would befit the old gentleman in black himself. His devilish looks matched his spirits, for he cared nothing of the canons of society and made no secret of it. Unlike most men of his class, he had been many things before his distant uncle died and left him this title and a fortune that allowed him to disregard gossip about him.

Priscilla had heard that he had once been an actor and a thief-taker for Bow Street as well as possibly one of their quarry. She was not sure what to believe about him other than that she was happy to see him.

When she said as much, he offered his arm. She put her hand on it. He picked up his coat and escorted her into the front room.

Most of the cloths had been lifted from the furniture, but a writing desk set between the two tall front windows still slept beneath its blanket. However, the dust had vanished from the mantel and the mirror over it. The light green settee was placed properly in the middle of the flowered carpet, and the wooden chairs faced it. When she noticed cobwebs weaving a fleecy pattern on the top of the door leading to the rear parlor, she made a mental note to remind Mrs. Moore to have them tended to.

"You may as well come out and join us," Priscilla said when she saw the drapes beside one window fluttering as if with a breeze.

Her older daughter, Daphne, who shared her blond hair and blue eyes, poked her head out of one side, and Leah, several years younger and with hair the same light brown as her brother's, looked out from the other. They wore expressions identical to Isaac's guilty one.

"I trust," Priscilla said, "at least one of you spoke of

your uncertainty about Neville tipping your brother over the railing.''

''I did,'' Leah piped up, earning a scowl from her older sister.

''Because you wanted to try it yourself,'' Daphne added.

''How do you know? You were not even here.''

''I know you, and—''

Again Priscilla held up her hand. She wanted to silence the brangle before it could begin. ''I am getting a very clear picture of the sequence of events.''

''Perfectly harmless events,'' Neville said, and, when her daughters grinned, Priscilla suspected he had winked at them.

''Fortunately.''

He laughed. ''Do not be so downish, Pris. Nothing happened.''

''Save that Lady Apperly must have thought I had lost my mind when I almost ran her and her dog down.'' She smiled as Leah began to giggle. Motioning for them to sit, she rang for tea.

Neville graciously sat her on the settee. With another of his roguish smiles, he kissed her cheek lightly, but something pounded deep inside her. Something she had not expected to feel again after Lazarus died. Now the man he had considered his best friend, even though many believed Neville Hathaway an odd companion for a parson, was eliciting the same delight from her.

Her fingers started to rise of their own accord to tilt his cheek and his lips toward hers, but they froze in midair as he turned and kissed Daphne as chastely in greeting. Glad he had his back to her, for she did not want him to see her silly reaction to his kiss, which obviously meant nothing more than the greeting between old friends, she listened to the girls prattle about what they had been doing since they last saw him more than two months earlier.

When Neville sat beside her on the settee, he drawled, "You are looking lovely . . . as always."

"Such a reluctant compliment."

"Not at all reluctant, but you must own that it becomes boring when I say the same thing each time we meet."

She laughed. "Then it is a habit you should watch with more care. You were closer to the truth when you said I looked windblown."

"Rather, I said you appeared winded."

"Because I hurried around the backs of the houses when I discovered the front door locked and screams coming from within." She watched her younger daughter squirm as she asked, "Was there a reason you had the door bolted?"

"Of course," Neville answered. "You must know me well enough by now, Pris, to recognize I always have a good reason for what I do. I wanted to avoid having someone walk in and let Isaac's collection escape into the street."

"I believe there are plenty more insects in the back garden."

"As well, I did not want to chance being startled and dropping the boy on his head. It would have made a horrible dent in your tile."

"And in his head!" Daphne averred.

Leah jumped to her feet. "I will be careful, Uncle Neville, if you hold me upside down."

"Enough," said Priscilla before her younger daughter began bouncing about the room like a monkey. "Daphne, take your sister into the back parlor while I speak with Neville about news from here on Bedford Square."

She thought one of her daughters might protest, but they went without comment, not looking back when the dark-haired maid June brought in the tea tray and set it on a nearby table. That warned her the servants' conversations had been overheard by more than Isaac. Or, and this was even more likely, he had hurried to share every detail, adding a few gruesome ones of his own, with his sisters.

When she looked back at Neville, all traces of humor had vanished from his face. He waited for the door to the back parlor to close and for her to pour the tea, then said, "When I got your message, I did not expect to arrive to find you out paying calls."

"I went to offer my condolences to Mr. Lampman, who lives on the other side of the square." She took a sip from her own cup, then set it on the table beside her. Her stomach was roiling too much, and she would be unwise to put anything in it, even tea. "His coachman was found dead this morning, and I know Mr. Lampman appreciated his many years of service and camaraderie."

He frowned. "What is bothering you, Pris? You never sound like a tutor unless you are deeply distressed."

Coming to her feet, she motioned for him to remain where he was. She could not stay seated while she thought of what she had learned in the past hour. "Mayhap it is nothing more than I have been infected with the servants' fears."

"Your servants are afraid?" He placed his cup next to hers, then leaned forward, propping his elbows on his knees. "Of what?"

"The coachee was the third servant to die in less than a month on this square." Holding her hand up as he started to speak, she said, "Spare me the arguments about coincidence and bad luck. I have said much the same myself. Yet the idea that these deaths are somehow connected is troublesome."

"There was talk when the second one died of no apparent causes," he said.

"You know about this?"

"Not of Lampman's coachman, but I had heard about the other two." He smiled coldly. "You know very little stays unsaid among the Polite World and those who serve them. There was some discussion of this at a musicale I attended at Lady Whitley's last week."

"You? At a musicale?"

"Why do you look so amazed? You know I appreciate good music."

"But not the stuffiness of one of Lady Whitley's musicales. I suspect music was not the only entertainment for the evening."

"There were cards."

"Ah-ha!"

"Don't sound like a chiding parent, Pris."

She closed the door to the hallway when she saw a shadow beyond it. Having June overhear and carry her worried words to the rest of the servants would add to the uneasiness in the house.

Coming back to the settee, she sat beside him so she could say quietly, "Forgive me. My emotions are a-jumble in the wake of this. I assured Mrs. Moore and Gilbert that these deaths were not at all related, but they seem to believe they are. And I find I can see why they would believe so."

"Isaac said there is talk in your kitchen about returning to Stonehall-on-Sea."

"We have only arrived!"

"I thought you were not coming to London before the Season was over."

Priscilla was glad for the chance to smile. "I grew tired of listening to Daphne plea to come here so she might enjoy the Season if only vicariously."

"The girl has grown even since I last saw her only a month or two ago."

"Not quickly enough if I am to judge by her opinions. I

agreed to pay this visit to London only if she recalled she would not attend any functions other than those for young people. She is persistent in her requests to be fired-off next year, even though she is still quite young."

"You are going to have young men filling the square as soon as she is launched into the Season." He gave her a warm smile. "Just as you did when you set off on your first Season, I wager."

"Then you would lose whatever you wagered, Neville."

"Beef-heads the lot of them were, then. If they failed to have the good sense to see you were unlike the frail flowers blossoming throughout the Season, you were fortunate they did not fall at your feet, professing their undying devotion."

"I daresay you consider that a compliment."

"That it was, and I believe it was well due to you." He cocked his head and appraised her as if he had never seen her before.

She tried to ignore the pleasure glowing softly inside her when his gaze returned to her face. When Lazarus had been alive and the three of them were enjoying a comfortable conversation in this very room, Neville had teased her with the same gentleness he showed her daughters. He granted her no quarter, however, in a debate on some political issue or the myriad plans to keep Napoleon from invading England. For many years, he had been her friend. That was what made these new reactions to him so odd and intriguing.

"I guess you will do," he said, startling her out of her thoughts.

"Do? For what?"

"As my guest at a soirée tomorrow evening. Would you like to go?"

"Neville, we are only just arrived, and I have been so busy putting the house to rights."

He smiled as he stood and walked to the door. He opened

it slightly, and she knew he wanted to be certain no one was on the far side, listening, even though they now were speaking of nothing that would be inappropriate for the servants to hear.

"And that is the exact reason," he said, "why you should join me at Burtrum's house. As he lives on the other side of the square, it would not be an onerous journey after your trip to London, I collect."

She laughed as she rose. In spite of their light conversation, she could not rid herself of the disquiet that seemed to hang over the house as that gray cloud had. "On *that* you would be correct."

"Only that?"

"I would be wise not to answer that question, for then you will spend the next hour regaling me with a list of each time you have deemed yourself to be correct."

He rested his hand on the door frame. "Mayhap, although that would not be my choice of how to spend an hour with you, Pris."

"Recall where you stand." She slapped his hand off the molding that had been cleaned that morning. "Your bear-garden language has no place in a home with children."

"My language?" He pressed his fingers to his dark green waistcoat. "Pris, it appears you have mistakenly granted my words a meaning they did not have."

"Uh-huh." She folded her arms in front of her and arched an eyebrow.

As she had expected, he laughed. He enjoyed these verbal jousts as much as she did. When Lazarus had been alive, he had marveled at how she and Neville could parry with words as quick and honed as a rapier.

"So will you join me at Burtrum's gathering?" he asked.

"I would rather not."

Neville frowned when Priscilla brushed aside a ladybird

that had crawled into the parlor. She could not hide her anxiety from him, for it was displayed vividly on her face. Her cheeks had lost the high color painted on them when she had stormed up the stairs. Now, beneath the golden wisps that showed no sign of fading even though she must have seen her thirtieth birthday more than a half-decade ago, her skin was blanched. Its pallor warned that even as she was talking to him about other matters, her thoughts were riveted on the three recent deaths on the square.

"Do you have other plans for the evening?" he asked.

"No."

"I thought you had returned to London to rejoin the activities." He had to own he preferred the light purple gown to the black mourning she had worn the last time he saw her. "If I am mistaken . . ."

She smiled and put her hand on his arm but pulled it back before he could lay his own over it. " 'Tis nothing like that. It is simply that I paid a call at the Burtrums' on my way back from Mr. Lampman's house, and I found Lord Burtrum's son barely endurable."

"If I had known you would give your neighbors a look-in with such alacrity, I would have sent word to warn you about Cecil Burtrum. He is worse than his father. Burtrum the Elder is insufferable, although he does gamble with rare spirit. The son does not even have that redeeming virtue, for I am not the only one who believes the word *boring* was invented with him in mind."

"Boring?" She shook her head. "If he had been only boring, I would have tolerated it. Rather, he was heartless in his comments about the coachman's death. After all, the man was found on his steps."

"Really?" Neville digested this fact and wondered if it had any relevance to his suspicions.

"Do you think I would hoax you about something like that?"

"Forgive me, Pris. I was not questioning you, only reacting to the information."

At a knock and a throat being cleared, Neville stepped aside so a footman could enter the room. The young man glanced at him, but Neville could not guess what message he was trying to convey.

"Yes, Layden?" Priscilla asked.

"A message for you, my lady. Your aunt, Lady Cordelia, wishes you to know that she will be calling tomorrow afternoon after her arrival in London."

"Thank you, Layden," she said with more aplomb than Neville suspected he could muster. When the footman bowed his head and took his leave, she sighed. "I had no idea Aunt Cordelia was coming to London too."

"No doubt she heard you were here and wished to see how you fared."

Her nose wrinkled as she laughed. "Neville, when did you become my aunt's advocate? You know she finds you totally unacceptable company for me and the children. If she is coming to call, it is most likely to make sure that Isaac has not been wasting his time at Langley Academy."

"Is she still trying to convince you to send him to a school of her choice?"

"She is still trying to convince me that *she* is a better arbiter of what is the best way to bring up the Earl of Emberson." She rolled her eyes. "Thank heavens she did not chance upon you holding Isaac over the railing."

He laughed. "I vow to be on my best behavior if I encounter her while coming to escort you for the soirée." When she regarded him in amazement, he asked, "You have changed your mind, haven't you?"

"Yes, but how did you know?"

"If I were in your shoes, I would be grateful for any excuse to cut Lady Cordelia's call short, even if it meant allowing Burtrum to play host to me."

"You make her sound like an old dragon."

"She is not that old."

When she smiled, he drew her into conversation about her trip from the south. Yet, he could not help noticing how, again and again, her gaze went toward the front window, which gave her an excellent view of Burtrum's front steps. No matter how much she demurred, she believed the three deaths were somehow connected.

Just as he did.

Chapter Three

Upon his arrival at Priscilla's house the next evening, Neville was relieved not to find Priscilla's aunt there. He was even more pleased to discover from one of the footmen that Lady Cordelia had postponed her call, deciding she needed time to supervise her household, which she believed, in spite of their experience, was incompetent when dealing with reopening her house on Grosvenor Square.

"Uncle Neville!" called Isaac from the first floor, peering over the railing and waving as if he feared Neville would fail to see him in the brightly lit hallway.

Climbing the stairs, Neville smiled. "I see you do not look the worse for your afternoon yesterday of helping Gilbert."

"He took Mama quite at her word and worked me all afternoon." He held up his hands, which were stained with black. "He had me polishing boots first. After that he sent me to wash dishes for Mrs. Dunham. Even after washing every dish in the dashed house, my fingers still are covered with bootblack."

"You must consider it good training. After all, an earl might find himself needing to polish his own boots on short notice one day in order to avoid shaming his title."

Isaac pondered for a moment and then grinned. "Now I know how to do it well. Fudge, I never considered that."

"Exactly." As he turned to go to the front parlor, where he was to wait for Priscilla, he added, "You might want to watch your language in front of your mother. She will not take kindly to hearing you say 'fudge' in front of her or your sisters."

"But Leah says it all the time!"

"When your mother is nearby?"

Again Isaac was silenced by the question. His intense expression showed that he was deeply considering what Neville had said. Leaving the boy to contemplate his advice, Neville walked into the front parlor.

Priscilla was not there, but he knew she would be soon. She was not the type of woman who kept a man cooling his heels while she spent time making sure her hair was perfect. Like so many aspects of her, the need to be unfashionably on time was something she had learned as a parson's wife.

Neville sighed. He had thought, after so many months, that returning to this house on Bedford Square would not be difficult. Instead, it brought forth so many memories of Lazarus. Good memories of laughter and debate and an acceptance that he had never known anywhere else. He did not let himself be betwattled into believing the welcome was extraordinary, because neither Lazarus nor Priscilla had ever closed their doors to anyone.

"Not even your unparalleled Aunt Cordelia," he said aloud with a laugh.

From behind him, he heard, "Aunt Cordelia is here?"

He looked at the doorway. Priscilla had dispensed with her bleak mourning clothes, and he had to applaud the decision. This gown, which was the exact shade of her dark blue eyes, did not have all the geegaws of lace and ribbons favored by the pink of the *ton*. Instead, its simple, classic lines accented her own. With her golden hair drawn back to leave only a few strands to curl against her high cheekbones, she would outshine every woman in attendance this evening.

"No," he said, smiling, "your aunt is not here, so you do not need to panic."

"You know that I never panic, Neville."

"True."

"Do I meet your expectations?" she asked, and he realized he was still gawking at her.

"You look—" He laughed as she arched a brow at him. "All right, I will not say you look lovely, even though you do."

"And you appear to be at your best, Neville."

He looked down at his black coat, which he wore over a white waistcoat and breeches. Clothes were never of vital importance to him, a fact his valet, Riley, whom he had inherited along with the house on Berkeley Square, found unacceptable. So it had become simpler, when staying at the house, to let Riley choose what he would wear.

"I shall pass your compliments on to Riley."

She smiled, but there was no amusement in her voice when she asked, "Whom are you intending to impress tonight?"

"Why can't you believe it is you?"

"Because we know each other too well to be impressed by mere prinkum-prankum. Such fine clothes cannot conceal what we know to be the truth."

He laughed. "Listen to the lady using Town cant as if she never wandered more than a day's ride from Hyde Park."

"You are avoiding giving me an answer."

"I had hoped you would not notice."

"But I have. Whom are you trying to impress tonight?"

Realizing she would not let him change the topic, he said, "Burtrum is reputed to enjoy high stakes at the card table. If I am to face him across the flats, it behooves me to show him that I am not wary of such wagers."

"Something everyone knows."

"Mayhap for those I have already met while enjoying a night of gambling." He became serious. "Burtrum has been in London and on Bedford Square only for the past seven or eight months, so I have not yet encountered him at the table. I believe he is considering membership at Boodle's, but I have heard as well that Boodle's will not consider him."

"So you want to know the reason?"

"Yes."

"Why?"

"I would think that is obvious, Pris. Three deaths—all of them suspicious—on this square, where you and the children reside. The situation is worrisome. I want to discover what Burtrum might know of these incidents so you can take any steps necessary to keep the children out of trouble." His smile returned. "In this matter, at least."

She gave him a genuine smile at last. "I appreciate that, Neville. I have been making excuses throughout the day to keep the children within these walls, and, if my efforts and the reason for them were not so transparent, I suspect they would have rebelled against my edicts by now. While you speak with Lord Burtrum, I shall endeavor to find out what information the rest of his guests might have."

"Shall we?" He offered his arm.

"I thought you would never ask."

* * *

The brightly lit house on the other side of the square had its door thrown wide open. Nothing looked amiss as Priscilla was ushered inside by Neville. He had said nothing on the short stroll around the square, and she watched him appraising the entry of the Burtrums' house. There was no sign of anything being amiss. If she had not known of the odd collection of deaths on the square, she would have guessed everything was just as it had been any number of nights during the Season.

Until she noticed how stiff and brittle the butler and the footmen appeared.

One footman dropped Neville's hat, not once but twice. Another's hands shook so hard that he appeared to have taken a chill. She wished she had an excuse to ask them what was bothering them—even though she knew quite well, she might learn something from even a brief conversation—but Lord Burtrum's butler steered them with efficiency toward the stairs.

At the top of the staircase, Lord Burtrum was greeting his guests with a jovial smile that stretched the lines etched into his face. The black hair on his head was as bushy as his mustache. She doubted she had ever seen one so thick. A gold chain across his silver waistcoat marked the location of his pocket watch. As he bowed over her hand, she could not help staring at the thick gold rings on his fingers. Not just the signet ring that would have come down through the family, but others studded with gems. Even Aunt Cordelia wearing her finest could not have outshone this earl.

"I am so pleased you are able to join us, Lady Priscilla," the earl gushed in his booming bass voice. Although his words were polite, his gaze sweeping along her suggested she was a prize sheep brought to market. "I have been looking forward to the opportunity to meet you."

"And I have anticipated this chance to speak with you." That was the truth, because she had been curious if the father was as vexing as the son. Apparently, he was, for he showed a lack of manners, too, by ogling her openly.

"Good of you to escort her, Hathaway." Lord Burtrum's jovial smile widened to include Neville. "If you have a few minutes to spare from this lovely lady's company, I have something I would like to discuss with you."

Priscilla did not wait for Neville's glance in her direction before she said, "I see a friend I have not had a chance to call upon since I returned to Town. If you two gentlemen would excuse me, I shall leave you to your conversation while I embark upon one of my own."

Although she wanted to linger nearby to overhear what the earl might have to say to Neville, she knew Neville would tell her anything of import later. She walked into the front parlor.

By now she should have been accustomed to entering one of these homes that was like hers, yet different. The walls and the doors and windows were set in a pattern identical to her house on the opposite side of the square. Mayhap that was what made the different colors and furniture so glaringly wrong.

Lord Burtrum had excellent taste as many of the paintings on the walls were done with the skill of expert artists who had been newly embraced by the *ton*. But others, she had to own, seemed out of place among the masterpieces because they were inferior. Mayhap the earl saw something in the work that she could not. Or mayhap it was nothing more than the *ton*'s latest determination of style, a subject that had seldom mattered to her.

She took a glass of wine from the tray held out to her,

and nodded her thanks. The footman glanced at her, opened his mouth as if to speak, then hurried away. She watched him weave his way through the room and disappear through a doorway at the back.

Curiosity teased her. How peculiar! If he had something to say to her, he needed only to say it. It could be that he had not wanted to speak when others were likely to overhear. Yet what could he say that would be troublesome if it was overheard?

Priscilla chided herself. She was letting her anxiety cause her to look for disasters where there were none. The butler and the footman downstairs had appeared on edge as well. No doubt the servants in this house were as agitated as the ones in hers. Lord Burtrum may have ordered them to say nothing of the incidents.

Or mayhap his son had. She frowned. The earl seemed to have more concern about those around him than his annoying son had shown the previous day during her call. If she spoke with Lord Burtrum, she might ask—in a most roundabout way—about the distress his servants were revealing. There must be a way to ease the fear so a cloud of apprehension did not hover over the square.

"Lady Priscilla!" The exclamation was not a shout, but it seemed so in the room when the conversation had abated at the very moment the words left Jerome Wayland's mouth.

Priscilla wanted to groan. Mr. Wayland, a solicitor, had rubbed poorly against her since their first meeting almost three years before. Mayhap it was because, even when Lazarus was alive, Mr. Wayland made no secret of the fact he would like to rub against her in a far more intimate way. If she had given the bothersome man as much as a single thought in the past year, it would have been the hope that he had convinced some unfortunate woman to be his wife and would be so happily married that he would have forgotten his infatuation with her.

That clearly had not happened, because the tall, undeniably handsome man rushed to her side, almost bowling over a pair of dowagers who looked daggers at him. His hasty apology, tossed over his shoulder, meant little when he did not slow until he reached Priscilla's side. His ruddy hair had receded since they had last spoken, but his eyes were eagerly admiring her. The action that had been pleasing when Neville had looked at her was disagreeable now.

"What a pleasure, Lady Priscilla! A true, true, true pleasure!" Grasping her hand, he bowed over it.

She drew it back before he could slobber onto her favorite lace mitts. "Good evening, Mr. Wayland."

Her cool tone had no more effect on him than it had in the past. He gushed about how well she looked and how wonderful it was to have her return to London and how sorry he was that she had suffered such a loss. The last comment was said with haste and not a great deal of compassion when he saw his compliments were gaining him no favor in her eyes.

"Thank you, Mr. Wayland," she said, slipping in the words when, at long last, he took a breath. "If you will excuse me, I—"

"A beautiful, beautiful, beautiful woman like you must be excused anything." He grinned, and she saw he had lost a tooth. She wondered if it had been knocked out when, after discovering the solicitor had been flirting with his wife, an irate husband gave Mr. Wayland a facer. Now, *that* was a most agreeable thought, although she could not slap his cheek when he had said nothing outrageous . . . yet.

"Thank you."

As she was about to walk away, he grasped her hand again. She looked from it to his smile without comment.

Even he was not so obtuse that he could dismiss her cool expression.

Hastily he dropped her hand. Her hope that he would accept her dismissal was doused when he asked, "Will you join me for a drive in Hyde Park on the morrow, my lady? It would give me so very, very, very much pleasure."

"I am otherwise obligated tomorrow, Mr. Wayland."

"The next day?"

"I am otherwise obligated then too."

"Then the day after that?"

How persistent and pesky could one man be? She was tempted to ask him that, but she would not let his common manners persuade her to act the same.

Before she could reply, a man behind her said, "Wayland, allow me to deprive you of this lady's company for a few minutes."

Priscilla looked over her shoulder and drew in her breath. She had not guessed Cecil Burtrum would be her savior. In spite of his unfeeling comments yesterday, she preferred his company to Mr. Wayland's. She put her hand on his proffered arm and bade the solicitor a good evening. This would probably not be the last time she must deal with the persistent Mr. Wayland, but now that she knew he was attending this gathering, she could be watchful and attempt to avoid him.

"You looked as if you wished to be done with the conversation," Cecil Burtrum said, pulling her attention back to him. He bowed over her fingers.

She was about to reply with her thanks. Then she realized he was eyeing her with an interest she had not expected a man of his relatively few years would exhibit for a woman who was a decade his senior. Bother! She drew her hand out of his. She had not thought any man could be more obnoxious than Mr. Wayland, but Cecil Burtrum clearly wished to try.

"I am glad I have the chance to speak with you again," she said with a tight smile. *Glad that I shall know to watch both myself and my daughters when you are about.* It was a most ungenerous thought, but the son seemed to have inherited his father's delight in gaining a reputation as a bang-up prime. She did not wish Daphne to become caught up in such a fast life.

"As I am most elated to have the opportunity to speak to you, my lady. I fear my conduct was not what it should have been during your call yesterday. I was quite unsettled by the events of the day, but I should have welcomed you more graciously."

"I understand."

"Thank you. I thought you might from what my father has said about you."

"About me?" She wished she had not let the words escape from her lips.

"Yes, but his words were only the most complimentary, I can assure you." He lowered his voice. "You are not seeing any of us at our best."

"That is understandable."

He looked past her, and his smile became sincere. She said nothing as a slender brunette and a tall, thin man paused beside them. There was no doubt the woman was related closely to Cecil Burtrum. The shape of her face was identical, although its lines had been softened into more feminine curves. She wore no jewelry other than a pearl ring on the fourth finger of her left hand.

"Have you met my sister, Eleanor?" Cecil's smile wavered as his voice grew brittle. "And her fiancé, Malcolm Drake?"

As Priscilla greeted them, she wondered as she had so many times how two hearts could lead obviously opposite people into falling in love. Lady Eleanor Burtrum, an attractive brunette, took control of the conversation, barely taking a breath between each spurt of words. If Mr. Drake had a tongue behind his teeth, he had no chance to use it, for he seemed required only to nod in agreement with whatever Eleanor said.

But Eleanor was a gentle prattler. She did not speak of anyone in a derogatory tone. Rather, she tried to persuade Priscilla to share her excitement about her upcoming nuptials. It seemed one of the family within these walls recognized the parameters society insisted upon. A pulse of sympathy rushed through Priscilla. Such a family was indeed a burden, and it was easy to understand why the young woman was eager to be married and away from it.

"Are your children here in Town with you?" Eleanor asked.

"Yes," Priscilla replied, startled when Eleanor gave her a chance to answer. "If you have some time amid all your wedding plans, I know my eldest, Daphne, would be so pleased to have you call. She is almost of an age to join the Season, and she could benefit from your experiences." She laughed. "My experiences, she believes, were an eternally long time ago."

"You have a daughter of such an age?" Eleanor pressed her hand over her mouth and flushed.

"Do not look chagrined. Your question was meant kindly."

"Yes, yes . . . I mean, I would be delighted to spend some time with your daughter." Her smile returned. "It shall be a pleasure."

"Thank you. I know Daphne will be eager to have you call when you have the opportunity. Wedding preparations take so much time."

Mr. Drake said quietly, "But a hiatus from the hullabaloo of the wedding would be welcome, wouldn't it, Eleanor?"

His long, thin face was neither handsome nor dignified, but it displayed his emotions clearly. He was very tired of the wedding plans.

The cut of his green coat and the polish on his low boots beneath his tan breeches labeled him as plump in the pockets. He had been introduced as *Mr. Drake,* so Priscilla guessed he was combining his wealth with Eleanor's family's title in a match that was bound to bring benefits to both families. A not uncommon occurrence, she knew, from the number of such couples her late husband had joined in marriage. A marriageable daughter could be salvation for a family long on tradition and short on money.

Surprised that Mr. Drake had spoken after standing silently for so many minutes, Priscilla started to reply. Then she saw Mr. Wayland walking toward her. She bade Eleanor and Mr. Drake a hasty farewell, then scanned the room. There must be *someone* she could speak with before Mr. Wayland cornered her.

She smiled when she saw Neville and another man near the rear doorway. Although she knew she would be wise to allow him to speak with the guests without her intrusion, as he always seemed to be able to elicit such interesting information from those conversations, this was an emergency.

''Ah, Pris,'' Neville said, glancing past her. ''I believe you have a friend. Wayland looks aghast that you are evading him so obviously.''

''If you say anything,'' she replied lowly, ''I shall invite him to speak with you.''

''No need for threats.'' He raised his voice. ''Allow me to introduce a friend. Lady Priscilla Flanders, this is Robert Peel. Peel, my friend Lady Priscilla.''

''Good evening,'' Priscilla said as the red-haired man took her hand and bowed politely. She recognized the name.

Robert Peel was involved with the always uneasy situation in Ireland.

"My pleasure, my lady." He smiled shyly.

"So, Peel, are you staying at your family's home on Upper Grosvenor Street?" Neville asked.

Mr. Peel shook his head. "No, I have quarters at Fife House, near the river. Those are far more convenient for meetings and discussions with the prime minister. You should call some evening, Hathaway. We have lively discussions."

"I will do that." He chuckled. "On a night when you look as if you have slept at least once in the past week."

"Concerns for the troops on the Peninsula are taking much of our time." He smiled, this time with more self-assurance. "But we are already planning methods to get them men and supplies in ways that may surprise not only the French, but our constituents here in England."

"That is wonderful news," Priscilla said. "Anything to bring the war to an end sooner."

"On that we agree."

Neville asked in a tone that was purely conversational, "Is Burtrum interested in such issues?"

"Burtrum?" Mr. Peel grimaced. "Lord Burtrum, mayhap, but his son? No. Cecil Burtrum talks of only three things—his wine, his snuff, and the women he hopes to seduce." He turned to Priscilla. "Forgive me, my lady."

"You can say," Neville answered before she could, "anything in Priscilla's hearing that you would in mine." He chuckled when she frowned at him. "Or almost anything."

"Then let us speak of something that is sure not to bother Lady Priscilla."

"Such as why you are here, Peel?"

He smiled. "You know why I am here. I have heard about the chain of deaths here on Bedford Square, and I am curious.

I own that I am glad to see you here, Hathaway. What have you learned?''

''Nothing, although Priscilla has.''

''Me?'' She laughed uneasily. ''The only thing I have learned is that every servant on the square fears he or she will be the next victim.''

Mr. Peel sighed. ''This is a matter best left to professionals. It is our misfortune that we do not have any concerted arrangement in London to tend to such crimes. Bow Street does an admirable job, but they are too few, and their best are constantly called away to protect the Prince Regent and his companions.''

''And the watch is useless,'' Neville said. ''Unless you have a keg of ale that needs emptying.''

As the conversation continued, Priscilla saw Neville scrutinize the room. She knew what he sought, but wondered why he expected to find it with such ease. No one was going to step forward and announce he or she had had a hand in these mysterious deaths.

After Mr. Peel took his leave to return to his office, Neville slipped her hand through his arm. He led her toward the door.

''We are being followed,'' he said quietly.

''Followed?''

''Don't look back.''

She ignored his warning when she saw how his eyes twinkled. Glancing over her shoulder, she saw Mr. Wayland trailing them at a distance that was just far enough for him not to overhear what they said but within earshot if they raised their voices and invited him to be part of their discussion.

''Poor Wayland,'' Neville said with feigned compassion. ''I fear you have cut him quite to the quick with your unfeeling words.''

"Nonsense. I did no more than bid him a good evening when our host's son sought me out."

He gave an emoted sigh that reminded her how he had spent several years as a thespian. "When a man is as bemused by love as poor Wayland, even such an *adieu* is shattering. You know, Pris, you have the most particular effect on men."

"Now you are talking arrant nonsense."

"Am I?"

"Yes, for 'tis long been clear, from your refusal to cling to the canons of society, that I have no effect whatsoever on you."

"I wouldn't say that."

Priscilla knew she should send a scathing retort back at him, but as she saw the strong emotions on his face while his mouth curved upward in a smile, words disappeared from her mind. How many times had she seen his smile? How many times had she been furious with it and him—and herself—because he had tripped her the double while teasing her? So many times, but none of those smiles had possessed the warmth of this one.

No, that was not true. When he had bade her and the children farewell in Stonehall-on-Sea after the to-do there earlier in the spring was brought to a satisfactory ending, he had been wearing this smile. Then, it had suffused her with a pleasant longing. It did the same tonight. A longing to spend time with him far from the curious eyes of their friends, her household, and her children.

As she walked with him into the corridor beyond the parlor, she watched his hand settle over hers on his arm. He stroked her fingers and paused. She looked up at him as he murmured her name.

"Yes?" She wished it did not have to be a question, but an answer.

"I missed you while you were in Stonehall-on-Sea." His intense gaze swept along her face, and she wondered if he was seeking something there.

"We would have welcomed you to pay another call."

"There is the problem."

"Problem? What problem?"

He smiled. "Sometimes, it would be pleasant to have my call be only on you and not your whole household."

"Why, Sir Neville, you could turn a girl's head with such fancy words!" She hoped the teasing would serve as a barrier between him and her arms, which wanted to draw him closer.

"I was not intending to have you turn your head, Pris." His palms were coarse against her cheeks as he framed her face. "Certainly not away from me."

As his mouth lowered toward hers, she closed her eyes to savor his kiss. Would it be as dangerous as his reputation or as tender as his friendship?

Priscilla did not learn, because he released her as his name was called. When he turned, she saw a footman rushing toward them.

"Sir Neville," the man in bright red livery said, "I am sorry to intrude, but it is an emergency."

Neville glanced at her, and she saw his face harden into the expression he wore whenever trouble came near.

"Will you come with me, Sir Neville?" The footman's face was so gray, Priscilla feared he was ill.

"Of course." He offered his arm. "Pris?"

"It might be better if the lady remains here." The footman gulped, and his face became a sickish shade of green.

"You should hasten to take us wherever it is you are intending to," Neville said, impatience entering his voice. "I doubt if Burtrum would appreciate you being sick on his fine carpets."

"On his fine carpets . . ." The footman spun on his heel and, with a wave to follow him, hurried along the hallway.

When Neville drew her with him, Priscilla whispered, "If this house is as much like mine as it appears, he is leading us to the room I use as a study."

The footman paused by the door, then stepped aside, clearly not wanting to enter.

Priscilla understood why when she saw Cecil Burtrum lying on his right side halfway beneath a table. Beside him, the rug was sprinkled with snuff and stained with wine. She took one step toward him, but Neville pushed past her.

He knelt and tipped the man onto his back. Putting his hand to the pulse point on Cecil's neck, he leaned forward so his ear was close to Cecil's gaping mouth.

"Have you sent for a doctor?" asked Priscilla, looking at the footman.

"There is no need." Neville's voice was strained as he whispered, "Pris, he is dead."

Chapter Four

Priscilla put her hand over her stomach and fought not to let its roiling contents rise. "Are you certain Cecil Burtrum is dead, Neville? He might be only foxed."

"Even when one is intoxicated, one's heart continues to beat." Neville stood and wiped his hands on his breeches. "And he is already growing cold."

The footman gulped and groped his way toward a nearby chair.

Neville guided him to one near the window and sat him there. Gently, he said, "Take slow, deep breaths until your head steadies."

That was advice Priscilla needed to take for herself. She stared at the young man who clearly had been enjoying a glass of wine and a pinch of snuff before returning to his father's guests. The wine was oozing in a broader circle from the upended glass, and not a flake of snuff remained in the box.

"We should send for the constable," she said.

Neville put his hand on Priscilla's shoulder as he came to stand behind her. "You are thinking as if you are still in Stonehall-on-Sea. Here we could send for the Foot Patrol or, better yet, to Bow Street. I think this is something that would interest Thurmond."

"Who?" She tore her eyes from the horrendous sight to look at Neville.

"John Thurmond. He has been with Bow Street for two decades now."

She nodded. "Then we should send for him." Looking at the footman, she asked, "Do you think you are able to send a message for Mr. Thurmond to come here?"

The footman pushed himself to his feet. Although his knees shivered, he said, "Yes, my lady. I am able to do that." He started toward the door, then paused. "Should I alert Lord Burtrum first?"

"Lord Burtrum doesn't know?" She had assumed the earl was prostrate somewhere with his grief.

"No, my lady." Again he gulped. "I did not wish to upset him if there was nothing really wrong." He cast a guilty glance at Neville. "From what I have heard about you, Sir Neville, I guessed you would know if he was dead."

If a corpse had not been on the floor in front of them, Priscilla would have laughed at Neville's astonished expression. He should know—as she did—that no servant was unaware of what the *ton* might pretend had never happened. Neville's disreputable past must be known belowstairs on every square in Mayfair.

"You need to send for Lord Burtrum and Lady Eleanor immediately," she said. "They need to know what has happened here."

"But, my lady—" He shuddered.

Taking sympathy on the lad, she ordered, "Just send them here. I will speak to them of what has happened."

"Thank you, my lady." He scurried out the door.

"You did not need to do that, Pris," Neville said as he knelt again next to the body. "It shall not be easy to tell them that Burtrum is dead."

"I know. I learned, as a parson's wife, that bringing bad news to someone is never easy." She took a steadying breath. Other than the body on the floor amid the wine and snuff, this study offered an elegance that matched the rest of the house. Paintings were displayed on the walls, and on shelves instead of the books that crowded her study.

She walked to a painting of a shepherdess flirting with a goat-footed man. It had been done by a skilled artist, for each fiber of the shepherdess's skirt seemed real. Wishing she could find a way into the painting and away from the horror here, she sighed.

Knowing she was being silly, she asked, "Do you think it is possible he was taken ill, and he came here so as not to distress anyone at the gathering?"

Neville snorted. "You are forgetting whom you are talking about. Cecil Burtrum would never have spared his father's guests a moment of his distress if he was stricken with some ailment and thought he might get compassion from some of them."

"I hope you do not plan on saying such things when his family arrives."

"*You* are the one who volunteered to speak to them, not I. While you do that, I am going to consider what has happened here."

"He was here alone, one can assume."

"You should not assume anything, Pris." He tilted the dead man's head one way and then the other. "There are signs of pain on his face, but there is no sign of a blow to the skull. But that does not reassure me no one baked his bread."

"Murder?" She shook her head. "Be careful what you say. Everyone on Bedford Square is jumpy enough already."

"You cannot disregard the facts."

"I am not. I am saying that murder is not the only way a man can end up dead on the floor."

He looked up at her with a wry expression. "That is true, but if I have ever met a man more worthy of coming to such an ignoble ending than Burtrum, I cannot remember when."

"Speaking poorly of the dead is not a good habit to develop."

"I have lots of bad habits. One more will make no difference." He reached toward the wine that had stained the carpet.

She caught his arm before he could touch it. "Take care, Neville. The wine might be the very thing that brought his end."

"You believe he was poisoned?"

"I cannot disregard the facts," she said as he had. "An otherwise healthy young man now is dead."

"And that asks the question of exactly who might have wished him dead." He stood and wiped his hands on one corner of the cloth covering a tray on the table. It must have held the glass of wine. "I suspect the list is intolerably long, for the rather loathsome sort tends to garner many enemies."

Priscilla was about to reply, but heard footsteps coming toward them. A pair. Bother! This would be simpler if she could speak to the Burtrums one at a time and offer them individual sympathy. Not easier, for she did not relish the idea of going through the explanation twice, but simpler.

Neville took her hand and gave it a squeeze. She smiled at him, glad that he was here to bolster her with his common sense and knowledge of the darker aspects of human nature. Facing the door, she took a deep breath, releasing it just as the footsteps slowed.

Eleanor appeared in the doorway along with Mr. Drake. Her tone was impatient as she asked, "You wanted to see me?"

Before Priscilla could answer, the young woman's face paled. Eleanor stared at her brother on the floor. She let out a screech that surely could have been heard by the Thames, and then she screamed again and again . . . and again. She pushed past Priscilla, almost knocking her from her feet. She tried to squeeze around Neville to get to her prostrate brother, but he stood his ground.

"Stay where you are," Neville ordered quietly.

When she paid him no mind, thrashing her hands at him like a maddened Don Quixote trying to joust with a windmill, he glanced at Priscilla.

She understood what he did not want to say. Taking Eleanor by the arm, she drew the young woman to the chair where the footman had been sitting. She tried to convince Eleanor to do the same. Crying uncontrollably, she bounced back to her feet and rushed past Priscilla.

"No!" Priscilla caught her and shoved her back onto the settee as gently as she could. "You must stay away from him."

"Cecil has swooned. Someone should help him!"

Priscilla put her hands on either side of Eleanor's face and turned it toward her. "Listen to me. He has not swooned."

"Then he is ill!"

"No, he is not ill."

"Then—?" Eleanor stared at Priscilla, disbelief in her wide eyes.

Priscilla nodded.

With a shriek, Eleanor collapsed back onto the cushions.

"How could you tell her so heartlessly?" demanded Mr. Drake as he elbowed Priscilla out of the way.

Rubbing her side and not looking at Neville, who would be glowering to see her treated so, Priscilla said, "I answered her questions, Mr. Drake. You don't expect me to lie to her, do you?" She looked toward the door. "Did the footman return with you?"

"He is on his way to find Lord Burtrum." Mr. Drake chafed his fiancée's wrists in hopes of reviving her. "How did this happen?"

Neville said as he bent over the corpse again, "Your guess is as good as ours. We found him here like this."

If he said more, Priscilla did not hear it. Eleanor came awake and began to shriek until it made Priscilla's throat sore just to listen to her. All efforts to calm the young woman were futile.

A shout cut through Eleanor's hysterics. Lord Burtrum plowed his way into the room.

"What is this hullabaloo?" he demanded. "I—"

Neville caught the man by the arm before he could topple onto his son. Sitting Burtrum on a chair by the door, he reached for the bottle in the middle of the table. He paused and looked at where Priscilla was trying to decrease the level of Lady Eleanor's banshee screeches. He then glanced at the wine staining the carpet blood-red. Could Priscilla be right? Had someone poisoned the younger Burtrum's port? He must take care that no one drank from the same bottle.

Taking the bottle, he placed it beneath the table beyond Burtrum's body. He called for wine to be brought for the earl and his daughter. Seeing Priscilla's wan face, he hoped whoever brought the wine would think to bring a glass for her as well. If not, he would urge her to take a bracing swig from the bottle. He knew she would not give in to vapors, but she was almost as colorless as the corpse.

Abruptly, Burtrum surged to his feet. He waved his hands toward the door. "All of you, go home. Now!"

"Burtrum," Neville said quietly, "you may want to keep them here until Thurmond has a chance to speak with them."

"Thurmond?" He whirled to jab a finger in Neville's chest. "How dare you send to Bow Street without my permission!"

"I believe *that* gave me permission." He pointed to Burtrum's son. "Don't you want to know the truth about your son's death?"

"Death . . ." His face crumpled, but it reformed into a scowl as he grasped Neville's arm.

Neville shook him off. "Get control of yourself, man! You are doing nothing to help uncover the truth."

Burtrum seized Priscilla's arm, whirling her away from his daughter. When her shoe came down on his son's coat, she winced and choked back a gasp.

"See here, Burtrum!" Neville caught the other man's wrist and twisted it off Priscilla's arm. When she looked down at where Burtrum's fingers had left red imprints in her skin, he swallowed his fury. Burtrum was not in his proper state of mind just now. Yet, even the death of his son did not give him *carte blanche* to abuse a woman, most especially Priscilla.

"No, no, no," the earl said, almost shoving him and Priscilla out of the room. "I shall not have you all gawking at this. Go home."

"Go home?" He scowled. "Burtrum, even if you want to handle this alone, you need to think of your daughter. She needs someone with her to help her deal with what has happened."

"She has her fiancé to help her." This time, he *did* shove Priscilla.

As he kept her from falling, Neville opened his mouth to

remind Burtrum that no situation—even the death of his son—granted him the right to be so rude. He closed it when Priscilla shook her head. Sorry that she had manners when he would have gladly shown Burtrum the cost of being so discourteous, he nodded.

She slipped her hand through his arm as he led her away from the room. Their cloaks and his hat were waiting for them when they reached the entry foyer. Outside, carriages were receiving the guests, who seemed determined to flee as swiftly as if they had brought Burtrum's life to an unexpected end.

Quietly, Neville said to Burtrum's butler, "I trust you will recall the names of all the guests this evening."

The man nodded.

"When Thurmond arrives from Bow Street, send him without delay to the book-room upstairs."

Again the butler nodded.

A twinge of suspicion teased Neville, but Priscilla asked before he could, "You have sent to Bow Street for help, haven't you?"

"No, because Lord Burtrum—"

"Lord Burtrum be damned!" snarled Neville. He did not bother to apologize to Priscilla for his language. She would forgive him for speaking with frustration tonight. Pointing to the footman who had brought them to find Cecil Burtrum, he ordered, "I told you to send to Bow Street straightaway. Do so!"

The footman scurried down the steps.

"I want to be informed as soon as Thurmond arrives," Neville continued.

"Where will you be?" the disconcerted butler asked.

"Send word to Lady Priscilla's house. I will wait there for it."

"Yes, sir."

Neville tossed his cloak over his shoulders, then offered his arm again to Priscilla. He was not surprised her fingers quivered on it, although she appeared quite composed. As he led her down the steps, he said, "You have been very quiet."

"I have been struggling to arrange my thoughts into some order."

"Do you think Cecil Burtrum's death is connected with the others?" he asked, seeing no reason not to be blunt.

She shuddered. "I hope not. If it is, we have a murderer on Bedford Square who is killing in no discernable pattern. And until we can unravel that bizarre puzzle, no one here is safe."

The square was so silent the next afternoon that Neville could have believed it was deserted. Even within Priscilla's house, the customary good spirits shared by her children and her servants had been curtailed. He had come here after paying a visit to Bow Street. The Runners had gathered no further information last night from speaking to the family and guests.

But on one thing Thurmond agreed with him completely. The earl's son had been murdered, for nobody could offer any other explanation why an otherwise healthy young man had cocked up his toes. That he was the fourth such victim on the square added to the mystery.

When Neville was shown to the study that was the twin of the room where Cecil Burtrum had met his end, he was not surprised to find Priscilla pacing from one end of the small room to the other. She paused when he entered.

"You look terrible," she said without a smile.

He rubbed the whiskers on his chin. "I suspect I have looked worse."

"I have no doubts about that." Her hands closed into fists before she forced her fingers to loosen. "Did you sleep at all?"

"No." Her hands tightened again, her fingers pressing into her palms. "What did you find out?"

"Nothing but that Bow Street shares our belief there is a murderer at work on Bedford Square."

"I had hoped they would have something more to say than that, although I discovered nothing new when I called at the Burtrums' an hour ago."

"I did not realize you were planning to call today."

"Eleanor had been so distraught, I wished to inquire about her. She sent word that she must stay by her father's side, for the man is overwhelmed with his grief." She unfolded her fingers, then clasped her hands in front of her. "I was able to speak to several of the servants, who assured me they saw nothing and no one out of the ordinary last night. Each of them mentioned how Lord Burtrum is completely inconsolable."

He frowned. "You seem to believe that his sorrow is something unusual."

"I don't, but they do."

"Why?"

"Apparently Lord Burtrum had another heir die. It was several years ago, and the situation was quite commonplace. The young man took ill and died very quickly. The earl was sad, but not grief-stricken as he is now."

"But he had an heir to spare then."

"He will gain an heir when Eleanor and Mr. Drake have their first son."

He put his hand on the back of a chair, hoping his calm pose would persuade her to let her shoulders drop from their stiff line. "Mayhap he has not given that any thought."

She went to the window overlooking her garden. "If you

stand here, you can see how it is possible someone might have come up the back of the house by climbing on the roof of the kitchen and—''

''Pris, you need to stay out of this investigation.'' When she faced him, astonishment in her eyes, he hoped she would heed what he had come here to say. ''Even you must own that things are different in Town than in a small village like Stonehall-on-Sea. There, you know everyone, and they trust you. Here . . .''

''Murder is no different in a small town than in a grand city like London.'' She regarded him with that pragmatic expression he hated, for it suggested he was a fool if he believed she would accept being wrapped in wool and put safely out of harm's way.

He did not believe she could be satisfied with that, but he wished—just once—she would be. ''You need to let Bow Street handle this.''

''I will . . . if you would agree to do the same.''

''Now, see here, Pris—''

''I can see quite clearly here, and I see that you are going to work closely with Bow Street and anyone you can find to solve what happened in that book-room.'' She turned her back on him to stare out the window again. ''Anyone but me. If you have not noticed, I did not leave my brain behind when I returned to London.''

''I know that, but I also know how worried you are for the children. That anxiety could discolor your usually discerning vision.''

''And you don't suffer from the same worry?''

Blast her! Any other woman would have succumbed to vapors upon finding Burtrum's corpse and would have retired to her bed for several days to recover from the traumatic sight. Although he usually appreciated her good sense and the fact that she did not swoon at the first sign of trouble, it would have been convenient for her to do so this time.

"Of course I do, Pris, but—"

She interrupted him once more, a sure sign of the depth of her distress. "If you are about to suggest that you can overcome such tendencies because you are a man, then I suggest you save your breath."

"I would never say that to you."

"But you would think it."

"Don't put words in my mouth that I had no intention of saying." He did not want her to guess how close she was to the truth, but he owed her the duty of being honest with her. Or, at least, somewhat honest. "Pris, our situations are different because *I* am not the children's mother."

"That I am anxious for their well-being makes me *more* determined to discover the identity of this murderer."

"A fact that will become well known if you persist in being so hardheaded and shortsighted."

He sighed as she walked past him and out of the room. He had insulted her as he never had before. Mayhap he was a fool not to be completely honest with her, but how could he explain that he did not want her becoming involved with this investigation because he feared it would make *her* the next target. She would have reminded him—quite rightly—that she already was in peril simply because she lived on this square.

Going to the window, he stared out. She was right. If the Burtrums' kitchen was built exactly like this one, it would have been possible for someone to scramble onto its low roof and then climb up to the study, where they had found Cecil Burtrum. No one at Bow Street seemed aware of that, which suggested the earl had not allowed Thurmond to investigate fully.

Neville heard light footsteps. Hoping Priscilla had

returned to accept his apology, even though he had no idea how he would express it without revealing the true course of his thoughts, he was startled to see Isaac peek around the door.

"You need not lurk out there," Neville said.

Isaac scampered in. "I can help you, Uncle Neville." The lad wore a broad smile. Did young Isaac think this whole mystery was a lark arranged especially for his holiday?

"Can you?" he asked, sitting so his eyes were closer to being level with the boy's.

Isaac nodded and perched on the very edge of the petit-point stool next to Neville's chair. "Yes, tell me what to do, and I shall do it."

"A grand promise, young man."

"I am an earl now." His thin chest puffed with pride as he smiled more broadly. "An earl should offer his help to those in need."

"That is true." Neville forced his lips not to tilt in a smile. Since Priscilla's father's death, young Isaac had reveled in the opportunity to assume the family's title. Not that the boy did not miss his grandfather, but Isaac had romantic ideas of how his life would change upon assuming the title. The fact that his sisters were not impressed and his mother still insisted he help with tasks about the house and study even more diligently than in the past had frustrated him.

Sharing the reality that a title could prove to be more bothersome than beneficial would further deflate the lad. Neville halted himself from rubbing the ring that had been a bequest from the uncle who had endowed him with the baronetcy. In the years since, Neville had endeavored to let the alteration in his status from disdain to welcome among the Polite World change *him* as little as possible.

"I will keep your offer of help in mind, Isaac."

"So what can I do to help?"

Choosing his words as carefully with the boy as he had with Priscilla, he said, ''I am not sure right now, but I will, as I said, keep your offer of help in mind.''

''I know you wish Mama would not poke her nose into this.''

''Eavesdropping at keyholes is not a good habit for an earl.''

Isaac would not be daunted now that he had embarked on this conversation. ''I did not need to listen. Your voices were loud.''

''Then you should not be paying attention to what your elders speak of privately.''

''I must.'' He stood and crossed his arms in front of him, reminding Neville of Priscilla's most stubborn stance. ''She is my mama, and, as the earl, it is my responsibility to keep every member of this family safe.''

''Safe?''

''Don't you want Mama to stay safe?''

''Yes, of course I do.''

Isaac's grin returned. ''It was a silly question.''

''Undoubtedly.''

''If she gets herself killed, then you two can't get married.''

Neville chuckled. ''Married? Leave the matchmaking to matchmakers, my boy. You are treading on hazardous ground when you begin such a journey.''

''Don't you like Mama?''

''Of course I like your mother. We have been friends since before you were born.''

''Don't you think she is pretty?''

''I cannot dispute an obvious fact.''

''So, if you like her and you think she's pretty, why don't you marry her?''

''That, Isaac, is another silly question.''

His hope that the lad would be silenced by his stern tone was for naught, as Isaac answered, "It is not a silly question. As often as you call here, you might as well marry her." The little boy's ears became a bright red, disclosing he had said something he had not planned to.

"Who told you that?"

"I should not say. I don't want to get anyone in trouble."

"A very good trait for an earl to cultivate," Neville said. The boy's answer was enough to tell him the truth. If it had been one of his sisters, Isaac would have told him straightaway. So it was likely that Isaac had either spoken with one of the upper servants or had overheard them discussing this.

"So if you do not want to marry Mama," Isaac asked, "why do you worry about her all the time?"

That question was not one he could answer with a quick retort. Its intensity warned him that Isaac was deeply concerned about keeping his mother safe.

Looking the lad directly in the eye, he said, "For the same reason you do, my boy."

"She is my mama."

"And she is *my* friend."

Isaac gave that some thought, then said, "I understand."

"I thought you would." He ruffled the boy's hair. "I vow that if I have need of your help, I will not hesitate to ask for it . . . as long as you promise me one thing."

"What?"

"You will not do anything on your own."

"But, Uncle Neville—"

"If you do, you know your mother is certain to get further involved in trying to keep you from getting too mired in this. If you want her to stay out of it, you must as well, until I seek your assistance."

Neville was unsure if the boy would accept such restrictions. When he himself was a lad, he would not have, but Isaac had been raised in a gentler household and had obligations Neville could not have imagined as a child.

With a wave, the boy abruptly rushed out of the room. Neville wondered what had caused him to race away, but understood when Priscilla came back into her study. Her face was even more rigid.

"I assume you heard the whole of it," he said.

She nodded.

"You are wearing a grim expression. Does the very idea of marrying me steal the twinkle from your eye?" He gave a feigned gasp of horror. "Or could it be that you fear breaking Mr. Wayland's heart?"

"Nothing about this is amusing, Neville, even though you seem to find it so."

He was instantly somber. "What is it?"

Priscilla never had met anyone who could shift from one emotion to another with such speed. Even when he was sincere, as she hoped he was now, Neville had a chameleon's gift to be one thing one moment, then another the next.

"Do not look at me with such dismay. I am not about to insist that you pay court on me." Before he could give her a quick back-answer, she raised her hand. "Heed me well, Neville. I know you are determined to find an answer to these deaths, but do not involve my children. Most especially Isaac. If Aunt Cordelia thought even for a second that I was allowing him to be imperiled in any way, she would use that as the very excuse she needs to persuade the family to let *her* oversee the rest of his life."

"Have you considered doing a bit of matchmaking yourself and finding that dragon another husband?"

"She says she has no interest in marrying again."

"She is overly concerned with the future of your son, the Earl of Emberson. As she acknowledges him as the preeminent member of your family, she certainly must be the first to own that she needs to heed his orders. If the earl insisted—"

She laughed. "Really, Neville, you have the most diabolical mind I have ever encountered."

"Hardly."

Following his gaze in the direction of the houses on the far side of the green in the center of the square, Priscilla lost all inclination to laugh. "I owe you an apology," she said.

"You owe *me* one?"

"Yes. I know your intentions are good ones."

"I have no intention of putting your children—or you, to own the truth—in jeopardy. Isaac understands that, for he accepted my stipulation that he must do nothing unless I seek his help. Do you understand it?"

"I am not nine years old, Neville. Please do not treat me as if I am."

"I will not treat you as if you are nine years old."

"Good."

"But," he said in the same solemn tone, "I still must ask you again to keep yourself out of this mess."

"I cannot, Neville. I am already a part of it."

"Because you were there when it was discovered Cecil Burtrum was dead?"

"No, because Mrs. Moore believes someone tried to break into this house last night."

Chapter Five

Cordelia Emberley Smith Gray Dexter should have been, as Neville had often suggested—sometimes in her hearing—born to a life in the theater. Even more than Neville, Priscilla's late father's sister liked to make an entrance that no one would forget.

That she was a striking woman, still thin and without a hint of gray in her hair, making her appear younger than her years, added to the impact. Her piercing gray eyes often peered at one through her quizzing glass, a warning she was not a woman to be trifled with or whose opinions could be ignored.

She had many opinions—all of which she held on to adamantly—but her most dearly held opinion was that Priscilla Flanders, daughter of the fourth Earl of Emberson, had married far below herself when she had accepted the proposal of a mere vicar. Such a woman could not be trusted—

in Aunt Cordelia's estimation—to raise the fifth earl to know his place in society.

And that fact she spoke frequently in Priscilla's hearing.

"My darlings!" she cooed as she came into the dining room and held out her arms as if she were about to scoop up all the children and hug them at once.

The children would be pleased their great-aunt was not staying at the house to insist they do their lessons and follow her dictates. They rushed to embrace her, for, in spite of her often cutting remarks, they knew she loved them dearly. Just as she loved Priscilla, although Neville had complained that he seldom witnessed any signs of that. Priscilla was glad he had agreed to believe her estimation of her aunt.

Priscilla noticed a man in the doorway. She recognized him as Dr. Summerson, a curate at St. Julian's Church. He had not been assigned there at the same time as Lazarus. She had met him when, as she had been leaving the Burtrums' on her most recent call, Dr. Summerson had been arriving to talk about the funeral.

He appeared to be a well-fed man with a decided tendency toward plumpness. What hair he had remaining was cut close to his round skull and was as gold as the quizzing glass hanging over the crucifix lying on the front of his dark waistcoat. When he lifted the quizzing glass to peek through it, Priscilla noticed the pair of heavy gold rings on his hand.

She wondered why Dr. Summerson was calling with her aunt, but she guessed she would learn soon enough. She waited until the children's exuberant greetings were over, then held out her hands to her aunt. Kissing her aunt on her cheek, she smiled. "Will you and Dr. Summerson join us for dessert, Aunt Cordelia?"

"I did not realize you had another caller." Her voice grew cold. "Sir Neville, good evening."

He bowed his head from where he stood by the dining

room table, but Priscilla caught sight of his smile. She hoped her aunt had not.

"Good evening, Lady Cordelia." He motioned to a chair on his right. "You are welcome to sit here."

"I did not know that you had assumed the place as host in my niece's household."

Seeing the children exchanging glances and knowing they could quickly dissolve into giggles, which would enrage her aunt beyond reason, Priscilla said quietly, "Aunt Cordelia, Neville is only trying to show you how welcome you are here."

"In *your* house!"

Priscilla signaled for two more plates to be brought, then looked at Daphne. Her daughter understood, because she sat and gestured for her brother and sister to do the same. They did not touch their forks, although Isaac stared wistfully at his cake.

"Dr. Summerson," Priscilla said as the curate walked toward the table, "what a pleasure to have you calling."

He handed his hat to Juster, who had followed him into the dining room. With his prize in hand, the footman hurried away, eager to be far from the inevitably sharp conversation between Aunt Cordelia and Neville.

"Lady Priscilla," the curate gushed, "I was so pleased when your aunt asked me to join her in calling here. I look forward to the opportunity to speak with you about your experiences with this parish."

"You are recently arrived at St. Julian's, Dr. Summerson?"

"About three months ago. Before that I served at a small parish in Berkshire." He drew out a chair for her aunt across from where Daphne sat and as far as possible from Neville. Apparently Dr. Summerson was a good judge of a situation, a skill a clergyman needed.

As her aunt sat, Priscilla did as well. While the guests' chocolate cake was served, Aunt Cordelia asked Isaac questions about his school. That he answered them with enthusiasm seemed to allay his great-aunt's apprehension.

"How are you doing, Priscilla?" asked Aunt Cordelia, reaiming her attention, much to Isaac's obvious relief.

"Well, as I assured you."

"I am not speaking of your health, Priscilla. I am speaking of what I have heard about a break-in here the day before yesterday."

Isaac said something around a mouthful of chocolate cake.

"Swallow before you speak," Priscilla said. While he did, she added, "Let me reassure you, Aunt Cordelia, there was no thief prowling through this house."

"My housekeeper was told by—"

She laughed lightly. "Gossip is often misquoted, as you have reminded me on many occasions. You need have no worries on our behalf." She jabbed at her cake with her fork, an excuse to lower her eyes so her aunt did not guess she was not being frank.

When her aunt mumbled something, then subsided, Priscilla was astonished. Aunt Cordelia must be less distressed about the rumors than the other events on Bedford Square. Before the conversation went in that direction, for she did not want to discuss the deaths again in the children's hearing, she turned the subject to events at St. Julian's. Dr. Summerson answered her questions with a smile, and she guessed he was as eager to speak of something other than crimes.

Gilbert came into the dining room with a bottle of wine for the gentlemen. He set it on the table with undue haste and made his retreat. No doubt to join the endless conversation in the kitchen about recent events. The servants must still be concocting theories about the deaths, and Priscilla vowed to speak to them as soon as possible.

"I believe this is our cue to withdraw," Priscilla said, motioning to her daughters and son.

Neville came to his feet as she did. "If you do not mind, I shall enjoy my port with you. Dr. Summerson?"

"Daphne, take Neville to the parlor."

"Yes, Mama." Her older daughter gave him a broad smile. "Neville, I have been waiting to tell you about my calls since I returned to Town."

"Aren't you coming too?" he asked, looking rather appalled at the idea of having to listen to Daphne's always long-winded descriptions of her calls to young girls who also yearned to be part of the Season.

"I will . . . later."

She was glad he understood without her having to glance at her aunt and Dr. Summerson. Or she thought he did until he followed her into the hallway as Aunt Cordelia asked Daphne about those calls. Her daughter would soon regret bringing up the topic, but Priscilla knew Daphne could deal with Aunt Cordelia as well as any of them could.

"Priscilla . . ."

She motioned toward where Leah and Isaac were waiting impatiently by the front parlor doorway. "You cannot escape listening to Daphne's tales by lingering here, Neville."

When he did nothing but nod, she saw her aunt had finished with Daphne and was walking toward Priscilla with a determined expression. Her younger children vanished into the front parlor. When Neville did the same, she let her sigh of relief ooze silently past her lips. As long as Neville was nearby, Aunt Cordelia would continue with her cutting remarks. Mayhap, if they spoke alone, Aunt Cordelia would relent. It was not likely, but Priscilla would try anything to bring peace back to her household.

When Priscilla motioned toward the rear parlor, Aunt Cordelia strode in that direction with an aura of purpose.

Dr. Summerson hesitated, then followed. A wise reverend did not chance offending one of his wealthier parishioners. Sympathy filled her at the thought.

Priscilla drew the door closed after she had entered the smaller parlor. The windows were narrower in this room, and she and the children preferred the front parlor, so there was little here to identify it as their home. The furniture was without a scuff left by Isaac's feet that always swung when he was trying to sit still. None of Leah's books were scattered about the room, although a hair ribbon, most likely Daphne's, drooped like a dying plant from the mantel.

Dr. Summerson had paused to look at a painting that showed the water garden at Emberson Park, the family's ancestral home. Aunt Cordelia was perched in the very middle of the white settee and was wearing the frown that needed no words to convey that she was distressed with Priscilla. Neville being a guest tonight was enough to send her aunt up the boughs, but Priscilla knew Aunt Cordelia was here to discuss Cecil Burtrum's mysterious death.

As she sat facing her aunt, Priscilla said, "I am glad you called, Aunt Cordelia." That was the truth despite how vexing her aunt could be. "It must mean your house is now in proper order."

"I wish you could say the same about yours."

"Within these walls, everything is as it should be. The trouble on Bedford Square has not invaded here."

"What do you intend to do, Priscilla? You cannot be thinking to remain here on Bedford Square when these tragedies are piling one atop the other."

She glanced at the curate, then back at her aunt. "I have been giving a great deal of thought about what I will do."

"Why does it require a great deal of thought?" Aunt Cordelia asked in her stern voice. Priscilla envied her aunt her inability to see any shades of gray. It would, Priscilla had decided, make life much easier for her, although far more difficult for those around her. "The answer is simple. You and the children must return to Stonehall-on-Sea. Without delay!"

"It is something, as I said, I have been thinking about."

"So why do you remain here?"

"It has been less than a week since we arrived, and only days since Cecil Burtrum's unexpected death."

Aunt Cordelia wagged a finger at her. "Unexpected? How can you be so shortsighted, Priscilla? One death is unexpected, two seem like a coincidence . . . but four? You must be thinking of our family's future. If something happened to Isaac—"

"Aunt Cordelia, I am equally concerned about my daughters' safety."

"I was not suggesting otherwise." She puffed up like a frog about to croak.

"I know. I know." She glanced at Dr. Summerson, and this time he came to sit in a chair at the end of the low table between her and her aunt. "We are all alarmed."

"That is true," Dr. Summerson said. "Everyone in the parish is upset over these events. Although this series of deaths has been focused on Bedford Square, who knows when it might explode somewhere else?"

Priscilla shivered. "I would rather not think of that."

"As I do not," said Neville while he crossed the room. He must have opened the door between the two parlors as silently as he was walking toward them. "There are enough suspects in the houses on this square. We do not need to compound the number by having a suspicious death on another street or square."

"You believe someone *here* has murdered those poor people?" Aunt Cordelia shook her head. "I will not believe that."

"Why? Because no one in the Polite World would do something so utterly impolite?" Putting his hands on the back of the settee where Priscilla sat, he chuckled coldly. "I can assure you, Lady Cordelia, that criminal thoughts do not rest solely in the hearts of the poor. I stand here as proof of that."

"Sir Neville, this is no time for your hoaxing." Aunt Cordelia stood, and Dr. Summerson leaped to his feet. "Think, Priscilla, about what I have said." She scowled at Neville. "Do not let others influence you as you have in the past."

Priscilla rose and gave her aunt a dutiful kiss on the cheek. Her aunt seemed happy with the promise that Priscilla and the children would call before— She glanced guiltily at Neville, for it was odd to feel uncomfortable about saying something in his company. She was unsure about her plans. Aunt Cordelia would be pleased to have Priscilla and the children return to Stonehall-on-Sea. Yet to go with this puzzle unsolved . . .

When her aunt and the curate bid them a good evening, silence filled the back parlor, broken only by the sound of the door to the street opening and closing.

"She believed you when you assured her that she was worrying needlessly about the theft here," Neville said quietly.

She sighed. "Lying to my aunt is not something I wish to make a habit."

"If you had been honest, even when your household suffered no more than a broken window and some missing foodstuffs, she would have become as hysterical as Lady Eleanor."

"I know." Sitting, she shook her head. "There is no way the broken window could be related to these deaths. Such things have happened before when there was a gathering on the square. A thief takes advantage of a house being quiet to practice his trade."

"Agreed. You would be wise to have your servants be very visible while you attend the funeral." He hesitated, then asked, "You are attending, aren't you? Or will you heed your aunt and leave posthaste?"

"Were you eavesdropping?"

"Of course." He chuckled. "Did you think I would leave you to that old tough without some line of defense?"

She tried to smile, but it was impossible. "I am staying to attend the funeral."

"And after that?"

"I don't know."

Priscilla doubted she had ever been to such a bizarre funeral service as the one for Cecil Burtrum. It was not being held at St. Julian's Church not far from the square. She had not expected the footman opening the Burtrums' door to redirect her and Neville to Lord Cagswell's house on the east side of the square. Neville just shrugged and walked with her along the square. At Lord Cagswell's house, which was twice the size of most on the square, they were ushered in to join the crowd of mourners.

"All of the people here are from Bedford Square," Priscilla said softly after she left her black cloak with a maid.

"Burtrum the Younger was not a member of any club, and he had not been in Town long."

"It appears you have been checking."

"The few questions I asked gained me few answers, because he seems to have been focused, as Peel said, on his wine, his snuff, and whatever woman he intended to seduce."

"How sad."

He nodded. "A sad life coming to a sad end."

Priscilla had to agree. Going into the crowded parlor, she said nothing as Neville went to speak with a man she knew only by sight. She guessed Neville would take advantage of this gathering to ask more questions.

"Lady Priscilla, thank you for coming." Malcolm Drake rushed to her and grasped her hand. "I had heard how Cecil was less than polite to you when you first called, and I wondered if you would attend."

"I forgave him, as I told him at the party that evening. Mr. Drake, I am perplexed about why the funeral service is being held here."

"Poor Lord Burtrum cannot bear to open his house to anyone." He sighed.

"Then why isn't the service at St. Julian's?"

"I know it seems odd, but Eleanor is insistent that we obey her father's wishes in this matter, and he wanted the service nearby so he did not have to reveal his grief to half of London."

"She is a devoted daughter," she said, for Mr. Drake seemed most comfortable with trite answers. She was curious why Lord Burtrum would think half of London would be standing between Bedford Square and St. Julian's, which was just a few blocks away. She did not want to upset Mr. Drake further, so she simply asked, "How does Eleanor fare?"

"As well as can be expected. I am sure you understand, Lady Priscilla, for you have buried your husband not so many months ago."

"Yes, I understand, but I wished only to ascertain why she is not here."

"She cannot bear to attend the funeral, for she clings to the hope that this is all just a horrible dream."

Priscilla frowned. "Mr. Drake, allowing her to continue

to think that is not doing her a favor. She must accept the truth and say her farewells to her brother. A funeral service offers that opportunity.''

''She is very fragile, and both her father and I agreed it would be best for her to remain in seclusion today.''

''Are his concerns for Eleanor why Lord Burtrum is not yet here?''

Now Mr. Drake scowled. ''Whatever are you speaking of, Lady Priscilla? Lord Burtrum is right over there.'' He pointed toward where the coffin was set in front of the hearth.

She glanced in the direction he pointed. Tears sprang into her eyes as she saw the earl draped over his son's body. He must be bidding his son a private farewell. She could recall too easily the grief and impotency of burying a loved one.

An arm around her shoulders gave them a tender squeeze. She did not have to look to know the arm belonged to Neville. He understood how attending this funeral service brought back memories . . . for both of them. Lazarus had been Neville's best friend, and the two men had welcomed her into that friendship, a gift for which she would always be grateful. Her husband had teased that she might have a civilizing effect on Neville and find him the proper bride so he would settle down and act as a baronet should. That she had failed on the former and not even attempted the latter had brought much laughter for the three of them to share.

''We should find a seat,'' Neville said so quietly she doubted Mr. Drake could hear him.

''Yes.'' She let him steer her toward the back row of the chairs arranged in Lord Cagswell's elegant parlor. She knew he wanted to be able to watch the mourners and gauge every motion they made. Although she doubted there would be any clue to the deaths during the funeral, she went along.

Priscilla selected a seat and composed her face into what she hoped looked like serenity. Every muscle was as stiff as ice.

When Neville sat beside her, he made no effort to look tranquil. His gaze followed every person who selected a seat, and she knew he was noting which mourners sat together and which were avoiding each other.

"They are dividing up exactly as they always do," she whispered. "Mrs. Lennon would never consider sitting near Miss Walters, and Lord Cagswell has yet to forgive Sir Stephen for beating him at a very-high-stakes game three years ago."

"Memories are long on Bedford Square."

"So it seems, even though everyone appears to want to forget what they were doing just before we discovered Cecil Burtrum was dead."

"Wise of them."

"Yes, but . . ." She looked around the room and realized that Lord Burtrum seemed to have vanished again.

She was about to mention it to Neville, but saw the earl hurry into the parlor and take his seat. At the front of the room, Dr. Summerson, resplendent in black robes, stood between the pair of long windows edged with pure white draperies. Beside him, a young boy rang a handbell three times, then three times more. There was a pause, and he gave it a final trio of chimes.

Priscilla pondered what else could be bizarre about this service. Not only was it being held in a neighbor's house in lieu of the deceased's home or the church, but the boy was ringing a handbell instead of the church's bells tolling the dead. Only the sprigs of rosemary set in a vase in front of the casket seemed familiar. She doubted if she would need rosemary to help her remember *this* funeral.

Her eyes widened when she saw Lord Burtrum's chair

was empty. She wondered where he had gone when his son's funeral service was about to begin. Tilting toward Neville to ask him what he thought of the earl's odd actions, she paused when Lord Burtrum slipped back into his seat. The man seemed as unable to sit still as her son.

She listened when Dr. Summerson began to read the service. She wondered how he had been assigned to St. Julian's when he seemed to have no gift for oratory. Each word was said with the same intonation as the previous one. He did not pause even to allow the mourners to participate in the service, continuing in the same monotone, forcing them to jump in where they could.

Priscilla shifted on her chair to see better. Again Lord Burtrum's chair was empty. In a hushed whisper, she asked, "Where is he *now*?"

"Who?" Neville replied as softly.

"Haven't you noticed how Lord Burtrum is here and gone and then back again after a few minutes?" She frowned, tapping her chin. "Do you think he is fortifying himself for the rest of the service?"

"He wouldn't be the first. Under other circumstances, I would guess he was sneaking off for an assignation."

"Neville!"

He wagged a finger at her. "Don't tell me that such an idea did not flash into your mind."

"Yes, but—"

"So do not play the priggish matron with me. If we are ever to gather together the pieces to solve this puzzle, you must be honest with me. Totally honest."

"And you shall be the same with me?"

He gave her his most rakish grin. "You hurt me by asking such a question."

"Hurt you? How?"

"By forcing me to lie to you, Pris."

She swallowed her laugh and almost choked on it. The mourners around them stared at her, clearly appalled she had found anything humorous during a funeral. Confound Neville! He somehow always appeared the pattern-card of propriety while making those with him fall prey to his tarnished manners.

Raising her chin and clamping her lips closed, she listened to Dr. Summerson bring the service to an end. She would have to apologize to Lord Burtrum and the curate, although she did not know what she could say without revealing the truth. Bother! This was a ticklish situation Neville had gotten her into, and he no doubt would enjoy every moment of it.

As he stood, Neville said, "The service's ending was far less dramatic than the dearly departed's."

"Really, Neville, can't you control your comments for just a moment?"

"I don't know. I never have tried."

Scowling at him, she retorted, "Why don't you try now?"

"Pris, what is bothering you so much that you don't like a little teasing?"

"I am at a funeral, for one thing."

His broad hand cupped her chin. "I know. Let's get out of here."

She wanted to agree . . . with anything he said when he touched her with such gentleness. Every fiber within her begged her to remain silent as she gazed up into his dark brown eyes and savored his rough fingers stroking her cheek. Every fiber but one, and that one noted Lord Burtrum slipping out of the room again.

Stepping away, she said, "After I pay my respects to Lord Burtrum."

If Neville replied, she did not hear him as she edged through the crowd. She *did* hear the comments in her wake, comments about rudeness and actions unbefitting a parson's widow. She ignored them and went out into the hallway.

A quick look told her the earl was not on this floor, so she went up the stairs. Invading Lord Cagswell's private rooms was something she did not want to do, but she needed to satisfy her curiosity about where Lord Burtrum was disappearing to and why.

She walked along the upper hallway. It was dusky because the draperies on the front windows were drawn. There was enough light to see that Lord Cagswell's housekeeper was not as attentive as Mrs. Moore. Several of the tables must have had small articles set on them, because squares and circles were clean among the dust. Mayhap the servants had been so busy getting the lower floor ready for the funeral that they had neglected this one. With the dirty, sooty air in London, even a day or two without dusting could leave such a coating. That the tables were being cleared probably meant the maids intended to clean before Lord Cagswell noticed.

Telling herself not to dawdle, she did not pause to admire the paintings on the walls or a sculpture of two young lovers entwined in an embrace that was set in the middle of a long table. She must ascertain where Lord Burtrum was, if he was even on this floor, and return downstairs before someone found her up here.

A form burst out of the murky shadows, and Priscilla almost screamed. She gave a shaky laugh when her gaze met Lord Burtrum's wide eyes.

If he had been drinking, he showed no signs of intoxication. She could have excused that if he were a man who could drink and drink and still appear sober. He was not, for he had been quite obviously foxed at the gathering at his house.

"Are you following me, Lady Priscilla?" he asked sharply.

"Yes."

Her answer startled him, because he stammered, "Y-y-yes? You own that you—that you were following me?"

"I fear I have lost my bearings within the house." She lowered her eyes as she had while being false with her aunt. She hoped she looked chagrined rather than trying to avoid letting him discover she was not being honest. "Lord Cagswell's house is far larger than mine, and I am embarrassed to say I have been unable to find my way back to the parlor. I had expected by trailing after you that I could return without anyone being the wiser to my misadventure."

Priscilla hoped he would believe her, although she wondered why he would. Even though this house was bigger than most on the square, the first floor was arranged in the same simple pattern with two large reception rooms and a room behind the stairwell.

He offered his arm. "Allow me to assist you, Lady Priscilla."

"Thank you," she said as she put her hand on it.

As if they had met under the most commonplace circumstances, Lord Burtrum led her toward the staircase. He kept more than a proper distance between them, and she had to take care not to brush one of the tables. He spoke about the paintings they passed, admiring their neighbor's selection.

"You have a great appreciation for and knowledge of art, Lord Burtrum," she said.

"It is a hobby of mine that brings me pleasure."

"I saw the splendid paintings in your house. I don't know when I have encountered such a marvelous array of recent paintings. You have obviously begun your collecting in the past few months."

He smiled coolly. "You might as well come out and ask your question."

"Excuse me?"

"You are wondering how I came upon the funds to purchase so many contemporary artworks."

"Lord Burtrum, I would never presume to inquire into your financial situation."

His face crumbled as he hurried to say, "Forgive me. I am afraid I am not myself at the moment."

Although she was tempted to say that he seemed more like himself now than he had been since his son's body was discovered, she would not be so coldhearted. "That is understandable. Ah, here we are at the stairs. Thank you for your assistance."

"You are welcome."

When he did not move, she hurried toward the first floor. She glanced up the steps, but he was no longer visible. He must have gone back to whatever he had been doing when she met him.

Priscilla went into the parlor and saw that many of the guests had already taken their leave. Were they bound for St. Julian's churchyard ahead of the body? That made no sense, but little had today.

"Where did you take yourself?" asked Neville as he came to her side. He settled her cloak on her shoulders. "Dr. Summerson is eager to be finished with the burial service."

"I told you. I wanted to pay my respects to Lord Burtrum."

"Then do so."

"But he is not here. He—"

"Not here? Pris, he is by his son's coffin."

She looked to where Lord Burtrum was once again leaning over the casket to give his son a final embrace. The idea of touching such cold, lifeless flesh cramped her stomach with disgust. "He was not there a moment ago."

"No?"

"I saw him upstairs."

"Odd."

"Yes. His grief at his son's death is genuine, but his other actions and reactions are so peculiar, I cannot imagine what he is thinking."

"I would rather not consider what he is thinking. A journey through Burtrum's mind is not one I wish to embark upon. The African interior would be more inviting."

"Mayhap that he is grief-stricken is the only explanation we need."

" 'Tis the only one *I* need, for I am eager to be done with this whole situation."

She regarded him with astonishment. "Neville, it is not like you to hide like a hedgehog from any gathering."

"Most situations do not include the death of four healthy people."

Lord Burtrum straightened and motioned for the lid to be lowered on his son's coffin. He did not look at anyone as he walked out of the room to lead the way to St. Julian's churchyard and the interment.

It was beginning to rain when Priscilla walked down the front steps. She was startled to see Layden running at an uncommon speed toward them. The footman's face was long with fear.

Neville did not give him a chance to speak where the other mourners might hear. Taking Layden by the arm, he drew the footman toward the garden in the center of the square.

She hurried after them. Even without being able to discern their words, she could tell whatever Layden was saying to Neville was dreadful.

"Tell me," she ordered when she caught up with them. Neville put his hand on her arm, and she let him pull her closer. She wondered what he believed she needed protection from, and she feared she already knew.

Layden stared at his toes. "It has happened again, my lady."

She did not want to ask, but she had to. "Another death?"

"Yes."

"Who?"

"No one from the square. The lad was found dead in Gower Mews behind the houses across the square from the house. Just like the others. Dead with no sign why."

Chapter Six

Neville walked around the body stretched across the road. It was covered with a wet and dirty blanket brought by two members of the Horse Patrol. They were discussing whether they recognized the young man and which crimes he might have committed.

When his name was called, Neville waved to the man walking toward him.

"Thurmond, what are you doing here?"

The man with the red vest that identified him as being employed by Bow Street looked down at the draped body. "I had gone to your house and was told you were calling on Bedford Square. When I asked an elderly woman—a Mrs. Lennon, I believe—I saw walking on the square where I might find you, she sent me here." He raised his eyes. "I can see why."

"This death has been reported around the square as another like the previous ones." He bent and drew back the blanket to reveal the battered body. "However, you can see he was struck by a carriage driving at a high speed."

"Last night or early this morning, I would guess."

Neville nodded. "I agree, because, if the lad had been seen, there would have been some sign of the carriage trying to slow."

"A tragedy, but a relief nonetheless."

"Yes." He tossed the blanket back over the body. Dirt and bits of leaves rose into the air before settling on the road again. "I have to own to being glad there is an obvious reason for this death."

"Unlike the others?"

"There is a reason for them, Thurmond, albeit not as obvious. All we need to do is figure it out."

"It may be more complex than you think."

"I am already thinking it is very convoluted."

Thurmond's eyes drilled him. "Have you given thought to the idea there may be more than one murderer at work on the square?"

"Yes, but not seriously." He frowned. Why hadn't he given that idea some credence when it had first popped into his mind after they found Cecil Burtrum dead?

"Then it may be time for you to give it some serious thought, Hathaway. Very serious indeed."

Neville entered the sitting room of Priscilla's private chambers, and Priscilla turned from the window to face him. With her hair pulled back with a ribbon at her nape and dressed in a simple wrapper that glowed in the moonlight sifting through the fog, she looked not much older than Daphne.

"I thought you had left for Berkeley Square," she said.

"I wanted to speak to Gilbert about having the servants

refrain from setting your household on edge by repeating rumors.''

''If you can halt them, that will be a miracle.'' She rubbed her hands together. ''But thank you, Neville.''

''You are welcome.'' He hated when they spoke like this. They were not polite strangers. Plunging ahead to break through the barrier so he could speak with her as he must, he said, ''I saw Isaac on his way to his room, and then I noted the light under your door.''

''So you decided to pay me a call here. That is outrageous, even for you.''

''I wanted to find out if you were having trouble sleeping too.''

''Yes.''

''And not just from the excitement of your dear aunt's most recent visit?''

She smiled as she perched on the end of her chaise longue and motioned for him to sit by the window. Her expression told him that he had succeeded in persuading her to lower that wall he had never seen before her return to Bedford Square. ''Aunt Cordelia can set off all sorts of alarms in my head, but 'tis not my aunt who is keeping me awake tonight.'' She laughed softly. ''Not just my aunt, I should say.''

He sat, glad the chair was not the delicate one by her desk. Leaning forward, he said, ''Dr. Summerson seemed very eager not to speak of the latest deaths on the square when I talked to him after the thief's body was delivered to St. Julian's. Not the proper attitude for a parson to have when his flock is in need of help.''

''He does not appear to be the type of churchman who considers himself a shepherd.''

''True. He thinks more of his own comfort than that of his parishioners.''

"You are judging him quickly." She laughed again. "Unless, of course, you have gone often to St. Julian's to observe him."

"You know how unlikely that is."

"Yes, because the roof was still atop the church when I passed by."

He chuckled, then grew serious. Leaning forward, he clasped her hands between his. "Pris, I have given the whole of this a great deal of thought."

"As I have."

"Don't interrupt me."

"I thought you were done."

"No, I have something very important to say."

Priscilla looked from Neville's stern expression to his hands that enveloped hers. They were weathered hands, for the years of the hard life he had before he became a baronet had left their imprint on him in many different ways. They were hands that were unafraid to strike out to protect him and those he cared about. They were hands perfect for cradling hers.

"What is it?" she whispered, uncertain with him as she never had been. Or was it that she was uncertain about herself and the effect his touch had on her?

He released her hands and, standing, curled one finger under her chin. Tipping her head up, he said, "I think you should take the children and leave Bedford Square as soon as you can."

"*You* think we should leave?"

"It might not be a bad idea. Stonehall-on-Sea should be very quiet now that its excitement is past."

" 'Tis not like you to suggest I run like a beaten dog instead of finding out the truth."

He put his hands on her shoulders, and she was astonished anew at the warmth that spread outward from his fingers as she rose. She fought to keep from reaching up to touch his waistcoat. Why was it getting more and more difficult to ignore this pleasurable sensation each time he was near? It was not as if she were oblivious to the truth of his past. Or, at least, what little he had revealed.

She knew many people could not understand why a vicar and his wife had welcomed this miscreant into their home years before the Polite World had opened their doors to him and his wealth-laden title. Even now, some—Aunt Cordelia among them—believed she was allowing him to be a bad influence on her impressionable children. Those people did not perceive how he had made her children and her laugh again as they had not since Lazarus died. He wrung every possible passion out of life and challenged them to do the same.

"What is it, Neville?" she asked again when he did not answer. "It isn't like you to agree with Aunt Cordelia."

"I do when she is right." He moved away.

She again had to fight her hands to keep them from reaching out to bring his arms around her. She must be far more tired and unsettled than she wanted to own even to herself. Otherwise, she would be concentrating on this conversation that she had not anticipated she would have with him.

"You believe Aunt Cordelia is right about us leaving here?" she asked. "What is disconcerting you so much that you want to banish us from Town posthaste?"

"The fact that we may have more than one murderer prowling through Bedford Square." He put his foot on the stool and peered out the window behind her. "I spoke with Thurmond from Bow Street during the investigation of that young thief's death. According to him, it seems highly unlikely that the person who put out Cecil Burtrum's lights also killed the servants."

"I have pondered that idea myself."

"I suspected you had. Little gets past your quick mind, Pris."

She smiled and patted his arm. "Save your compliments."

"But I like complimenting you. It makes your cheeks glow as pink as young Daphne's."

"But this is not the time for such fancies."

He nodded, again somber. "As always, you focus on the crux of the situation."

"I have been trying to." That was the truth, but she must not own that Neville was the reason she was having trouble concentrating on anything else.

"Pris, it is not cowardice to leave and take the children to someplace safer."

"So why does it feel that way?" She leaned her elbow on the back of the chaise longue and propped her chin on her hand. "Neville, would you leave?"

"Me? You know I revel in trouble."

"That much I have known for a very long time."

"A very, very, very long time."

She groaned. "If you are reminding me of Mr. Wayland's irritating comments in an effort to give me another reason to leave, please don't."

"I am sorry, Pris."

"Your apology would carry more weight if you were not grinning like a widgeon." Standing, she went to the bell in the corner. She rang it, then returned to sit on the chaise longue.

She had thought Neville would say something, either out of curiosity about why she was sending for a servant or gloating that she was at last doing something he wished. He remained as silent as the fog-obscured garden in the center of the square.

A knock came on the door quickly, and she guessed the servants were as restless as she and Isaac were. When she called for whoever stood in the corridor to enter, Mrs. Moore opened the door. The housekeeper's eyes widened for only a moment when she noted Neville in the room, then her face was once again placid.

"Mrs. Moore," Priscilla said, "please have the household prepare to return to Stonehall-on-Sea."

The housekeeper smiled broadly. "Of course, my lady. I know I speak for everyone when I say that we will be most pleased to leave Bedford Square." She turned to Neville. "If you have persuaded Lady Priscilla to take this course of action, Sir Neville, I thank you deeply." A flush coursed up her face, and she hurried to the door.

"A moment more, Mrs. Moore," Neville said.

She turned with obvious reluctance.

"What is being said belowstairs in other houses?" he asked.

Mrs. Moore glanced at Priscilla, then answered, "You talked to Gilbert."

"About not spreading unsubstantiated rumors among the servants. He was reluctant to tell me what the mood is in other houses." He smiled tightly. "Probably because he did not appreciate me giving him a dressing-down."

"They are saying there is a devil loose in Bedford Square. A devil who stalks his prey and strikes without anyone but the poor victim seeing him."

"That is true."

"Neville!" gasped Priscilla, setting herself on her feet. "Please do not frighten my household more than they are already frightened."

"I doubt if I can."

"Tea for three," Priscilla said to Mrs. Moore over the sobbing from the front parlor.

"Yes, my lady. Loud, isn't she?"

Priscilla glanced toward the parlor that was half hidden behind crates filled with what they were taking with them back to Stonehall-on-Sea. The past three days had been spent supervising this move she did not want to make. Her daughters were torn between relief and disappointment at the plans to leave.

This was not the time to think of that. She must focus on her guests. Eleanor had wept nonstop since she and her fiancé had arrived just as Priscilla was about to have tea with her daughters, while Isaac polished some pots as punishment for hiding Leah's favorite doll. Her son was not happy about leaving when the murderer had not been captured. Neither Eleanor nor Mr. Drake had wished to tell her what was amiss, asking instead to speak with her privately in the front parlor.

"Mayhap you should bring Madeira, Mrs. Moore. Mr. Drake may have need for something more bracing than tea." She gave her housekeeper a wry smile. "Or I may."

"Yes, Lady Priscilla." The gaunt housekeeper hurried away, her skirts wagging like a lizard's tail.

Priscilla kept that thought to herself. No need to insult Mrs. Moore with the rather fanciful observation. Everyone was too upset to find anything amusing.

Going into the parlor that was bright with sunshine and filled with the clatter of passing traffic, she was glad her callers had their heads bent together. Mayhap Mr. Drake could console Eleanor enough so her tears would dry and she would be able to share what was upsetting them.

Eleanor, as always, was the pattern-card of elegance from the high, beribboned bodice of her black silk gown to the straw bonnet tied beneath her chin with a ribbon that was a paler pink than her teary eyes. She looked every inch the daughter of an earl. Perfect ebony curls peeked from under her bonnet as she dabbed her eyes with a linen handkerchief. Her own lace-edged one lay, quite damp, in her lap.

Mr. Drake stared at her as if he feared he would forget what she looked like. He came to his feet when Priscilla entered the room. He wore a strained smile. When she motioned for him to sit, he waited until she had chosen her favorite rosewood chair. It faced the settee and offered her an excellent view of both her guests.

"I do appreciate your receiving us uninvited," Mr. Drake said, handing Eleanor another handkerchief. She dropped the sodden one atop the other in her lap.

Priscilla was curious how many handkerchiefs Mr. Drake had hidden beneath his coat, but replied, "I am always at home to friends."

"Thank you," breathed Mr. Drake, clearly relieved Eleanor's sobs had eased to a hiccuping whimper. "We are quite desperate."

"Desperate?" She gripped the arms of her chair when she heard the hysteria in his voice. "Why?"

"You must help us find him!" Eleanor jumped to her feet, shocking Priscilla. "It is unspeakably horrible. I cannot bear it a moment longer."

"Find whom?"

"It is beyond words! Who could do such a dreadful thing? They must be beneath reproach. Oh, my stars! You must help us find him, Lady Priscilla. You must!" She dropped back to the settee and hid her face on Mr. Drake's shoulder.

"Find whom?" she repeated, aiming her question at Mr. Drake, for it was clear Eleanor was in no state to answer even the simplest query.

The lanky man reached out a long arm and put it around Eleanor's quivering shoulders. "You must understand that this has been most unsettling for my dear Eleanor."

"I would be more than pleased to understand, Mr. Drake,

if you would be so kind as to explain to me whom you seek."

"My brother!" choked Eleanor as she shrugged off Mr. Drake's arm.

Priscilla stared at her, too astonished to speak. When she finally found her tongue, the arrival of the tea halted her next question. As Priscilla poured, Eleanor began to sob anew. Mr. Drake was glancing at the bottle of Madeira with the eagerness of a man who needed something to bolster him for battles yet to come. Setting a teacup in front of Eleanor, Priscilla served Mr. Drake a generous portion of the wine.

"Thank you," he murmured, gulping half of it down.

"You are welcome." She picked up her own cup and stirred it. Setting her spoon on the saucer, she said, "I am afraid I do not understand what you mean when you say your brother is missing."

Eleanor wiped the handkerchief along her cheek and sniffed rather ungraciously. Her weeping grew even louder than the rattle of wagon wheels in front of the house. What could be causing Eleanor to act so? Priscilla recalled Mr. Drake's words at the funeral. Eleanor had not attended because she did not want to own her brother was dead. Had she convinced herself to believe her brother was missing?

Priscilla placed her cup on the tray as Mr. Drake swallowed the rest of the Madeira. Immediately, she refilled his glass.

He leaned toward Priscilla and said in a whisper, although the only other one in the room was his fiancée, "We discovered this afternoon that Cecil's body is no longer in St. Julian's churchyard."

"Not there? Are you sure you looked in the right place?"

"Very sure, Lady Priscilla."

"But how can it not be there?" She swallowed the bile in her throat. "Could the body have been stolen?"

"Stolen?" he asked in astonishment. "Who would want a corpse?"

Regaining her equilibrium, she replied, "You would be surprised how many folks might. I can think of several situations worthy of investigation." She smiled gently and patted Eleanor's hand. "Please do not think I am dishonoring your brother's memory if I ask some questions."

Eleanor managed no more than a sniff, but Priscilla accepted that as an agreement to go on.

"Did your brother have any enemies who might want to desecrate his grave?" Priscilla asked.

Mr. Drake put his hand on his fiancée's arm when she swayed, but Priscilla thought he would be wiser to reach for his wine to bring some color to his pale face. "I cannot contemplate a single person known to us who would do such a heinous thing."

"Good. Can you, Eleanor, imagine a friend of either your brother's or your father's who might wish to play a prank on your family?"

Again Mr. Drake answered. "Such a person would no longer be a friend."

"True." She had never noticed his gift for spouting the obvious, mayhap because he seldom spoke when Eleanor was about. "There is also the possibility someone stole the body to obtain ransom for its return."

Eleanor's eyes widened. "How atrocious!"

Mr. Drake shook his head. "Anyone who knows the family well would know Lord Burtrum does not have the money to—"

"Lady Priscilla does not need to know everything about my family's private interests!" Eleanor gasped.

"I am afraid I do if you wish my help," Priscilla corrected her quietly.

"And Sir Neville's?" Eleanor asked.

"He is whom you should have contacted as soon as you spoke with authorities." She watched them exchange guarded looks. "You have contacted the watch or the Horse Patrol, haven't you?"

"For what purpose? They have done nothing to halt the deaths on Bedford Square." Her eyes snapped with fury. "The only matter they have brought to a close was the death of that thief!"

"Then you should have spoken with Neville without delay."

"I know, but . . ." Again Eleanor looked at Mr. Drake.

Priscilla did not intend to waste time learning why Eleanor was reluctant to seek Neville's assistance herself. Rather, she said, "If there is even a single aspect of your lives that might give a clue as to why Cecil's final rest has been disturbed, I will need to know it to share with Neville. That may enable us to figure out what has happened."

"I know what has happened!" Eleanor's voice grew shrill. "My brother's body is missing."

"Please calm yourself, Eleanor. How do you expect me to help when you are shouting?"

Eleanor gripped Mr. Drake's sleeve. "Oh, do let us leave, Malcolm. I cannot bear to be treated like this. *I* have done nothing wrong."

"Of course not, my dear, dear Eleanor," he crooned. He looked at Priscilla. "Oh, do tell us there is another alternative to the loathsome scenarios you have outlined."

"There is, but I fear you will like it no better than the others I have posed. That is why I have left it to the last." She watched both of them closely. It was an idea she did not want to give voice to, but she could not ignore the possibility simply because it was distasteful.

"Speak of this last scenario, Lady Priscilla," urged Mr. Drake. "Speak of it, and give us hope that my dear Eleanor's dearly departed brother can soon be returned to us unharmed."

"He *is* dead, Mr. Drake. There are few things that can do him more harm." She folded her hands in her lap. "However, one of them is, unfortunately, the final alternative I have to offer to you."

Eleanor asked, "Which is?"

"The resurrectionists."

"Resurrectionists?"

"Bodysnatchers, Mr. Drake," she replied, watching him closely. Odd that he should not recognize the term. Lazarus had been furious about the resurrectionists' forays into churchyards, although there had not been any problems at St. Julian's . . . until now. "They disinter bodies in the depth of the night and sell their unsavory harvest to unscrupulous medical professors for dissection."

Eleanor gasped, put her hand to her bodice, and promptly fainted.

As Mr. Drake caught her before she could fall from the settee, he cried, "Lady Priscilla! My dear Eleanor is too delicate to hear such horrifying things."

"So I see." Priscilla rose to ring for Mrs. Moore. Bother! She disliked the smell of *sal volatile*.

Mrs. Moore rushed in and took one look. "I shall bring the smelling salts straightaway, Lady Priscilla."

Priscilla went to the settee to untie Eleanor's bonnet. Too late, she realized, for the straw had broken when the young woman collapsed. She glanced at Mr. Drake. He was so wan, she feared he would faint next. She did not relish the idea of having both of them senseless in her front parlor.

"More Madeira?" she asked.

"How can I enjoy something when my dear Eleanor—"

"You need to fortify yourself to assist her through this trying time, Mr. Drake."

"Yes, thank you." He needed little encouragement and did not wait for her to serve. He grasped the bottle and splashed what remained in his glass. Again it vanished in one gulp.

"Please bring another bottle of Madeira," Priscilla said when the housekeeper brought the small flask of smelling salts.

Eleanor was restored to her wits with a choke and a gasp. Priscilla drew back before one of the young woman's flailing arms could strike her. Letting Mr. Drake soothe Eleanor, Priscilla took the tray with more Madeira and a trio of glasses from Mrs. Moore. The housekeeper rolled her eyes as Eleanor began to weep again, and Mrs. Moore took her leave swiftly.

Priscilla filled two glasses and held them out to her guests. When neither took one, she put both on the table in front of the settee.

"Oh, Malcolm," moaned Eleanor, "do let us go."

"You cannot blame Lady Priscilla for the actions of others," he replied.

"But even to speak of them—"

He hushed her by grasping her hands and pressing them to his lips. "My dear Eleanor, you must be strong if we are to save your brother from such an appalling fate." He looked up his long nose at Priscilla. "Isn't that true?"

"You must be strong. That is most definitely true." She saw no reason to add that if Cecil Burtrum had become the victim of a resurrectionist raid on St. Julian's churchyard, his corpse was, in all likelihood, already under study in some hidden workroom.

Mr. Drake picked up a glass. "Drink this, my dear Eleanor. It may ease your despair somewhat." To Priscilla, he asked, "May I speak with you while my dear Eleanor recovers?"

"Of course." She led the way to the front of the room. Sitting on the windowseat, she said, "Say what you do not want Eleanor to hear."

"No, no, no," he corrected her hastily. He gulped, his Adam's apple bouncing like a cork on the sea. " 'Tis not that I wish to have secrets from her. I seek only to ease her despair."

"Of course," she said again.

"May I be honest with you?" he asked, shifting from one foot to the other as if standing on hot coals.

"Always telling the truth is an excellent practice."

Mr. Drake clasped and unclasped his long fingers. "As you may know, my dear Eleanor and I are to be married in two weeks. The banns were read on Sunday last at St. Julian's."

"Are you suggesting there is now a change in plans?" She did not add that she considered it in poor taste for the wedding not to have been rescheduled before now.

"My dear Eleanor cannot bring herself to be happily joined to me in matrimony when her brother may have suffered such an appalling fate."

"If you will allow me to be forthright, Mr. Drake—"

"Oh, please do."

"Cecil's present location means little to him at this point."

Color flashed on his sallow face. She could not guess if he was outraged or trying to restrain a laugh.

"I think only of my dear Eleanor's fragile constitution," he said. "The strain of this horrible situation is too much for her. I shall not expect her to add the excitement of a wedding to it, for I fear it will overmaster her."

"But?"

"But, if I may be forthright, I do not wish this wedding to be delayed." He glanced over his shoulder, but Eleanor was too busy pouring his Madeira into her glass to notice him. "It is my good fortune that my dear Eleanor accepted my suit. With her brother's death, the heir to her father's title can be my first son."

"You are, indeed, fortunate." She tapped her chin. "Let me speak with Neville and see what we might do to help."

He grasped her hand and pumped it vehemently. She withdrew it with the greatest difficulty. As he hurried to apologize, she shook her head and turned back to Eleanor, who had regained her composure as well as a pretty pink in her cheeks. Brought on, Priscilla guessed, by the Madeira.

As Eleanor rose, the young woman said, "Please give any information you and Sir Neville obtain only to me or Mr. Drake. I shall not have Father bothered by this."

"Lord Burtrum doesn't know of his son's disappearance?" She wondered if she had ever met a more peculiar family.

"No, and I wish to keep it that way. Father has enough to worry about already."

Priscilla nodded. This family was determined to protect each other, which was a good sign for their future happiness. However, it made the task of finding Cecil Burtrum's body more complex.

As soon as Eleanor and her attentive fiancé had bade farewell and taken their leave, Priscilla rang for Gilbert. While she waited for her butler, she sipped what little remained of the Madeira. She hoped Mr. Drake, in the wake of the amount of wine he had consumed, was fit to walk around the square. Eleanor was so upset, she might leave him on the walkway.

She grimaced when she saw the pile of damp handkerchiefs on the settee. She would have Mrs. Moore arrange for them to be laundered and returned to Mr. Drake.

"Lady Priscilla?"

She smiled as she heard the very correct voice of her butler.

"Do come in, Gilbert." She waited until he came into the room. "I need a message delivered posthaste."

"To the curate of St. Julian's?"

She smiled. "Are you listening at keyholes again, Gilbert?" She never had caught him at such an act, but could guess no other way he could be privy to everything that was discussed in the house.

"No, my lady. It was unnecessary when the door was open." No hint of amusement or apology filled his answer.

She withdrew a sheet of paper from the desk in the corner and scribbled a quick message. It did not have to say much. Neville would understand straightaway. Folding it, she handed the page to Gilbert. "This message is to go to Brooks's."

"To Sir Neville?"

"Yes. And, Gilbert?" she asked as he walked to the door.

"Yes, my lady?"

"Please have whoever delivers it impress on Neville that I mean every word I wrote."

He nodded.

Priscilla went to the window and stood there until she saw Juster leave the house, striding in the direction of St. James's. She hoped he would not take long.

Chapter Seven

"All right, Pris. Why did you send for me?" Neville walked through the shaft of moonlight bleaching the front parlor carpet. Reaching beneath his blue waistcoat, he pulled out a slip of paper and read:

Neville, come with all haste. Something very interesting has happened.

He chuckled. "You knew I could not resist such an oblique message."

"True, although I thought you would be here long before this." Priscilla motioned for him to help himself to some of the port she had had Gilbert bring in after she tucked the children into bed. She poured coffee for herself and took a slow sip.

"My horse pulled up lame, and I had to stop at Berkeley Square to tend to him."

"Will he be all right?"

"He looks better than you do, Pris. What is going on?"

"Late this afternoon," she said quietly, "Eleanor Burtrum and her fiancé came to ask me to help them find Eleanor's missing brother."

"Missing? How could he be missing? He was put to bed with a shovel three days ago."

"Exactly."

Neville lowered his port and grinned like a fox about to enter a yard of hens. "You are hoaxing me. Is the whole of this your way to repay me for teasing you at the funeral?"

"No, I am telling you the truth. I doubt I could make up such a tale on my own."

"This *is* most interesting," he said, his brow wrinkling in concentration. "Do you suspect this is the work of resurrectionists?"

"Certainly. Who else would be interested in absconding with a corpse?"

"Before you returned to Town, I met a chap with a traveling circus down near—"

She raised her hands. "Spare me the details about some new friend who leads an abominable life."

He chuckled. "Those friends of mine have proven helpful in the past."

"I hope they shall this time. We have but a fortnight to find Cecil Burtrum's body, or else Eleanor's wedding to Mr. Drake will have to be postponed."

"I doubt they will delay when they were going ahead with the wedding in spite of a death in the household. This marriage has its advantages for both of them. And Burtrum? What does he think of this?"

"Eleanor said he knows nothing of what has happened to Cecil's remains." She rested her elbow on the chair as she held her cup near her lips. When she saw how it trembled, she set it on the tray.

"So she wishes to keep him ignorant? Why?"

"She wishes to spare him from the truth."

"A fine daughter." Leaning back, he drew a large cheroot out of his pocket.

"Neville, you are not at Brooks's."

"By Jove, Pris, most women enjoy the scent of a fine cigar."

She smiled. "Rather, you should say they endure it in hopes that the gentleman's company will be pleasurable."

He put the cigar away under his coat. He tilted his glass to his lips, then smiled. "Excellent vintage." Without a pause, he added, "It *is* most curious that Eleanor would make such a request to keep her father from hearing that his son's body is missing, but not without precedent with that family."

"True." She sipped her coffee again, grateful for the memory of its warmth when a chill ran up her spine.

"Shall we go, Pris?"

She smiled as she looked past him to the window. Night obscured the square. "The hour seems perfect for a call on anyone who might be alive within St. Julian's churchyard."

He picked up the cloak she had draped over a chair. His grin became malevolent as he hunched and cackled. "And anyone else who might be lurking about."

A warm breeze off the Thames contorted tendrils of fog clinging to the ground as Priscilla stepped from the carriage by the gate to St. Julian's churchyard. She stared up at the steeple, which stretched far above the Corinthian columns along the front of the church. Its top was silver in the moonlight struggling to sift through the fog. In the distance, the clatter of wheels was a familiar, comforting sound, but the street in front of the churchyard was deathly silent.

Neville went to the gate on the far side of the walkway. "The churchyard is this way."

"I know."

"Sorry, Pris. I know you do." He glanced around. "I want to have this done with quickly."

"I agree. Your carriage—"

He pointed to a shadowed form by it. "Yon lad will keep it from being stolen in exchange for a tuppence or two."

"Very generous of you."

"It will buy him a pint, and that is all he cares about." He held out his arm. "Ready?"

"How can I resist such a tempting promenade?" she asked in the same ironic tone he had used. "I have long yearned for the chance to wander about a deserted churchyard after dark."

"Let's just hope it *is* deserted."

Priscilla ignored the shiver oozing down her back when, as Neville opened the iron gate, it creaked like an old man's bones. He held his other hand beneath his coat. She knew he would not come out at this hour with nothing to protect them, but she hoped he would have no need for a pistol.

The grave markers gleamed eerily in the dim light. A few low bushes clung to the wall surrounding the churchyard, and a stone structure, which she knew was a crypt, was set in the shadow of the church. A dog howled, and she flinched.

"Someone step on your grave?" Neville asked.

"Not amusing." She looked about. "I thought there would be a watchman. Resurrectionists would have been able to slip out easily with Cecil Burtrum's body."

"The watchman probably is sitting within the church's porch." He tugged on her arm. "Or sleeping there. We can— Blast it!"

"What is it?" She grasped his arm.

He grimaced. "Calm yourself. It is nothing save I stepped in something that would ruin your delicate slippers. I suggest we watch where we step."

"There is a lantern in the carriage."

"No need."

Priscilla was about to ask what he meant, then she, too, saw the light of a lamp bouncing toward them. A man as bent as the trees trying to grow in the shadow of the church edged around the gravestones.

"Who goes there?" His voice squeaked as rustily as the gate.

"Are you the watchman?" Neville asked, waving to invite the man closer.

"Aye." He did not move from where he stood behind a tall stone cross.

"What's your name?"

"Johnson."

"A conveniently common name."

"Neville," Priscilla interjected quietly, "please allow me to speak with Mr. Johnson." Bother! Neville could rankle an archangel. Couldn't he see the man was half frozen with fear? But of what?

"Go ahead," Neville said with a grumble. "I think I'll look about."

"Take care," called Mr. Johnson. "Look where ye step."

"Is there an open grave?"

"No, dogs."

Priscilla hid her smile behind her hand as Neville looked with a rueful grin from the watchman to his boots. "Do go, Neville, so I might have a cordial conversation with Mr. Johnson."

"I will, but not far. Scream if you need anything."

"And you'll come running?"

"I shall run, at any rate."

She chuckled as she lifted her cloak and skirt out of the grass and picked her way to where Mr. Johnson watched her as warily. She should have known to wear her high-lows. This damp grass—and she did not want to guess what else had been dropped in it—was sure to ruin her slippers.

"Mr. Johnson, may I speak with you?" She edged toward him as if he were a frightened pup she needed to coax closer.

" 'Bout what?"

"I am Priscilla Flanders. My late husband was assigned here at St. Julian's. I am searching for—"

"Ain't 'ere."

"What ain't—I mean, isn't here?"

"What ye be searchin' fer."

"I know that, Mr. Johnson." She gave him what she hoped was her most serene smile. He was not as old as she had guessed, although he was bent. Wisps of dark hair fell into his face, and his clothes stank. "I have not come to accuse you of anything."

"The m'lord there"—he glanced at where Neville was squatting between the stones—" 'e thinks I done wrong."

"No, that's just his way. May I?" She pointed to a stone bench.

"Aye." He pulled a cloth from a pocket somewhere in his tattered breeches. When he wiped the bench, Priscilla suspected the filthy cloth was putting more dirt on the seat than it removed. "Make yerself comfy, m'lady."

She sat and folded her hands over the reticule in her lap. "Mr. Johnson, I am in dire need of information, and I believe you may be just the man to help me."

"If I can, m'lady."

"Do you work here every night?"

"Only three out of each seven. My brother-in-law 'as the other nights."

"Have you seen any people coming into the churchyard after dark? Other than the gentleman and myself, I mean."

"Lor', don't be askin' 'bout that, m'lady." He crouched even lower.

"Then you have seen someone?"

He shuffled his feet and stared at the ground. "Aye."

"Bodysnatchers?"

"'Ow—?" He gulped. "Worse thing I ever seen, m'lady." He waved his hands as if spirits were floating around his matted hair. "Dark beasts they be. Climbed right into the grave just as easy as ye please. Shoveled out the dirt and went 'bout their business."

"Can you describe them?"

"Describe them?" He shuddered. "Low creatures. Wore nothin' but rags and dirt."

"That would describe a good portion of the people in London. What about their faces? Did you see anything to—"

"Didn't see nothin', m'lady. Don't want to see nothin'. Bad sort they be. Wouldn't doubt they would've put me in that grave and closed it up if I'd come closer."

"Mr. Johnson, if you see them return, would you please send word as soon as possible to me at Bedford Square?"

"If Dr. Summerson finds out I done that, 'e—"

Her forehead wrinkled in bafflement. "I would think any of the churchmen here would be eager to put a stop to such sacrilege."

"Scared they be too."

"Of the resurrectionists?"

"Aye." He nodded so fervently, she feared his head would bounce off his shoulders. "Said to stay far from 'em. Just wants to keep it quiet, 'e does."

"It shan't stay quiet if more bodies are stolen. The families shall be in an uproar and demand answers."

"Let the families ask all they want. Won't do nothin' to

stop them sackers. They take wot they want and ain't nary a soul livin' 'oo can stop 'em.'' He seized her hand, shocking her at his boldness. She forgot that as he added, ''Do ye understand, m'lady? Nary a soul livin' can stop 'em, 'cause they'll kill anyone who gets in their way.''

Neville swore under his breath, then aloud. He was unsure what he had expected to discover here, but it certainly was not *this*.

''Neville?''

He stood as Priscilla emerged from the shadow cast by a tastelessly ostentatious gravestone. In the years he had known her, she never had failed to surprise him with her courage and kindness. Mayhap that was why they were such good friends—opposites attracting and all that silliness.

''Over here,'' he called back. ''Watch for the third stone from where you are. It wobbles. Nearly tipped me into more of this blasted dog—onto the ground.''

Her low laugh reached him. ''You need not curb your language for me. I have heard far worse, I am sure.''

''I'm not.''

Again she laughed as she came to where he stood. He discerned, now that she was closer, a honed edge to the sound. Priscilla had discovered something unsettling. She would tell him when she deemed the time right or necessary.

''What did you find?'' she asked.

''Wagon tracks, boot prints, and the hoofprints from a single horse.'' He tipped his low-brimmed hat back on his head. ''Odd thing, Pris. The horse and the wagon did not seem connected in any way. I would guess our resurrectionists were pulling the wagon to keep from garnering attention in the middle of the night.''

''Without a horse, they would be dismissed as common

peddlers." She shivered. "Pity the poor soul who thinks to peek into the wagon and see what they have to sell."

"And our friend Johnson? What did you unearth with him?"

"Really, Neville, this is no time for your ghastly sense of humor."

"On the contrary, everything about this is ghastly. Why should my questions be any different?"

"Our friend Mr. Johnson is scared nigh to death. If he knows anything—which I most sincerely doubt—he will not share it, for fear the resurrectionists will repay him by making sure he is put under the earth and stays there."

He shook his head. "No, they would slit his throat and sell his corpse for a pound or two."

"I suggest you keep that fact to yourself. To know that would make him even less willing to talk."

"He knows that when the churchyards are guarded too closely or the graves are made untouchable by some odd contraption, the resurrectionists turn to murder to gain their product for the surgeon-anatomists."

She put her hand on the low wall. "You speak with the authority of one who knows much about these despicable vultures."

He opened the gate. "Don't ask what you don't want to know, Pris." Closing the gate behind her, he asked, "Where next?"

"The obvious person would be Dr. Summerson or one of the others here at the church."

"You think Dr. Summerson will be more willing to risk his corporeal being to reveal the truth?"

"Would he risk his immortal soul with a lie?"

"Possibly."

"Neville, you are growing even more cynical."

He glanced down at the ruined shine on his boots. "It

comes from being dragged away from a winning hand to trudge through a churchyard in search of something long gone."

She hooked her arm through his. "Do not be petulant. Come. Let's see what the curate can tell us. With a bit of the good fortune you have been boasting about, we may have the answer before the bell tolls midnight."

The door to the curate's office was near the end of a narrow hallway. A pair of lanterns offered no more light than Mr. Johnson's had in the churchyard, for every bit of the glow was dampened by the wood on the walls and floor.

Neville arched a single brow when they stopped in front of the door that was marked with large gold letters: *Dr. Henry Summerson, Curate*. "One would wonder what glorious trinkets his superiors have decorating their offices, if a mere curate may aspire to this."

"Please do not estrange the man before I have the chance to ask a single question," Priscilla returned, straightening her shawl.

"I vow I shall have manners as fine as anyone at court."

"Better, I trust."

He knocked on the door. A mumbled answer came from behind it. "I shall assume that was a request for us to come in."

Priscilla did not share his optimism when he pushed open the door and motioned for her to enter. The chamber, which was not much larger than a cloakroom, was buried in a blizzard of papers that stuck to every surface and rose in piles like albino stalagmites. Bookcases against the wall on both sides of the single window spewed more sheets to drip to the floor. Only a small square of floor was visible in front of what might be a table or a desk. She did not bother to discern which as she looked at the man rising from a chair behind it.

Dr. Summerson had a single page attached to his elbow from where it had been resting on his desk. His pate glistened in the light, and he was hastily rebuttoning his waistcoat. As blindly as a mole, he squinted at them.

"Do we have an appointment this evening?" he asked. He bent to flip through the pages of a book open on top of the papers before him. "Oh, dear me, my secretary is lax at recording such appointments, I fear. Do allow me to ring for some tea."

"That is not necessary," Priscilla said.

He glanced toward the window. "Ah, I see. The hour is late. Mayhap you would wish something else? Have you supped, Lady Priscilla? Or is it too late to send for food?" He rubbed his hands together. "Dear me, I forget what time we were given to order supper from the church's kitchen. They make rules and forget to tell us." As if he had abruptly remembered he had callers, he repeated, "Do we have an appointment this evening?"

"No, Dr. Summerson." Neville scooped up an armful of papers from a chair and smiled at Priscilla. When she sat, he continued. "However, we have a matter of the greatest urgency to discuss with you."

"We read banns every Sunday." He gave them a beneficent smile. "The schedule has been set for this week. Or so I believe. I can check. I would not say for sure. If—"

"We have no desire to be married," Priscilla said when she saw Neville's appalled expression. Even the hint of marriage connected with his name had this fascinating effect on him. It was most amusing as well as something she should recall the next time he started acting high-handed with her. She could think of several misses who would not be averse to being seen on the arm of a baronet whose well-laid pockets more than made up for his wicked reputation.

Then her smile faded. What once had been a joke no

longer seemed funny. Could it be that *she* was thinking of marriage and Neville at the same time? That was more ridiculous than anything she had ever thought of. Wasn't it? He did not want to get married, a fact he had made mightily clear. She needed to contemplate her children's future, not her own. Telling herself it was the stress of the events at Bedford Square betwattling her, she started to answer.

Neville beat her to it, frowning as he said, "Dr. Summerson, we wish to speak of a funeral that—"

"Forgive me." He rushed around the desk like a chubby piglet. Grasping their hands, he said, "You have my condolences at this time of loss. I despise the idea of another death on Bedford Square, where there has been so much tragedy already. Was this a sudden thing, or was it expected?"

"It was, indeed, an extraordinary and most unexpected loss," Neville answered as Priscilla pulled her hand out of the curate's cool, sweaty grip. "Are you always in charge of funerals, Dr. Summerson?"

"Dr. Horwood, my superior here at St. Julian's, marries, and I bury."

"How progressive of you to split the duties like that!"

The day had been long, and Priscilla did not care to spend the evening listening to Neville bait the poor curate, so she said, "Our loss is not as you might expect."

"How is that?" asked Dr. Summerson.

"I think it would be better if you sat."

Dr. Summerson looked from her to Neville. His skin became a sickly shade of gray as he nodded, but he did not move until Neville brought another chair from beside an overflowing bookcase. Dropping heavily onto it, Dr. Summerson said, "I am sitting."

"Obviously," Neville muttered.

Priscilla fired him a reproachful glare. An ally was never

gained through cruel comments. Affixing a smile in place, she said, "Dr. Summerson, we are here on behalf of Lady Eleanor Burtrum to—"

With a moan, he jumped to his feet. His coattails whipped at Priscilla as he whirled to scurry behind his desk. "I cannot speak of that unspeakable matter."

"Why not?" Neville asked in a reasonable tone even Priscilla found irritating. "I trust *you* have nothing to hide about this abominable situation that has left an earl's son's body missing."

"Of course not." He raised both of his chins. "The bishop has asked us to say nothing until we have the facts."

Neville put his hands on the papers stacked on the table. "The facts are that you have a band of resurrectionists preying on your churchyard. One body is missing. Or have there been more incidents?"

"Six, I believe." He sank to his chair. "Oh, dear me, whatever shall we do?"

"I would suggest we work together to put an end to these grave robbers." Priscilla stood and smiled again. "Dr. Summerson, Sir Neville and I wish to help Lady Eleanor. *You* have the records of your churchyard, and you know which graves have been disturbed and who was resting in them."

"Those records cannot be seen by the laity without my superiors' permission."

"We shall wait," Neville said as he sat in the chair the curate had vacated, "while you send a messenger to obtain that permission."

"Then there are the families to be considered."

Priscilla began, "Lady Eleanor—"

His tone was chiding. "My dear Lady Priscilla, as you should know from your own experiences here at St. Julian's when your husband was alive, things are not that simple.

Although the Burtrums are your sole focus, they are not the only family I must concern myself with. I would need to procure authorization to speak to each of the families before I could give you as much as the name of their recently departed."

"Yes," she returned, "those who are recently departed from the churchyard are our primary interest." When the curate winced, she continued. "Forgive me, Dr. Summerson. I am afraid gracious words fail me when confronted by such nefarious acts."

"It has been a trial for all of us." He pulled out a handkerchief and wiped jewels of sweat from his nearly bald pate.

Priscilla glanced at Neville and saw he was staring at the gems glittering on the curate's rings. She was not sure if they were genuine, but Neville would know.

When Neville opened his mouth, she hurried to ask before he could say the wrong thing to Dr. Summerson, "So the graves that have been disturbed are of the recently dead?"

"I am not sure."

"But you said—"

"Excuse me," Neville said. "I don't wish to interrupt, but, Dr. Summerson, are you asking us to believe you don't know which bodies have been stolen?"

"The reports on the matter are here." He looked anxiously about the cluttered office. "Somewhere."

"And was Johnson the watchman each time a body was stolen?"

"No." Dr. Summerson scowled, and Priscilla knew he had owned to something he had not intended to reveal. With a sigh, he said, "You may as well know that Johnson is recently hired. He was, however, the watchman when Lady Eleanor's brother's corpse was lifted from the earth. Avery, I believe, was here the other nights."

"Avery? His brother-in-law?" asked Priscilla.

"Mayhap. The two chaps share an abhorrence for work and an affinity for sleeping on the job, so they may very well be related."

From the corner of her eye, Priscilla saw Neville make a motion. She knew what he wanted. She was to keep Dr. Summerson talking while Neville checked surreptitiously around the office. She would do her best, although the curate was trying to look past her to see what Neville was doing.

"Dr. Summerson," she said, coming closer to the desk. As she put her hands on its top, she made sure her elbows were caught in her cloak. That spread the fabric out like the dark wings of an avenging angel.

"Yes?" His piqued tone revealed she had blocked his view.

"I understand your obligation to your superiors."

"You do?" His myopic gaze settled on her, and, when his nose rumpled like an old sheet of paper, she guessed he was trying to bring her into focus. Mayhap she need not worry about him seeing Neville's prying, after all.

"Of course." She gave him a smile. "As a parson's wife, I know how delicate these matters can be."

"That is very understanding of you, Lady Priscilla. Now, as you comprehend my quandary, I must ask you and Sir Neville to excuse me. I have reports that must be finished before the bishop's visit next month."

"We would be delighted to leave." Hearing the rattle of papers, she raised her voice slightly. "We will leave as soon as you answer a single question."

"A single question? That is all you wish to ask?"

"Just one." She held up a gloved finger and smiled. "After all, Dr. Summerson, surely you could cause no damage or transgress one of your superiors' rules by answering a single question."

He pondered for a moment, then said, "All right. Ask what you wish, and I will answer it."

"How long has this grave robbing been going on?"

He recoiled from her abruptly sharp question. "Lady Priscilla, I should not—"

"Dr. Summerson, you gave me your word you would answer this question." She put her hand to her bodice, taking care she kept her elbow out to prevent the cloak from dropping back to her side. She wished Neville would hurry. Not that looking for anything in this mess would be a quick or easy task. "My late husband, the Reverend Dr. Lazarus Flanders . . . I am sure you have heard of his good works even if you never had the chance to serve with him."

"The Reverend Dr. Lazarus Flanders? Of course. He is well spoken of here at St. Julian's."

She grasped his hand and squeezed it gently. "Oh, Dr. Summerson, you honor me by recalling my husband with such generous praise. As my late husband was fond of saying, the clergy must keep its word to those who look to it for guidance, for how else would the parishioners learn the value of an honest pledge?"

Behind her, she heard Neville clear his throat. He had found something of interest and, no doubt, had secreted it beneath his cloak. Neville had as few compunctions about stealing from a churchman as he would from a highwayman. It was time to depart, so they might look more closely at what he had discovered.

She did not let her gaze shift from Dr. Summerson's round face. When it became an unhealthy tint of red, she resisted smiling. She recognized the expression of a man who had been thwarted.

"Very well, Lady Priscilla," the curate said in a clipped voice. "I shall keep my word and tell you that, as I recall, these incidents have been taking place over the past three months."

"So far apart?" asked Neville, coming to stand beside her.

"A single question was what I said I would answer. I bid you good evening."

Neville's smile did not waver. "Dr. Summerson, you need to be aware that these occurrences will not stay a secret. How do you intend to protect the other graves if you keep this quiet?"

"No more questions!"

Priscilla flashed the curate a sympathetic smile and patted his arm. "Of course not. You have suffered enough already, I suspect. What with these horrible robberies and the rumors spreading through the parish."

"What rumors?"

"Dr. Summerson," she said, feigning shock, "I thought we had agreed to no more questions. Sir Neville and I shall bid you good evening now. I trust you still have a donations box for the poor at the back of the church."

"Yes, but—"

She held up her hand to halt his question. Opening her reticule, she said, "Good, then I shall make a donation. Small though it must be, it may be of help. As the wife of a parson, I know too well how rumors can affect the attendance at services. If the *ton* does not come and tithe, there can be little hope of maintaining a church. Such a sad, sad thing."

"The attendance and the collections have been thin for the past few days." Dr. Summerson blanched. "If this continues—"

Priscilla patted his arm. "Do contact me, Dr. Summerson, as soon as you hear from your superiors. We want to change this unfortunate trend with all due haste."

''Yes, yes. I shall speak to my superiors on the morrow.''

Holding out her hand, she let Neville draw it within his arm. ''Thank you and good evening, Dr. Summerson. I look forward to hearing from you before the week's end.''

Neville held his laugh until they emerged from the church and onto the street, which was deserted save for the carriage. After paying the lad as he had promised and two shillings more at Priscilla's insistence, he handed her in and sat next to her.

''Excellent!'' he said with a chuckle as he drove them back toward Bedford Square. ''You planted the right seed of discontent in that man's less than fertile mind. Without the generosity of the *ton* who attend his services, he might soon be without his golden ornaments.''

''I wanted him to realize he needs our help as much as we need his.'' Glancing over her shoulder, she shuddered. ''If I had an ounce of intelligence, I would have turned down Eleanor's request to involve myself in such a ghoulish task.''

''But you have an ounce of intelligence, Pris. You saw how amusing traipsing about graveyards after dark could be.'' He pulled a slip of paper from beneath his cloak and handed it to her.

''What is this?''

''A list of the current members of the church. Now, if our friend Summerson fails to garner us permission to speak to the families of the *recently departed*—''

''Refrain from using that term, if you please.''

He laughed again as he turned onto Bedford Square. ''It is perfectly appropriate. However, I shall use it only when it garners us what we need, and what we need now is to talk to others who have had family graves violated. Even if Summerson refuses or is incapable of getting us the information, we can contact the families ourselves.''

She flipped through the half dozen pages. "The list is rather long."

"Then I suggest we start at dawn."

"Dawn?" She shook her head. "No one will receive us at such an hour."

"Many of the names are not of the *élite*. We can start with the servants and work our way up the stairs."

She sighed. "Let us hope we can gain more specific information from Dr. Summerson or Dr. Horwood."

"That would be the simplest, but things seldom work out that way. Pris, we are avoiding a question neither of us wants to consider."

"If the bodysnatching is related to the deaths here on the square?"

"Exactly. It adds a darker motivation to these deaths if they are being killed to provide product for bodysnatchers."

"Dr. Summerson said the bodies have been taken over the past three months, and these deaths have all been within the last month."

"I know you may find this hard to believe, because you were married to an honest clergyman, but *I* find it hard to believe that Summerson is being totally honest with us." He halted the carriage in front of her marble steps.

"I find neither difficult to believe." Smoothing the cloak over her skirts after he had handed her out, she said, "While you put the carriage away, I will scan this list. There might be some hint to point us in the right direction." She started up the steps. Something leaped toward her from the shadows. "What in perdition—?"

"Priscilla!" Neville shouted.

He grasped her arm and jerked her back. A crash of wood on marble echoed around the square. The wood splintered. Priscilla ducked beneath her cloak, but a sliver struck her arm. She heard Neville curse as he released her. Broken wood was scattered on the walkway and into the road, but most of the object remained intact.

"Oh, my," she whispered. "That looks like—"

"A coffin lid," he finished.

"A warning?"

"Most likely." He straightened and looked in both directions along the empty street. "I would say our fortune is about to take a turn . . . for the worse."

Chapter Eight

"I will hear no argument on this, Pris," Neville said as he handed his hat and cloak to Layden, whom Priscilla had already instructed to clean up the front steps. "This situation has taken a darker turn, and I will not have you or the children put into danger."

"You will receive an argument if you are about to suggest that the children and I leave without delay for Stonehall-on-Sea. St. Julian's was Lazarus's church, and I will not have its fine reputation blemished further."

He smiled tautly. "I was not going to suggest you leave London at this hour, when the night is half over. Haven't you learned that I am not one to waste my breath on futile discussions?"

"Then what are you suggesting?"

"I think I would like to confer about this with something strong at my side. I trust you have some decent brandy in the house, Pris."

Fear coursed its icy finger down her spine, for it was unlike Neville to own to being even this unsettled. With a great deal of effort, she kept her voice even. "Certainly. Layden, please ask Juster to bring some brandy for Sir Neville and some coffee for me to the study."

"The study?" Neville asked as they climbed the stairs, taking care not to make any loud sound that would wake the children.

Again she shivered. If her children saw the broken wood on the steps, they would be more frightened than they ever had been.

"Pris?"

It took her a moment to recall his question. "I thought there would be less chance of one of the children wandering downstairs and into the study."

His arm curved around her shoulders, and she leaned her head against him. So frequently she had asserted that she did not need anyone's help, that she could handle every crisis on her own. Tonight had shown her how mistaken she was. As his fingers massaged the tight muscles along her upper arms, she wanted to close her eyes and lose herself in his embrace. She had never realized how she could close out the world when Lazarus opened his arms. Nor had she guessed how much she missed that haven.

Neville was not Lazarus, for he would toss her from that haven if he thought it was in her best interests—or his. No, that was unfair, because he would battle any dragon to protect her and the children. Even if that dragon was Sir Neville Hathaway.

When he sat her on the chair by the desk and lit the lamp so it glowed off the dark red walls, she grasped his hand before he could walk away. He looked from it to her, astonishment in his eyes.

"Don't pace," she said.

"How did you know I was going to do that?"

She smiled. "Because pacing is what you always do when you are trying to sort out a problem."

Leaning back against the window frame, he said, "You know me too well, Pris."

The door opened, and Mrs. Moore with her hair under a cap and lines of sleep on her face brought in a tray. When she had set it on the table, she took one step toward the door before pausing.

"We are both fine," Priscilla said. "Some horseplay—"

"With the top of an eternity box?" Mrs. Moore reddened. "Excuse me for interrupting, my lady, but Layden said someone left its lid by the door and it almost toppled on you. That is not horseplay. That is a threat."

Neville nodded. "It would appear that way, Mrs. Moore, but a threat by someone who does not wish Lady Priscilla any harm other than setting her heart to a frantic beat. The worst that could have happened would have been a lump on her hard head."

"Thank you for another compliment," Priscilla said crisply.

"I thought the truth would soothe Mrs. Moore." He looked back at the housekeeper, who was scowling. "Has it?"

Mumbling something that sounded to Priscilla like *two of you* and *impossible,* the housekeeper left the room. She shut the door just loudly enough to make her opinions known without waking the children.

"Apparently she was not soothed." Neville picked up a cup and poured coffee into it. Handing it to Priscilla, he picked up the second cup. Filling it partway with coffee, he added brandy. He held up the bottle, and she shook her head. As much as she would have liked a bracing drink, she needed to have her faculties at their peak.

"You should refrain from jesting with Mrs. Moore. You know her sense of humor evaporates when she is upset."

"As does yours."

"Mine?" she asked, astonished. "If you believe I should find something amusing about people dying around us and bodies being stolen and someone trying to hurt me, you are—"

He put his finger to her lip. When she jerked back, a jolt sparking through her, he said, "I know very well what I am, Pris. Among other things, at the moment I am very worried." He pulled a chair closer to hers and sat. "You have two choices until you take your leave of London, Pris. You can stay at my house on Berkeley Square, or I will settle into your guest room."

"Why?"

"I think it is quite obvious that someone knows you are asking questions and wants to frighten you into stopping."

"They are wasting their time. I shan't stop until I know the truth."

He set his cup on the table. "Pris, I know that, and so do those who want to scare you. When this prank fails to send you scurrying back to Stonehall-on-Sea, the ones who perpetrated it will have to resort to other methods."

"Oh." She placed her cup next to his and folded her hands in her lap, hoping he would fail to notice how they trembled.

When he placed his broad hand over her clasped fingers, she raised her eyes to meet the anger in his. She did not quail before it because that fury was not aimed at her. Did the ones who had tried to hurt her on the front steps have any idea the peril they had incurred with their prank? She had seen a few, infrequent signs of Neville's temper, but those rare glimpses had been enough to let her know how powerful it was.

"I shall not be able," he said with the intensity she knew was impossible to argue with, "to leave you here to face those blackguards alone. You are likely to jump to the defense of one of the children without a cautionary thought. I know that, and so, I collect, do those who want to halt the questions. In fact, they may be counting on you doing exactly that."

"I intend to be careful and ask the children to do the same."

"Which may mean nothing."

"I am not sure I understand what you are trying to say."

"Yes, you do. You simply do not want to own that Isaac has a penchant for slipping away from the most observant adult set to watch over him, even you."

She could not halt her smile. "That is true, but that does not explain why you believe you can succeed where others, including his mother, have failed."

"Because Isaac wants to play a part in finding a solution to this puzzle. I have accepted his offer of help with the proviso that he does not attempt anything without informing me first."

"And you believe he will accede to that if something exciting demands his attention?"

"I believe he will try."

"Then you are as much of a fool as those bodysnatchers are."

"Mayhap, but sometimes it takes a fool to defeat a fool. So will you come to Berkeley Square, or shall I stay here?"

Knowing any answer she gave would incur a wrath far more powerful than any resurrectionist's—Aunt Cordelia's—she replied, "Let me give it some thought."

"Don't think too long, Pris. I am not sure how much more time these resurrectionists are going to allow you before they try to do more than scare you."

* * *

Isaac was missing.

Telling Neville that she had been right would be worthless, Priscilla reminded herself as she hurried down the stairs to discover if one of the footmen had found him. The boy could slip into the smallest hole and pull the diggings in after him to leave no sign of where he had been or what he had been up to.

She tried not to panic, but Neville's words from last night had repeated over and over in her head while she tried to sleep. The repetition had drowned out the conversation at breakfast that morning, even her daughters' complaints that they were going to miss the birthday hop for Lord Cagswell's youngest. Daphne had said at least a dozen times that she considered it unfair that she was being denied even this tame entertainment and how she would not be acquainted with a single soul when she was fired-off into the Season.

"Nothing yet, my lady," Gilbert said before she could even ask. He stood guard on the front door, and Mrs. Dunham would be watching over the back door. The cook never allowed anyone in or out of her kitchen without her knowledge. "Juster is going to check the stables on Gower Mews across the square."

"And Layden?"

"He is—" The butler was bumped forward a pair of steps as the door opened into his back.

"Isaac!" she cried as her son peered around its edge.

His face fell into dismay, and she knew he had hoped to skulk back in as unseen as he had snuck out. He glanced over his shoulder as if intending to scurry away.

Priscilla took him by the arm and drew him into the house just as Neville came rushing down the stairs with Daphne and Leah in tow. Mrs. Moore and Mrs. Dunham appeared at the top of the kitchen stairs.

After thanking them for their efforts, Priscilla shooed away the servants and her daughters. They all went quickly, and she was glad they knew she wanted to talk with her son alone. That Neville did not leave was no surprise. She doubted she could have budged him with a crowbar.

"Whatever have you been up to?" she asked, drawing off Isaac's coat that was as spotted with jam and crumbs as his face.

"Helping." He held his head high, and she knew he would be unrepentant.

Bother! Mayhap Neville was influencing the boy too much, for this pose was one she recognized too well. But, she had to own, *she* had been known to resist backing down when she believed she was right.

"Helping what?" she asked.

Neville said calmly, "Helping himself to scones and jam, if I am to judge by the colors splattered on him."

She scowled. He did not need to encourage Isaac. Her son was quite capable of finding trouble on his own. That was another way in which Isaac reminded her too much of Neville. She silenced the thought. It sounded like a comment Aunt Cordelia would make when she told Priscilla—as if Priscilla had forgotten from the last time her aunt mentioned it—that Neville should not be allowed to spend time with the children.

"Isaac, go and wash," she ordered. "Then change and return to join *us* for tea."

"More tea?" His eyes brightened, and she wondered how one small boy could possibly eat so much.

"We shall speak of your calls while we have our tea."

His excitement disappeared. When he looked at Neville, she was glad Neville did not give him any encouragement to resist her orders. This was the one thing her aunt did not understand. As much as Neville enjoyed joining the children to tease her, he never would undermine her authority with them.

As her son scrambled up the stairs, Priscilla followed more slowly. She was glad to see tea waiting for them in the front parlor. Even in the midst of the house being turned inside out in an effort to find Isaac, Mrs. Moore never would allow tea not to be served on time.

She sat and prepared a cup for Neville as she knew he liked it. No milk or sugar, but lemon. More than once she had been tempted to tell him such a cup fit his personality exactly, but she had resisted, knowing there might come the perfect time to tease him. Handing him the cup, she prepared her own tea while he sat facing her.

"Don't say it," Neville said.

"Don't say that I was right about Isaac's inability to restrain himself when he is caught up in what he sees as the excitement of these bodysnatchings?" She tilted one brow and took a sip of tea.

"I am glad you did not say it."

"Neville, I have managed to raise my children to their present ages only because I have learned to think as they do." She laughed. "Or mayhap it is because I have been able to recall the mischief of my own childhood. Yet, if that is the case, I would have guessed you would be a master at discerning their thoughts."

He laughed shortly. "One would think so."

"Mayhap it is because you are still involved in mischief, and—" Priscilla looked at the doorway, where her son was entering.

Isaac was almost clean. A spot of red jam was visible just below his left ear. She did not need to guess how it had gotten there. Left to his own devices, he would happily take such a large bite of bread or muffin that he left a trail of crumbs in an arc from one ear to the other. However, he had changed out of his stained coat and wore a clean shirt which was, for once, buttoned correctly.

"Come in and join us, Isaac," she ordered.

He inched toward them as if dragging a pair of elephants behind him. When he sat next to Neville, she was not surprised. Isaac would be, though, if he thought he and Neville were allied against her.

"Do tell us what you were doing," Neville said.

"Trying to find out some information."

"Never a bad idea."

Giving his mother a victorious smile that dimmed when she frowned, he reached for a cake on the tea tray.

Priscilla moved it beyond his reach. "I daresay you have enjoyed enough tea for one day."

"But, Mama—" He clamped his lips closed when hers remained stiff. Apparently he was learning how useless it was to argue with her. Now, if her aunt would only take a lesson from Isaac.

"Go ahead," Neville urged. "What tidbits did you discover during your calls?"

"The Burtrums are boring."

He laughed, and Priscilla had to smile. "Something you could have found out from a single call. Or did you hope to gain a consensus from the entire square?"

"A con—con—"

"A consensus," Priscilla said as she handed Isaac a half-cup that was filled with more cream and sugar than tea, "is a general agreement among a group of people."

"The con—whatever it is—is that the Burtrums are boring." Isaac lowered his voice as if he were about to reveal a great secret. "More than one person hinted that the family has been extraordinarily ordinary since their one ancestor was awarded his title by assisting King Edward the Third centuries ago."

"Therefore, you had no reason to be seeking tales about them and their private business."

"No reason?" He jumped to his feet, then sat back down quickly when Neville put a hand on his arm and shook his head. "Mama, Mr. Lampman's coachman died on their front steps and the earl's son in his study."

"I am quite aware of both of those incidents, Isaac. Even such incredible circumstances do not grant you leave to be sharing scan-mag with our neighbors in an effort to learn more about what goes on behind their closed doors."

"And," said Neville as he reached for a cake, "asking your neighbors about one another is a waste of time."

"Really?" he asked.

"Really. After all, haven't you learned that servants are the ones who know all the secrets?"

"Neville!" Priscilla gasped. "Why are you encouraging him?"

"Just stating the truth, and you do want me to be truthful with the children, I believe."

Priscilla wondered how he could be so unthinking at times. Isaac needed to be scolded and reminded to be courteous instead of being urged to gossip with the servants. As soon as the boy finished his tea and rushed off—most likely to harass Gilbert and Mrs. Dunham for what they knew—she told Neville that.

He did not have the decency to look chagrined as Isaac had, and she understood why when he replied, "Pris, I am trying to keep him close to home rather than wandering about the square."

"Oh." She poured more tea for both of them. "I owe you an apology."

"You owe me an answer. I used your guest room last

night, but I need to know if you are going to come with me back to Berkeley Square or allow me to stay here until this matter is settled. I know you no longer will consider doing the wise thing and return to Stonehall-on-Sea."

"You are right, and you may as well stay here, for you are as unwilling to be away from Bedford Square now as I am."

"Tongues will wag, Pris."

"I know that well, but my children have always been more important to me than my reputation."

He grinned. "We are not so different, after all."

"Egad! Pray do not insult me."

Priscilla laughed along with him, glad the humor stood between them and the truth. What the truth was, she was no longer sure, but she was, beyond doubt, glad to have him as a bulwark against what was happening in the square.

The sound of their laughter must have lured the children to the front parlor, because first Daphne and Leah and then Isaac came into the room. Soon they were giggling as Neville told them a wild story that Priscilla guessed had some connection, however slight, with an actual event.

She waited until he had finished before saying, "I am glad you joined us. I need to tell you something very important."

Daphne's eyes grew round. "Not another death?"

"No, no." Her clasped hands almost creaked as she tightened them. She did not want her children to guess every tiding was of tragedy. "I wanted to tell you that we are staying in London."

The children cheered, jumping to their feet, and the girls grabbed each other's hands while they skipped in a circle. Abruptly Daphne dropped her sister's hands and smoothed her gown, looking embarrassed at the very idea she had reacted so.

Priscilla hid her smile. She recalled that age of being

almost an adult but still not finished with being a child. Daphne wanted desperately to be welcomed among her elders. Curbing her natural enthusiasm was not the way to do it, because Priscilla wanted her oldest to retain the warmth that would be such a delight when she began the social events of her first Season. Nothing Priscilla said would be able to help Daphne find her way now, for her daughter held tightly to the belief that Priscilla wanted to keep her a child.

That, Priscilla had to own, was not totally untrue. She wanted to safeguard Daphne until her daughter was able to confront the *ton* without being shattered by its sometimes unintentionally cruel whims . . . and the occasional intentionally cruel ones.

"We must go shopping, Mama," Leah said, "to find a gift for the birthday party."

"That we shall. Do you have any idea what you might wish to give to Barbara Cagswell?"

As the girls debated what small remembrance they might give, she listened with a smile. This was the first time since the day of their arrival on the square that she had felt this was home. It was a precious feeling she wanted to savor for as long as she could.

She doubted she would be given too long a chance.

Chapter Nine

''Where are we going?'' asked Isaac, bouncing from one foot to the other in the Berkeley Square kitchen that was almost identical to the one in Priscilla's house.

Putting his finger to his lips, Neville motioned with his head toward the stairs. No one would come down them after he had asked his cook, Mrs. Quigley, to keep everyone away. She was accustomed to such strange requests. Not just from him, but from the previous baronet, he guessed, because she never did more than nod at such an order.

Neville picked up another handful of soot from the main hearth and rubbed it onto Isaac's coat. He would bring Mrs. Moore a bottle of his best wine to atone for giving the household extra work in cleaning this filthy coat. Mayhap he would bring her two if she would say nothing to Priscilla about this excursion. He had better make it a trio of bottles, because Gilbert's silence must be bought as well.

He was glad his servants were as loyal, for none of them

would own to having seen Isaac arrive here this afternoon, nor would they reveal they had seen what would appear to be a small chimney sweep leaving. Opening a door in a small room off the kitchen, he took a ragged coat off one of the pegs inside. He hastily closed the door when Isaac tried to peer past him.

"What is that?" the boy asked.

"A storage cupboard."

"Filled with all sorts of clothes?"

"Yes."

"In the kitchen?"

"Near the back door, to be more precise."

Isaac grinned broadly. "So you can change quickly, as you did when you were an actor?"

"Yes."

"When do you use those costumes?"

"When I need to." Walking to the back door, he motioned to the boy. "Come along. If we want to walk to Lincoln's Inn Fields and back before your mother returns from her errands with your sisters, we need to get going."

"Walk? Why don't we take the carriage?"

"When was the last time you saw a chimney sweep and a ragman riding in a phaeton?"

The lad's eyes twinkled.

Neville guessed his own also divulged his anticipation. A pinch of guilt he ignored with the ease of long practice. Priscilla had been insistent that safeguarding her children was of primary importance, so she would be furious to learn he had invited Isaac along today. Yet, he would challenge her to come up with another excuse to gain entrance into one of the workrooms of the surgeon-anatomists who bought the resurrectionists' wares.

Isaac was the perfect age to begin an apprenticeship in one of those ghoulish places, and the boy had a natural curiosity that would seem appropriate for someone who wished to study medicine. Acting as Isaac's guardian, Neville could ask the questions he needed to without arousing suspicion.

Or so he hoped.

The house looked no different from the others in the shadow of the larger buildings in the nearby streets. Neville found it amusing that the surgeon-anatomists did their illegal business within view of the Inns of Court. Or as amusing as he could find anything when he was about to enter one of their laboratories.

"You must remember that you are interested in studying with one of the surgeon-anatomists," Neville said as he and Isaac approached the house. No one had given a second look at them as they left Mayfair's fine squares and walked north.

"Will we get to see some cut-up bodies?"

He hid his smile. Priscilla had mentioned more than once that Isaac had a young boy's interest in things that made his sisters cringe. However, even a lad who was intrigued with insects and snakes, both alive and dead, might not be prepared for what was within this house. He was not sure if he was either.

"We may," he said. Putting his hand on Isaac's shoulder, he added, "Do not touch anything."

"I won't." He grinned. "But I am going to look at *everything*."

"If you need to leave, just say so."

"Leave? Why?"

"You shall see."

"Because of the corpses?" Isaac raised his chin with

pride. "It would be silly to be scared of something already dead."

"A good credo." He reached for the door. "Stay close."

The boy nodded, and Neville took a deep breath when he opened the door. He slipped through with Isaac right behind him. He wondered if the boy's bravado was cracking. He would not blame Isaac, for, as they climbed the stairs to the topmost floor, a reek reached out into the hallway.

Isaac gagged.

"Are you going to be all right?" Neville asked.

The boy nodded, even though his face was becoming a very sickly shade. He would not leave now, Neville guessed, because he would be determined to prove he could deal with whatever was inside as long as Neville could. That might not be too long unless he could inure himself to this stench.

Raising his hand to knock on the shadowed door on the top landing, Neville wondered how much the surgeon-anatomist had to pay the watch to keep them away from here. Mayhap not too much, because he doubted many people would come to this door willingly. He rapped on the door and put his hand on Isaac's shoulder as the boy began to bounce about in anticipation. A bit of excitement was good for their charade, but he did not want the boy to say the wrong thing and reveal the truth of why they were there. Even though Neville had not told him, Isaac must have guessed.

The door opened a crack, and the odor strengthened. Behind him, Neville heard Isaac cough. He fought his own heaving stomach. Even though he had accustomed himself to the open sewers of the poorest streets in London, this smell was far worse.

Somehow, he ground out past his clenched teeth, "Are ye Mr. Lofts?"

"Who is asking?" The voice revealed nothing about the man behind the door but that he was educated.

"M'name's Jones." He hoped Isaac would be able to fake a lower-class accent well enough to bamblusterate anyone in Mr. Lofts's laboratory. They had practiced on the walk over, and the boy had a quick ear. Now it would be put to the test. "I brought m'boy to ask 'bout 'im apprenticin' 'ere."

The door opened a finger's breadth farther. "Why are you asking about Mr. Lofts here?"

"Like I said, m'boy wants to apprentice with 'im."

"Step forward, boy."

Isaac glanced at Neville, then obeyed.

"How old are you, boy?" asked the voice.

"Nine, sir."

"Why do you want to apprentice with Mr. Lofts?"

"I want t'be a surgeon, sir." His smile returned as he repeated the story Neville had insisted he learn. His accent failed on a word or two, but Mr. Lofts might not notice. "M'ma died when I was a babe. Died of some sickness in 'er gut. I want t'learn enough to 'elp other folks."

Whether it was Isaac's apparent sincerity—and Neville reminded himself not ever to accept anything the boy said as the truth without a bit of questioning, because Isaac seemed to have skill at spinning a tale—or something else, the door opened wide enough so they could enter. Neville kept his hands on Isaac's shoulders as they walked through, not sure what they might find on the far side.

The inside was well lit, and, except for the odor, there was nothing out of the ordinary. The few tables set along the long, narrow hallway were well made and topped with books. Faded wallcovering suggested this house had once been far finer than it was now. Beneath their feet, the floor was worn but clean.

"I am Elihu Lofts," said the voice that had come from around the door.

"Thank ye fer lettin' us in." Neville appraised the man

in front of him. Lofts had the round, jovial appearance that he had not expected of a man who worked in this dreary, ghastly place and pawed his way through some corpse's innards. With his sleeves rolled up on his beefy arms and his apron spotted with blood, Lofts could easily have been mistaken for a butcher.

But the blood did not belong to a calf or a sheep or a chicken. It was human blood dried on his apron.

Neville swallowed hard. Dash it! He had prided himself on being able to withstand any set of circumstances and emerge with his composure intact. Here he was, acting as squeamish as a young miss confronting a spider. By his side, Isaac seemed to have forgotten his distress with the smell, because the boy was looking around with obvious interest.

"The lad wants t'learn to be a surgeon-anatomist," he said when he realized Lofts must be growing impatient waiting for his answer. "I 'oped ye might be in need of an apprentice to 'elp 'round 'ere."

"Who sent you?"

"Murray."

"Are you a friend?"

"I worked with 'im at various theaters around Covent Garden and in Drury Lane." Dash it again! He was having to reveal more than he wanted to.

Lofts nodded, seeming to accept the story that was too close to the truth.

Neville silently thanked Murray, who knew more about what went on in this section of London than the Horse Patrol and Bow Street combined. Murray had once worked at the theaters, but now was living with his granddaughter not far from there. After Neville had returned Isaac to Bedford Square, he would buy a few pints for Murray at his favorite tavern as well as give him an extra guinea or two. Such generosity would be returned the next time Neville needed information.

''This way,'' Lofts said.

The maze of rooms twisted together in a pattern that suggested the upper floors connected through several buildings. Most of the doors were closed, and Isaac was frustrated at not being able to see what was behind them.

They entered a chamber that was showered with sunshine from a pair of skylights in the roof. Two tables held bodies covered by soiled, stained sheets. More tables were pushed against the wall. Bottles of every size were arranged along them and on the shelves above.

''Boy, come away from there,'' the doctor said as Isaac peered at one bottle from every possible angle.

''Wot is it?'' Isaac asked.

''A heart.''

''A 'uman 'eart?'' His eagerness was becoming more macabre, in Neville's judgment, with every passing moment. Mayhap the boy would profess a true interest in studying surgery. Now, *that* would distress Lady Cordelia into apoplexy.

''It is a cow's heart,'' Lofts said. ''In spite of what is said about us, we use *every* source for our studies, not just cadavers.''

''Because ye cannot obtain enough corpses fer yer students?'' Neville asked, edging around a pool of something dark on the floor. It was not likely to be blood, but he was in no mind to ascertain its exact contents.

''The corpses do not last long, for often they are in sorry shape by the time they reach us. As they decompose, they no longer have any value as a teaching tool.'' He sighed and wiped his hair back from his spectacles. ''Then there is the matter of how short the duration is of our tenure in any one location. Corpses are notoriously difficult to move without anyone being the wiser."

"The chaps who bring them 'ere must be willin' to 'elp."

Lofts shook his head. "Resurrectionists are not reliable for such tasks. Once they have received their money for what they bring us, they vanish."

"Ye don't know where they go?"

"No, and I do not wish to. It is an unfortunate aspect of what I teach that I have to deal with them. I would rather never speak with one of them again."

" 'Tis clear ye'd prefer to obtain yer cadavers legally."

"Not only that. The resurrectionists are a low lot. If they were not stealing bodies from their graves, I suspect they would be finding other forms of criminal behavior to keep them busy and in gin." He turned to Isaac, who was now staring at another bottle. "So you are interested in studying surgery and anatomy, boy?"

"Yes!" There was such enthusiasm in Isaac's voice that Neville knew he must find something else to intrigue the boy before he blurted out the truth of this call in his mother's hearing.

"There is more than just the dissections we do here."

"There is?"

Neville interjected with a smile, although he was amazed how disappointed Isaac sounded at this information, "The whole of what 'e is goin' to study is somethin' 'e would learn while servin' as an apprentice, correct?"

"That is correct."

"Can I see one of the bodies?" asked Isaac.

Wanting to silence the lad, because Neville doubted his stomach could endure much more, he was glad when Lofts demurred with the explanation that he did not want to disturb the work his students had undertaken. At that last word, Isaac shot a grin at Neville.

Lofts looked toward the door, and Neville knew the time had come to ask the real questions that had brought them here.

Steering Isaac back through the workrooms, he asked, "Did any of these stiff ones come from St. Julian's churchyard?"

"St. Julian's?" Lofts's face became the pasty shade of one of his little science experiments. "Why do you think that?"

" 'Eard 'ow they be missin' a few there. The raffle-coffins 'ave been busy in the churchyard."

Lofts recovered his composure quickly. "None of our cadavers come from a neighborhood such as St. Julian's serves. These poor, soulless shells were taken from the most impoverished sections of the city. What they could not offer their fellow man during their brief lives—often made even shorter by the amounts of liquor they drank to ease their deprivation—mayhap they can offer now that they are dead."

"And they come to ye already pickled in the brine they drunk down."

Lofts looked at him, clearly uncertain if Neville was jesting or making an honest insight. "The liquor they swallow is so destructive to their bodies that it ruins them rather than preserves them."

"Uncle Nev—come and see this!" Isaac's guilty expression vanished as he excitedly pointed to a table.

Wondering what body part he was about to see this time, Neville strode over to the boy. Relief spread through him when he saw Isaac was studying some sharp instruments that were spread across the table's top.

"I would advise you not to touch those, my lad," Lofts said with a chuckle. "They are beautiful but unforgiving.

A single wrong motion, and you can lay your finger open instead of the flesh you are studying.''

''Fudge!'' breathed Isaac, staring at the instruments with awe.

Lofts faced Neville. ''Although the boy is showing an aptitude for study, I suspect something else is the reason for your call, Mr. Hathaway. Oh, I forget. It is Sir Neville Hathaway now, I believe.''

Neville saw no reason to lie. Letting his feigned accent fall away, he said, ''You are right, Lofts. How do you know?''

''I recall seeing your performance in *Macbeth* before you left the theater, and another play whose name I cannot recall at the moment.'' He smiled, but his voice grew colder. ''Your performance that day was far more realistic than the one today. Why are you really here?''

''One of the corpses missing from St. Julian's churchyard is a friend's neighbor. Or was, I should say.''

Lofts scowled. ''I had hoped you were making up that aspect of your charade. Ben Crouch and his lads do not work in that area.''

''Crouch?''

''Surely you have heard of him. He fancies himself the leader of the resurrection-coves, as his lads like to call themselves.''

''I *have* heard of him, but I had heard as well that he does not work in Mayfair.'' Neville searched his mind for every detail he knew about the man. It was not much more than Crouch's name, for the man stayed ahead of the authorities at every turn.

''He is smart enough to prey on churchyards where the people are less likely to seek help,'' Lofts said with a sigh. ''Yet someone is now stealing bodies from St. Julian's churchyard?''

"From what the curate said, there apparently have been as many as six bodies taken. If you are not receiving corpses from St. Julian's, do you know who might be?"

He shrugged. "There are several schools that teach surgery throughout London. Because of the laws forbidding dissection, all of them must keep hidden. Even I do not know the locations of many of the others."

"Who would?"

"I think that answer is quite obvious." His icy smile returned.

Neville did not silence his curse. How could he be so want-witted? The persons most likely to know the location of the schools were the same ones who provided the cadavers for study.

So he was right back where he had started. He needed to find some of the bodysnatchers and persuade them to be honest with him. An unlikely scenario, because he doubted any of them had had an honest thought in their lives. Unfortunately, the resurrectionists were the sole key left to open the door to the truth.

On the way back to Mayfair, Neville barely paid Isaac's chatter any mind. Neville sorted through the list of contacts he had, trying to decide which of them would be the most likely to know how he could contact a bodysnatcher. He would ask friends at Bow Street to see what they could tell him about Ben Crouch. Then, if necessary, he would seek out the watch in the City. Checking at a few of the churches in the destitute neighborhoods might gain him information, for those pastors must be as eager as Dr. Summerson to put an end to the thefts. Mayhap he would check with Murray again. The old man might have further information.

Someone knew where the bodysnatchers hid when not doing their nefarious work. He needed to find that person and persuade him or her to talk.

By the time they reached Berkeley Square, Neville had a list of a half dozen people who would be good to start with. He hurried Isaac into the house, not wanting any of his neighbors to catch sight of them. Mr. Bulwyn would keep him busy for hours answering questions about any topic the old man could think of, and, if he chanced to meet Lady Harriet, she would have spread the news of his being dressed fantastically in his rags throughout the square and beyond before his front door was closed.

It was vital that Priscilla did not learn how he had taken Isaac to call on Lofts's laboratory. If she found out, she would be—

"Where have you two been?" asked Priscilla from the stairs leading up from the entry foyer.

Isaac muttered something that sounded like one of Neville's favorite curses. Mayhap the boy's words resembled it because Neville was thinking the exact same phrase as Priscilla came down the steps.

He shot a scowl at his butler, although not even Stoddard could have kept a determined Priscilla out of the house. Neville wondered if the man had even attempted to do so. Stoddard had inquired about Priscilla several times since her husband's death. The butler admired her and had mentioned more than once that such a lady would be a good influence on *this* household.

"Well?" asked Priscilla as she paused on the bottom riser, her hand on the walnut banister. The gilt on the niche in the wall behind her was dimmed by the sparks of fury in her eyes. "I cannot believe that you are hesitating, Neville. Why? Because you are trying to concoct some falsehood to feed me?"

"I don't lie to you, Pris."

"Often."

"Not often." He smiled as he crossed the dark marble

foyer. Looking back, he saw Isaac had remained by the door, appearing as unwilling to move as the statue of a lad and his dog that was set in another niche next to him. Neville motioned, and the boy shuffled toward him with the enthusiasm of a felon coming to the bar.

Priscilla's nose wrinkled. "You two reek. Where have you been?"

"Asking a few questions."

"Where have—? Oh, no, Neville!" Her eyes grew wide. "Tell me you did not take my son to the lair of a surgeon-anatomist."

"I could tell you that, but I would prefer to be honest with you."

She stared at him for a moment, then said, "Stoddard, will you take my son somewhere and clean him up so he no longer smells like rot?"

"Yes, my lady." The butler edged around Neville and took Isaac by the arm.

"Mama!" The boy pulled away. "Don't get into a brangle with Uncle Neville. I asked to go with him."

"I am sure you did." Priscilla's voice did not ease from its stiff tone. "Neville, while my son is being cleaned enough so I can take him back to Bedford Square, I would like to speak with you."

"May I remind you that I do not endure scolds well?"

She met his eyes squarely. "And may I remind you that you promised me you would not allow my son to put himself in any sort of danger?"

"He was in no danger, Pris. I would not have taken him if I thought there was any peril to him."

Instead of replying sharply as he expected, she turned on her heel and walked up the steps past the paintings and sculptures the previous baronet had collected. He heard her angry footsteps above his head as she strode to his front parlor. Swearing again did no good. This conversation must be held, and delaying it would only add to her ire. He had, he must own, never seen her fly off the hooks like this.

Priscilla faced Neville as he entered the front parlor. Her nose wrinkled at the stench of his clothes.

"Do you want me to change into something less aromatic?" he asked.

"I believe this conversation must be held posthaste." She did not relent from her indignant stance as he scowled at her.

Sitting on the elegant gold brocade settee, she waited for him to cross the thick navy carpet that was several shades darker than the blue walls. More sculptures, some of them in quite passionate poses, were scattered throughout the room. She knew they had been selected by his uncle, who had bequeathed him this house along with his title, and she was unsure if they remained here because Neville enjoyed them or because he could not be bothered by something as mundane as decorating his house to his own taste.

Continuing her thoughts aloud, she said, "I had come to assume I could trust my children with you. I did not want to be proved wrong, but your actions this afternoon pointed out that I might be."

"I assure you that Isaac was never in the slightest bit of danger."

"When I came home from shopping with Daphne and Leah," she went on as if he had not spoken, "I was astonished to learn Isaac had left Bedford Square with you. Believing you might have brought him here to keep an eye on him while you gathered what you needed to stay with us, I followed. Imagine my shock when I discovered you two had left dressed like *that*!"

"Who told you?"

"Does it matter? Will you berate that person for being

concerned enough to be honest with me about my own son's whereabouts?''

He rested one hand on the molding around the door, and his eyes narrowed as if he dared her to ring a peal over him for what she had asked him not to do at her house. ''I told you. The boy was in no danger, and I did not have to drag him to Lofts's.''

''Of course he was eager to go on an adventure with you. On the other hand, you are a man and should have known better than to take him to that abominable place.''

''He offered the excuse I needed in order to make the visit without Lofts becoming even more suspicious.'' He pulled up a wooden chair and sat. ''Pris, Lofts was quite shocked with the idea that someone was harvesting bodies from St. Julian's. The ones he has received were from much poorer parishes.''

''So he believes.''

She saw her answer had surprised him. And that surprised her. Usually Neville saw the possibility of conspiracies. The visit to the surgeon-anatomist must have unnerved him more than he wished to own.

''You cannot use Isaac to help you again,'' she said when he remained silent. ''Not him or any of the children.''

''Because of Lady Cordelia?''

''Why are you even asking, when you know that is one reason why. On her latest call, she was asking question after question about Isaac's school, for she still believes he should attend the school she selected for him.''

His mouth twisted. ''She needs something to fill her time other than attempts to discredit the choices you have made for your son.''

''I agree, but the fact is that she sees it as her obligation to interfere.'' She closed her eyes and sighed. ''And the fact is as well that she would be horrified if she learned where you had taken Isaac today."

"How will she know? I have no intention of speaking to her of this, and I know you have none either. Isaac avoids her as much as he can because she asks him about the lessons she believes he should be doing even while on holiday."

"But he does not avoid his sisters. You can be certain that he will want to share with Leah every detail of the visit, making it as gruesome as possible. Leah has the inconvenient habit of prattling when my aunt is within earshot. A single word spoken at the wrong time, and Aunt Cordelia will pounce on this incident to use with the rest of the family in her argument that I am obviously inept at raising the current Earl of Emberson." She came to her feet. "Neville, I will not allow anyone or anything—even bodysnatchers—to persuade someone to take my son from me."

He stood. "You know I would not let that happen."

"*You* would have nothing to say about it." She regretted the words as soon as she spoke them. She did not want to be angry with Neville, and she did not want him angry with her, but— She was not sure what the "but" was in her thoughts.

"I understand." His face became as hard as the marble floors. "If you will excuse me . . ." He walked toward the door.

She longed to call him back, if for no other reason than for him to explain to her why she was suffering from guilt as strong as if *she* were the one who had broken a promise. She bit her lip to keep from speaking his name.

When he left, she sank to the settee again. She popped back to her feet when he strode back into the room and toward her.

He clasped her by the shoulders and said, "By all that's

blue, Pris, you are going to make me apologize to you, aren't you?"

"Not if you do not wish to," she whispered.

"You probably have no idea what I wish to do right now." His gaze swept over her as he stepped back.

She gasped, unable to silence the sound. His eager perusal revealed exactly what he wished to do. She should say something—*do* something—but she was frozen as if she had become another sculpture in the room. That now-familiar, enticing fire surged through her as she tried to clear her mind of the images of those erotic sculptures in embraces she should not be wanting to share with him.

"However," he said when she did not reply, "I will content myself with only an apology, Pris. If you think I broke the vow I made to you, I am sorry. I do not think I did, but I would rather be wrong than have you flurry your milk over me."

She stared at him for another long while, then began to laugh. "If that is your idea of a heartfelt apology, you need to put more effort into your apologizing skills."

His hand curved along her face as his expression remained serious. "All my effort is, at the moment, being expended on something very different." He moved away again before she could do more than gasp again. "If you will give me a few minutes, Pris, I will change so I can escort you and young Isaac back to Bedford Square." He walked out of the room.

"Don't change," she whispered, although he could not hear her. "Don't ever change, Neville."

Chapter Ten

The letter was delivered just after midday. Juster brought it to Priscilla's study, where she had been replying to a note from the vicar in Stonehall-on-Sea. The Reverend Mr. Kenyon, who had taken over St. Elizabeth's after Lazarus was sent to London, worried about his parishioners, so she had promised to write him about their safe arrival. That she had taken so long was the reason she was so eager to finish it.

"From St. Julian's," the footman said as he held out the folded page. "From a Mr. Knight, who is Dr. Summerson's secretary."

"Interesting," said Neville, who must have followed Juster to her study.

She had to agree. Thanking Juster, she opened the letter and scanned it as Neville closed the door.

"Is it the list of the families that have had bodies stolen?" he asked.

She looked over the page. "Patience, please."

"How can I be patient when we have waited days for this information?"

"Patience, please."

With a grunt, he strode across the room. He poured himself a cup of coffee but did not take a drink.

She gave him the letter. "It appears Dr. Summerson was mistaken. There are not, according to this, six bodies missing. The number is five. Even though the deaths have taken place over the past month, you will note that the bodies have been stolen from the churchyard in the past fortnight."

"So I see." He handed the letter back to her. "Knight was very thorough, because he even mentions the unnamed thief who was found in Gower Mews. His zeal at trying to help us halt the bodysnatchers shows he is as frightened as Johnson."

"Agreed, for Dr. Summerson suggested it would take weeks to obtain approval from the families involved."

He laughed shortly. "It is our good fortune that Knight is more afraid of the resurrectionists than he is of Dr. Summerson. He is being honest instead of telling us the thefts had been going on for several months."

"True." She stared at the list. "Isn't it unusual for the bodies to be left in their graves so long before being taken? Some of these must have been lying undisturbed for two weeks or more. I would think the surgeon-anatomists would want specimens that are very recently dead." Lowering the page to her lap, she said, "That is one of the reasons why, I have assumed, the resurrectionists prey on the poor. They are buried very quickly, and their families do not have the ear of a member of Parliament, either Lords or Commons."

"Then why has this churchyard suddenly become a target?"

"Location? St. Julian's is convenient to the neighborhood where you found Mr. Lofts's laboratory."

"Which would make sense if he had received corpses from St. Julian's churchyard, but he assured me he had not." He smiled. "Don't say it, Pris."

"Say what?"

"That he might have lied to me or that the resurrectionists might have lied after stripping the bodies of any valuables that could identify them. I am quite aware of that."

"I am sure you are. If the reason is not location, what do you have to suggest?"

He sipped his coffee. "I have nothing new to suggest at this point, because, even with Knight's information, I do not have enough specifics to draw any sort of conclusion."

"Are you leaning toward the idea that the deaths and the stolen corpses might be intimately related?"

"Yes, but such a diabolic plot is difficult even for *me* to envision. While I am keeping it as a possibility, I am considering others as well."

Tossing the piece of paper onto the table next to her chair, Priscilla sighed. She felt the same, but had hoped Neville had taken note of something she had missed.

"We are going about in circles and getting no closer to the truth," she said.

"Which is most likely right beneath our noses."

"This is beyond frustrating."

He set down his cup and brought her to her feet. "Don't sound so down-pinned, Pris." His hands cupped her elbows.

She raised her own fingers and stroked the hard line of his jaw. When he bent closer to her, she thought he whispered her name, but the sound was muted by her pulse thundering in her ears. She stared at his lips approaching hers.

A throat cleared, and Priscilla slid away from Neville as color rose up Juster's face. Glad that she could not see her reflection in the glass to his left, she was unsure what she would have done if she had seen her cheeks were as red as the footman's.

They might have stood like this—the footman discomfited at interrupting and she unsettled at how easily she had given in to her yearning to sample one of Neville's kisses—much longer if Neville had not asked, "What is it, Juster?"

"Th-th-this . . ." He cleared his throat again and began anew. "This message was delivered to you from Lord Burtrum's household, Lady Priscilla, with the request for an immediate answer."

Priscilla tore her gaze from the footman to glance at Neville. He arched a brow, and, for once, she could not guess what that irreverent expression meant. Now was not the time to ask. She went to take the letter from Juster.

"I knocked, my lady." He swallowed hard. "I should not have opened the door without permission."

"You did nothing wrong. Thank you for delivering this."

Priscilla stared down at the sheet of paper. She did not doubt Juster's assertion. As thunderous as her heartbeat had been, she understood why she had not heard his knock. What astonished and unnerved her was that *Neville* had not heard it either. Had he been as lost as she in the anticipation of their kiss?

"What is Burtrum or his daughter asking you to do now?" Neville asked, his voice again honed.

Keeping her back to him, she hoped he did not see her fingers quivering as she opened the letter. "This is an invitation to join them this evening." She faced him. "The family is in mourning! Why would they be hosting a gathering at their home when they did not have the funeral there?"

"They are an odd lot."

"Juster," she said, "tell whoever waits that Sir Neville and I accept the invitation."

The footman nodded and hurried away.

Neville took the page and read it. "If one did not know there had been a death at that household—two, actually, if one counts the coachee's death on their front steps—one would see nothing amiss with this invitation. I wonder what Burtrum is up to?"

"What makes you believe Lord Burtrum planned this gathering and not his daughter or Mr. Drake?"

"A good point, Pris. However, I do not believe either of them would make a move without Burtrum's blessing. Lady Eleanor is too eager to gain her father's approval and Drake too eager to gain the family's title for the son she may give him."

"Agreed." She walked to the window and looked across her garden. Rain fell lightly, creating a mist that obscured the stable. "Neville, I cannot keep from thinking that the answer is right here on the square, and we are overlooking it."

"These are your neighbors. Do you know them?"

"Some better than others."

"Which one do you believe capable of these crimes?"

She laughed wryly. "Several of them if provoked."

"Then the question is what provocation would lead one of your neighbors to kill the others. Burtrum the Younger was, as Isaac said, quite a boring fellow. He might have been obnoxious, but, because he kept to himself most of the time, it seems he did not offend too many."

"Other than me."

"I thought of that, but I believed you should be left off the list of suspects in these crimes."

"Thank you."

He laughed. "If you keep using that sarcastic tone, you may get yourself on someone else's list."

"This is no time for jesting. It has been almost a week

since his death, and all the deaths among the servants took place about a week apart."

"So we are due another?"

A chill seeped through her as she said, "Yes."

Priscilla glanced at Neville and saw his smile was stiff as they entered the front parlor at the Burtrums' house. He must have taken note, as she had, that the guests were from households that had lost someone in the past month. A shiver oozed down her spine. Even more ghoulish than Lord Burtrum having a soirée so shortly after his son's death was the fact that everyone here, save for her and Neville, were dressed in unrelieved black. Even Mr. Lampman was present. She had not heard that he had returned to Bedford Square.

"Quite a collection of crows," Neville said quietly.

"I suspect a collection of ravens would be a better description."

He chuckled as he drew her hand within his arm. "I trust you will curb such comments while we are here."

"I will endeavor to."

Mr. Drake, ever eager to please those around him, hurried to greet them. "I am so very glad you could come this evening."

"Why?" asked Neville bluntly.

"I fear grief has undone Lord Burtrum's mind. Do you know what he has arranged for this evening?" He answered his own question with "A séance!"

"A séance?" She could not keep from adding, "You must be joking!"

He shook his head. "Lord Burtrum believes we might find an answer to these mysterious deaths by talking to the dead."

"It will be a very short, very one-sided conversation," Neville said.

As Mr. Drake rushed away to welcome Sir Stephen Wright, Priscilla said, "I am leaving. I do not wish to be a party to such moonshine."

"Ah, Pris, stay and see what we might learn."

"Learn? This is nonsense, Neville." She scowled. "I cannot believe you wish to be part of this skimble-skamble."

"During my time in the theater, I discovered it was wise to be superstitious."

She folded her arms and regarded him with the expression that worked so well with Isaac. "Really?"

"Really."

"When it was to your benefit?"

"Of course." He put his hand on her tightly crossed arms. "Pris, do not look at me as if you were my tutor chiding me. You know you don't really want to go when there is a chance we might find an answer."

"From a séance?"

"From Burtrum's guests' reaction to a séance."

Priscilla stared at him, then lowered her arms. "I do hate it when you are right."

He gave her a smile, but she noticed he was struggling to keep it on his face as Lord Burtrum welcomed them and introduced a short, round woman he called Mrs. Egbert. She was dressed in clean but shabby clothing and appeared no different from the many women who could be seen shopping at Covent Garden or the Smithfield Market.

That this ordinary woman could speak to the dead strained Priscilla's imagination, but she did not resist when the guests were instructed to sit around a table. She saw how Eleanor hesitated before sitting, and guessed the young woman was uneasy about this too.

No one spoke as Mrs. Egbert took the last chair and asked

them to join hands. On Priscilla's left side, Neville's hand was warm and steady, the complete opposite of Mr. Lampman's, on her right. She was tempted to ask if Mr. Lampman was more disturbed with the idea that the woman would not be able to contact the dead . . . or that she would be able to.

"Silence," Mrs. Egbert ordered. "We must await the signal that those who have gone before are willing to speak to us."

Nothing happened. Priscilla did not dare to raise her eyes from the white linen tablecloth because she feared she would start laughing if she looked at the expectant, frightened faces around the table.

A chair scraped, and Sir Stephen started to stand. "This is arrant nonsense, Burtrum. If we—"

A soft rap-rap-rap came from the table.

Priscilla shot a furious scowl at Neville, but he shrugged his shoulders and squeezed her hand to remind her that he could not be making the sound. But he was, she was certain, when she saw the flicker of amusement in his eyes. She simply did not know how.

"Is it the dead, Mrs. Egbert?" asked Lord Burtrum.

The woman's face was as pale as the tablecloth. She tried to speak, but choked as the soft rapping began again.

Mr. Lampman dropped Priscilla's hand and covered his face. "Make it stop!"

The sound, like the clip-clop of a carriage horse's hooves on the street, continued.

"Make it stop!" Mr. Lampman shouted.

"I can't!" Mrs. Egbert looked at Lord Burtrum in desperation.

"Can't you halt it, Mrs. Egbert?" asked Neville, his voice suggesting that he was querying about a matter no more outlandish than the weather. "I thought you were in control of this séance."

"Make it stop!" Mr. Lampman jumped to his feet.

Priscilla rose and put her hand on his quivering arm. Locking eyes with Neville, she wanted to warn him to halt whatever he was doing before Mr. Lampman swooned. There was no need, she realized, when the noise faded. A noise made by Neville's knee, for he shifted in his seat, stretching out his leg. His prank would have been uncovered with ease if they were not so on edge.

Neville stood. "This nonsense has gone on long enough. If this was your idea of a jest, Burtrum . . ."

"No!" The earl came to his feet and reached for a bell. "I was assured this woman could truly help us."

Priscilla did not believe him, for he refused to look at his guests while he waited for a servant to come and escort Mrs. Egbert out of the house. When she saw Lord Burtrum press something into her hand, which was almost hidden beneath a paisley shawl, Priscilla wondered if he was paying her for her efforts or to be silent about what had occurred or both.

"I think it is time we took our leave as well," Priscilla said.

"Not yet, Pris." Neville's eyes were slitted as he watched their host speaking with Lady Traverson, in whose house the youngest victim had worked. "I would like to hear what Burtrum has to say in the wake of this folly."

She knew she would not budge him until he had satisfied his curiosity. Mayhap she should use the time for the same purpose. Seeing Eleanor across the room, she wondered how she might persuade the young woman to speak with her privately. It was a needless worry, because she had taken no more than a few steps before Eleanor almost ran over to her and pleaded with Priscilla to come with her to where they could talk without being overheard.

As they entered the garden behind the house, Priscilla doubted Eleanor could have found a better place for a clandestine conversation. Not only was the ground and every leaf damp from the day's rain, but she had to draw in her skirt so it did not catch on a sharp branch or who knew what else in the neglected garden.

"Thank you, Lady Priscilla, for taking time to speak with me," gushed Eleanor. "I know it is damp out here, but I thought it the best place to talk." She looked around with a smile. "I like to come here."

"Why?"

"This garden has been a great interest for my father since we moved to Bedford Square. He spends much of his time here, especially since Cecil's death."

"Really?" Priscilla closed her mouth when she saw Eleanor's shock. She was not sure why the young woman was astonished, when the garden was overgrown and tangled, a sure sign of indifference rather than hours of attention. Other than a few pots with new plants that had little hope of thriving when they were set beneath the leaves of dead plants, everything appeared to be past saving.

"I know it looks forsaken, but it was much worse when we first moved in. Father works hard here. As I said, the garden gives him comfort."

"He spends that much time in the garden and it looks—so unmanicured?"

"You must not judge it by its appearance, Lady Priscilla. Unlike the sedate gardens we are accustomed to, Father's garden has exotic plants that have come from all over the world, ones that you would not see elsewhere in England."

"What sort of plants?"

"I don't know. You would have to ask Father." She grasped Priscilla's hands. "I do not want to speak of gardens.

I have wanted to call on you, but I did not want Father to be suspicious."

"Why would he be suspicious of you calling on me?"

Eleanor opened her mouth to answer, then a sheepish expression filled her eyes. "He would have no reason to be suspicious. 'Tis nothing more than my own disquiet, I fear, and my eagerness to find out what you have learned."

"I fear I have nothing to tell you."

"But you said you would ask Dr. Summerson about . . . about . . ."

"I know," she said, trying not to let her sigh reach the young woman's ears. She had to have sympathy for Eleanor, who seemed to be the only one in this household to be genuinely distressed by her brother's death.

She had no chance to say more, because she heard, "What are you doing out here?" Lord Burtrum strode toward them like an avenging knight on his charger. "Eleanor, you know I do not want others wandering through my garden."

"I am sorry, Father. Lady Priscilla wished to speak with me about her suggestions for re-creating the garden that was here before."

Priscilla kept her face from revealing her amazement that Eleanor was lying to her father. Was she trying to protect her father as she had with the horrible news of how her brother's grave had been disturbed? Or was she trying to keep Priscilla from being the focus of Lord Burtrum's rage?

"You should know better!" he snarled, his eyes bright with fury. "You must leave now."

Priscilla wondered why he was so adamant, but doubted she would get an honest answer when he was angry. She edged around a pot where fresh plantings poked from beneath a shroud of dried leaves. She had no chance to discover what was strong enough to grow in the weeds and dying plants, because Lord Burtrum herded her and his daughter into the house.

He slammed the door behind them and twisted a key in the lock. With another glare at Priscilla, he stormed away.

"Forgive my father." Eleanor sighed as she walked with Priscilla back toward the front parlor. "Since Cecil's death, the garden seems to be the only thing to comfort him. My efforts have been worthless."

"I am sure he appreciates what you have tried to do."

Eleanor waved away her words. "You are kind to suggest that, but it simply is untrue. I fear the very sight of me reminds him of the son he has lost." She dabbed at her eyes with a soggy handkerchief she withdrew from her bodice. "You must forgive Father. He is so distraught over Cecil's death."

"That is understandable. It has been a shock for your family. Have you told him about—?"

"No!" She grasped Priscilla's hand again, but dropped it when Priscilla drew back at the touch of the wet handkerchief. "Lady Priscilla, please reassure me that you have said nothing to my father of what happened at St. Julian's churchyard."

"I told you I would not, and I would not break such a promise."

"But you did you tell Sir Neville, didn't you?"

"Yes, but he will say nothing to your father or anyone who might speak to your father of this subject."

"And you trust him to keep his word?"

"I would not have spoken to him of this otherwise."

"Good." Eleanor walked into the parlor, heading directly for her fiancé.

Priscilla stepped aside as a woman more than a decade older than she came out into the hallway. Priscilla greeted Lady Traverson.

"Oh, Lady Priscilla, I had thought you had come to your senses and left already." The gray-haired woman's mouth was set in a frown that deepened the lines all along her plump face.

"I had hoped to speak with you."

"About the death of my tweener?" Tears flooded her eyes but did not fall.

"Lady Traverson, I know how distressing this has been for you."

"There had not been a funeral on this square since your husband's passing, Lady Priscilla, and now there have been four in such a short time, as well as the death of that thief found behind my house." She shuddered.

"I have been hearing the most disturbing rumors."

"As I have." When Priscilla said nothing, Lady Traverson continued, dropping her voice to a conspiratorial whisper, "The worst of the lot is that young Burtrum was poisoned."

"Really?"

She nodded, her chins vibrating in emphasis. "Did you know his father has sown many varieties of exotic plants in that garden of his? If someone was well familiar with them, then one could have been used in the young man's wine."

"That is possible, but it does not explain the other deaths." She glanced at the parlor. "Or are you saying your tweener was given poisoned wine as well?"

Lady Traverson sighed. "I would not have guessed the girl was one to steal sips from her betters, but it is the only explanation I have."

"Yet no one else in your house has sickened."

"I had every open bottle disposed of as soon as I learned of her death."

"Why? She was the second to die, and, at that time, there was no reason to believe she had been poisoned."

"My housekeeper suggested it after revealing the girl had

been involved with Sir Stephen's butler, even though he was old enough to be her grandfather. Although it seemed unlikely, Mrs. Orton asked me to consider that the girl had killed herself because she was in mourning or—'' Lady Traverson's voice trembled. ''Or because they had a pact to die like Romeo and Juliet.''

''Both were possibilities.''

''Until Mr. Lampman's coachee was found dead.'' She drew a handkerchief from her bodice and wiped away a single tear from either eye. ''Jarvis was a loyal servant and treated everyone on the square with respect, unlike some of these new servants, who seem to consider themselves the equals of their betters.''

''My servants are very anxious about what may happen next.''

''Mayhap you should speak with Sir Stephen and Mr. Lampman. They may be able to tell you something to give solace to your household. I am afraid I have none to offer.''

Priscilla went into the parlor as Lady Traverson hurried down the stairs. Seeing Sir Stephen balancing one elbow on the mantel as he glowered into his glass, she decided she might not get a better opportunity to speak with him.

He listened to her for only a second. ''Lady Priscilla, why are you asking about this? Isn't this a matter better left to the authorities?''

''Sir Stephen, I want answers to reassure my own household staff,'' she said as she had to Lady Traverson. ''They are unable to concentrate on their tasks since Cecil Burtrum's death. I have lost count of the dishes and china figurines that have been broken because they are fumble-fingered.''

His impatience straightened his lips. ''The answer to his death is obvious. Someone put something deadly into his wine. I don't understand why you are continuing to pry into this, when the answer is right in front of us.''

"But the answer is not in front of us. It does seem self-evident that he was poisoned, but who would have done such a thing?"

"*That,* Lady Priscilla, is one of the matters that should be left to the authorities to uncover." He looked back down into his nearly empty glass, and she knew she was being dismissed. She was surprised when he added, "I have spoken with them on several occasions in an effort to discover the truth about why my butler Grant was killed. I would like to have a few words with his murderer, who may not realize how difficult it is to replace a well-trained butler."

Priscilla bit back the words she should not speak. Was that all Sir Stephen was upset about? Replacing his butler with another who understood his peculiarities? She crossed the room before she could not restrain the words any longer.

What a waste this evening had been! She had not learned anything she had not already known. She hoped Neville had had better luck in uncovering the truth.

Chapter Eleven

Neville looked over his cards to the money in the middle of the table. It was enough to buy a fine horse. When Burtrum added twenty guineas to the pile, Neville hid his astonishment. It seemed strange for so much money to be hazarded by a man who was marrying his daughter to Drake for the blunt in his pockets. Glancing at Drake, whose face was expressionless, Neville wondered if it might be as simple as Drake had agreed to cover his future father-in-law's losses this evening.

Burtrum looked at him, a triumphant smile on his lips. It wavered when Neville placed a matching amount on top of Burtrum's coins.

Almost a week had passed since the disastrous séance at Burtrum's house. When another invitation had arrived at Priscilla's door, this one for an evening of conversation for the ladies and cards for the gentlemen at Mr. Parkman's home, Neville had been intrigued by another opportunity to observe the residents of Bedford Square. Their host showed every sign of being an encroaching mushroom, for he agreed with everything anyone with a title had to say even if it was contrary to a statement he had just concurred with. A slender man whose mustache brought to mind a mouse's whiskers, Mr. Parkman was welcome among the *ton* because he was an excellent host and had the wealth to entertain them grandly.

Even this small room had gold trimming the frames around paintings. A pair of ceramic lions imported from China had been created by an accomplished artisan, if Neville was not mistaken.

Burtrum's triumphant smile vanished when the pot was won by someone else. Before Neville could speak, Burtrum was grinning again and placing another twenty guineas in the middle of the table.

"Very daring," Drake said with a surprising chuckle. He placed twenty more guineas on the pile.

Neville hid his amazement. Mayhap Drake had more to him than his money. There was only one way to find out. He tossed thirty guineas atop the others.

Drake deflated as if he had been popped with a pin, and he said nothing more as the evening unfolded. His losses were not great, but he seemed to sink more deeply into his seat with every passing minute.

In contrast, Burtrum was jubilant in spite of reckless wagers that were costing him the money he had brought to the table. He was drinking as heavily as he was betting, and he seemed determined to engage Neville in conversation. Whether he was aiming to cause Neville's concentration to flounder or the brandy had loosened his tongue, it soon became too vexing.

Neville stood. "I believe I shall bid you a good evening, gentlemen."

"It is early!" The protest came, not surprisingly, from Burtrum.

"I promised Lady Priscilla that I would escort her home before midnight." He put the disdain in his voice that the men would expect to hear. "She needs to rise early for something with her children. Good evening."

Coming to his feet, Burtrum grasped the table to keep from wobbling. Neville had not guessed the earl had swallowed so much of Parkman's excellent brandy. Burtrum draped his arm over Neville's shoulder and grinned. Doubting if the man could walk far by himself, Neville let Burtrum lean against him as they went to the room where the ladies were gathered.

He smiled as he looked across it to where Priscilla was speaking with Lady Eleanor. The young woman was—for once—not piping her eyes, a pleasant change. He could not fault her for her grief, but he found it difficult to believe she could be so overmastered when her father seemed to have recovered from his sorrow with such alacrity. Then, scolding himself, he recalled how Burtrum did not know that his son's corpse had vanished.

And he would much rather enjoy the beguiling sight of Priscilla dressed in a creamy dress that added a rich glow to her golden hair. He watched her hands emphasizing her words and recalled them stroking his face. *That* had been most unexpected, although he could not lie to himself and say he had never imagined her touching him with such tenderness. The kiss on her cheek when he had greeted her upon her arrival to Town had whetted further his craving for her lips. He had battled with that yearning since he had last called in Stonehall-on-Sea. Her fingertips, gentle and inviting, had revealed that even though she would miss her late husband for the rest of her days, she was ready to welcome another man's attentions.

"That is a grand sight," said Burtrum, his words slurred. He was slanting now against the wall. "Two lovely ladies."

"Yes."

"Shall we?"

Not sure what Burtrum meant, Neville went with him when he reeled toward his daughter and Priscilla. This drunkard should not be inflicted on Priscilla, even though she would be able to handle him with her usual aplomb. When Drake trailed close behind, Neville guessed he was as determined to protect Lady Eleanor from whatever her father might do or say while in his cups.

Priscilla's smile did not alter as they approached. She greeted Burtrum and Drake as graciously as if she had been awaiting the opportunity.

Beside her, Lady Eleanor edged toward her fiancé. Was she afraid of her father? That made no sense, because she had proved herself to be a devoted and dutiful daughter in trying to protect Burtrum from the truth about his son's corpse.

Priscilla must have noticed the motion too, because she said, "We will try not to fill you gentlemen with ennui, but Eleanor and I had one more matter to discuss about her upcoming wedding." She smiled at Drake. "Mayhap you should not heed this, Mr. Drake. A bridegroom is not to know what his betrothed is wearing until she arrives at the church."

"She will be a lovely bride," Burtrum said with an embarrassing burp. He draped an arm around Neville's shoulders again and gave a drunken laugh. "I have just the jolly. You must join me and Eleanor for a ride in Hyde Park on the morrow, Hathaway. A man can be bamboozled by the shadows at night, but in the bright sunshine you shall see she is even more beautiful than you guessed."

Neville looked from Drake's scowl to Priscilla, who was

trying not to laugh. Did Drake believe Burtrum was trying to renege on his agreement to give him his daughter? Burtrum must be floored if he believed Neville was eager to pay court on his daughter, who had not hidden her discomfort with him.

Only by promising that he would take a drive with them in the Park—"but not tomorrow, because I regret that I have other plans already"—was Neville able to put an end to Burtrum's comments. That it was true he had another appointment the following afternoon made it easier to feign regret. When Drake and Eleanor eased away, he was relieved when the earl followed, still prattling about whom they would see in the park.

"Now, that was interesting," Priscilla said, smiling. "I had not guessed you were considered a proper husband for the earl's daughter."

"Nor had I."

"What happened while you were playing cards?" She listened as he explained, then laughed. "Now I understand."

"Do not fret on my behalf, Pris. I have slipped through the hands of busybody matchmakers before."

"I know, but I doubt you have met one as determined as Lord Burtrum. Apparently he was satisfied with Mr. Drake until you proved that your pockets are full of lard."

He shook a finger at her. "If you have been up to your usual tricks—"

"Me?" She laughed. "Neville, I did not need to say anything to anyone. All the ladies have been abuzz with whispers about the high-stakes game you gentlemen were enjoying in the back parlor. When you topped Drake's bet and won, you brought into the earl's fuzzy mind the idea of making you and your fortune a part of his family."

"I should suggest he let the idea go immediately."

"Even if he acceded, Neville, I doubt he will recall it on

the morrow. Mayhap he will forget his intentions to leg-shackle you to his daughter."

"Pris, you are a most bothersome woman sometimes."

"I know." She gave him a smile he knew she had borrowed from him. He had never guessed how aggravating it could be.

Priscilla toed off her slippers one at a time and then sank back on the settee. The hour was not late for those accustomed to the *ton*'s schedule, but she was exhausted.

When Neville sat beside her, she drew up her feet and moved so she could rest against the settee's arm. That allowed her to look at him and keep a respectable distance between them, something she had endeavored to do since she had been ready to succumb to his seduction in her study.

"What do we do next?" she asked. "I must have been asked several times tonight where I thought the murderer would strike next."

"He or she is overdue."

"Mayhap he or she has been busy elsewhere."

"Doing what?"

"Digging up corpses."

"Kill them and sell them? A handy operation." He rubbed his eyes and yawned. "Sorry, Pris, but I found sleep impossible last night."

"I know. I heard you pacing. What were you thinking about?"

When he hesitated on his answer, she regarded him with astonishment. Neville did try to shelter her from the darkest sides of human nature, even though she had told him again and again that she was well aware of them. She wondered what thoughts of villainy had kept him from sleeping last night.

He answered as if she had asked that question aloud, "I am trying to figure out the best way to contact Ben Crouch. Every venue I have attempted has been blocked."

"Ben Crouch? The resurrectionist?"

"Why do you sound surprised?"

She smiled. "To own the truth, I had assumed you would have spoken with him by now. No other of his ilk is as well known in London."

"The man is dashedly elusive when one tries to pin down a meeting with him." He gave her a frown. "By all that's blue, Pris, I am doing all I can to get to the bottom of this."

"I know you are." She put her hand on his arm. "Forgive me if I suggested otherwise. After watching what I said so closely all evening, I fear I spoke out of turn now. Do you have a new idea of how you might meet with him?"

"Better than that. I believe I have set up a meeting with the man tomorrow."

"Excellent. When are we leaving?"

"*We* are not leaving. *I* am meeting Crouch. It will be rough where I am going."

"I realize that, and I need enough time so I can change into something more appropriate for our call."

"Didn't you hear me? You should remain here. Even if I acquiesced to your going with me, 'tis unlikely you have anything appropriate for *this* call."

She smiled. "Do not be certain of that, Neville. I have been making a few plans of my own that seem to parallel yours."

He grasped her arms, his eyes flashing as if they were afire. "Tell me that you were not foolish enough to consider going . . . going where I am going on your own."

"Of course not." She shrugged off his hands and jabbed a finger into his chest. "I had intended to ask for your help.

I had not guessed you would seek Isaac's help and disdain mine."

"It is not that I disdain your help, but where I am going is no place for a lady."

She laughed shortly. "Mayhap you have forgotten that as a vicar's wife I have been in all sorts of homes, high and low in character."

"I never forget that you were a vicar's wife, Pris."

Her fury vanished. "I know you don't."

Neville was not astonished that Priscilla could read his thoughts. She always was insightful, but, in this case, she shared his grief. If Lazarus were here, he would have laughed at Neville's uncharacteristic attempt to safeguard her. Lazarus had owned, more than once, that nothing short of a command from King George himself would halt Priscilla once she believed she was doing the right thing.

"If I do not take you with me," he said, "I suspect I shall turn around to find you shadowing me, but, Pris, you cannot let a hint of the truth escape and reveal that you do not belong to that low world."

"I am prepared. When your friend from Drury Lane sent over garments for your call, I asked for another, more feminine set to be delivered as well."

"He should have known better than to have them brought here."

"A crown or two helped persuade him otherwise."

He grimaced. "A pair of crowns on top of what I paid him? He has profited well from this errand."

"If you were concerned about that, you could have arranged for clothing for me when you did for yourself."

"I thought, just once, you would see the wisdom in being patient."

"Why should you expect that of me when you have never been patient?"

That was a question he could not answer. He knew by this time tomorrow he would wish he had.

''Mama, you do not need to escort us back around the square.'' Daphne held the prettily wrapped box containing the handkerchiefs she and Leah had picked out for Barbara Cagswell's birthday gift.

''Yes, she does,'' Neville said.

Daphne's eyes grew wide, but she did not argue.

Priscilla gave her daughters each a kiss on the cheek when they reached the Cagswells' door. She said with a glance toward the butler that the girls should remain there until she and Neville returned. As they went in, she saw Neville slip something into the butler's hand.

''You do not need to bribe someone to do their job,'' she said as she and Neville went back to her house in the unseasonably warm sunshine.

''That was a guarantee he would not forget your instructions.'' He smiled coolly. ''Although I doubt if anyone could forget the danger prowling through this square.'' As her door opened, he added, ''Do hurry, Pris, and change. We do not have much time to meet our soon-to-be new friend.''

''I will meet you in the kitchen.'' To Gilbert, she added, ''Remember. If anyone calls, neither Sir Neville nor I are receiving guests this afternoon.''

''I remember, my lady.'' His face seemed even bleaker than usual.

It did not take Neville long to redress in the ragged clothes his friend Morton had obtained for him from the theater. These were far worse in appearance than anything he had in his storage room on Berkeley Square, for they smelled almost as bad as Lofts's workrooms.

He ignored the servants' stares as he went down the stairs

to the first floor. He paused at the top of the lower stairwell when he heard Lady Cornelia's unmistakable voice from the entry foyer. Dash it! Nothing about this was simple. Motioning to the redheaded maid, he sent June to alert Priscilla. Then he tiptoed back into the shadows as Gilbert brought a most insistent Lady Cornelia to the parlor to wait for Priscilla to receive her. When he reached the kitchen, he breathed a sigh of relief.

"What is that smell?" asked the cook as she came into the room. "I—oh, Sir Neville!"

"We will be leaving shortly, Mrs. Dunham."

"We?"

Quick steps coming down the stairs answered the cook's question better than Neville could have. Mrs. Dunham's eyes grew round and her mouth gaped when she looked past him.

Neville turned and was speechless, a condition he never thought would afflict him. He had not imagined that Morton would send a costume like *this* one for Priscilla. Although he was unsure which show had included a harlot dressed in a gown that had tattered lace edging a deep décolletage, he doubted Priscilla could have played the part. She might wear the frayed gown that revealed more of her ankles than a lady should, but she possessed an aura of refinement she could not rid herself of. Even though her hair was tangled around her face, its rich gold refused to be dimmed.

"You are looking exceptionally horrible," she said as she entered the kitchen. Cocking her head and setting her foot on a stool, she leaned toward him. "Are ye lookin' fer some company, gent?"

Mrs. Dunham laughed, then clamped her lips closed.

He rested one hand on the table and smiled. "Gent? Ain't no gent."

"So I have heard." She laughed, sounding no older than her son.

"But you, Pris, are most unquestionably a lady." He chuckled. "May I suggest a few smudges to dirty up your face?"

"As you did with Isaac?"

She went to the kitchen hearth, squatted, and reached for some of the soot. He followed. Blocking her hand, he sprinkled soot into his. He dipped two fingers into it and ran them across her left cheek. When she laughed, he did the same to her right cheek. She dabbed spots down his nose and on his chin.

He caught her hand, sending a dark cloud of ashes around them. He traced one line that was visible on her palm. When her fingers quivered beneath his, he said, "You have a very long lifeline, Pris."

"I had no idea you could read palms." Her voice was as unsteady as her hand.

"I have all sorts of skills that come in handy when I need them."

"Do you?"

Her breathless question swept his own breath away. He reached to tilt her mouth beneath his but drew back his hand. Being late for the meeting with Crouch might mean they would never be able to speak with the resurrection-cove again. Yet, he did not stand and step away. Letting this opportunity to kiss her evaporate like clouds on a sunny day seemed an even greater loss.

She rose and held out her hand to him. He took it. There would be another chance. Another chance soon. He would make sure of that.

* * *

Priscilla wondered how long she could hold her breath so she did not have to smell the odors coming from the open sewer along the street. Mayhap it was not intended to be a sewer, but it had become one. When something poured from an upper floor of a house, she pulled Neville out of the cascade.

"Watch where yer steppin'," she said in the broadest accent she could concoct.

Neville's eyes sparkled with amusement, and she was glad his good spirits had returned. He had been silent since they had left her kitchen, where she had been sure he was about to kiss her. She almost had stated that if he wanted to kiss her, why didn't he just do so? Then they could concentrate on this meeting. She could not say that, feeling abruptly as shy as a young miss at her firing-off.

"Don't be scoldin' me, woman," he retorted. "I'll walk wherever I please."

"Walk through chamber pots if ye want, ye slow-top!"

Laughter came from the steps, where people even more ragged than they were sat and gossiped. One woman was nursing her baby while her other breast was exposed over her lowered gown. She called, "If ye don't want 'im, dearie, I'll take 'im." She eyed Neville boldly. "D'ye want a sample?"

"No, thanks," he said, slipping his arm through Priscilla's and hurrying her along the street.

"You are blushing!" Priscilla laughed. "I never thought I would live to see the day someone caused you to blush."

"I do not blush."

"Then your ears have been burned from too much time in the sun."

He grumbled something under his breath and steered her along the uneven street.

Priscilla lost any inclination to tease him more when he

opened the door of a house that looked as if it could tumble into rubble at the first breath of wind along these cramped streets. What was inside was recognizable as a public house only because a keg was set in one corner and men were refilling mugs at it. Other men sat on benches against the walls. Through another door, several tables were visible, but no one sat there.

Following Neville through that door, she winced when she stepped into something she hoped was only sour ale. She went with him out of that room and into another that had no windows. Even as she blinked, trying to see in the darkness, he grabbed her hand and led her out a door she had not noticed. They were in a courtyard that was even more overgrown than Lord Burtrum's garden. A tug on her hand sent her hurrying after him as he climbed some teetering stairs that she hoped would not crash to the ground beneath them.

He opened the door at the top and gave her a shove inside. She was about to protest, when she saw a man at the small table that almost filled the room.

"Sit down," Neville hissed as he put a hand on her shoulder. Raising his voice, he said without a trace of accent, "And be quiet."

"Wot's she doin' 'ere?" asked the man, whose face was disguised by the shadows. He shifted forward when Neville closed the door, for the only light was a candle set directly behind him. It left his face in silhouette.

Neville threw a leg over the bench and sat. His foot clunked against something, and she realized the table was set on another keg when he grabbed a mug and filled it with foamy amber. "Are you Crouch?"

"Aye. Ye be 'Athaway?"

"Yes."

"And 'er?" He pointed at Priscilla.

"A friend."

The resurrectionist chortled. "If I 'ad a friend like that, I wouldn't be bringin' 'er 'ere. Too many lads would be glad to pay 'er a few pennies to lift 'er skirts."

"That is her business. Mine is with you."

Priscilla hid her smile. No one who met Neville for the first time was prepared for the verbal jousts he enjoyed. It gained him an advantage he would not relinquish.

"So, Crouch, tell me about this business at St. Julian's churchyard."

"M'lads 'aven't been there. You 'ave my word on that, 'Athaway."

Although Priscilla wondered how much value a body-snatcher's word had, she remained silent when Neville nodded. He had some reason to trust Crouch, and she had to trust Neville.

"If your lads have not been harvesting corpses there," Neville said as he stuck a finger into the foam so it would dissipate more quickly, "then you must know whose lads are."

"No idea."

"Do you expect me to believe that the inimitable Ben Crouch has no idea of the identity of his rival?"

" 'E's like a ghost 'isself." Crouch tilted back his mug of ale.

"The way he slips in and out of a churchyard?"

"Aye." He finished the ale with a gulp. He struck the mug against the table, then threw it at the wall. It bounced across the floor. "The Ghost is wot m'lads call 'im."

Priscilla picked up the mug as it rolled back against the bench. Refilling it, she put it on the table.

Crouch grunted his thanks, then said, " 'Ad them workin' together. Then 'e comes along, and 'e's got them thinkin' of goin' out on their own. Wot's a man to do when 'e can't negotiate a livin' wage from 'is work?"

"Livin' wage?" Neville chuckled darkly. "An odd choice of words."

Crouch regarded him with eyes that should have belonged to a serpent. "Joke as ye wish, but the truth's the truth. Most of the lads will accept three guineas for a large and less for a large small or a fetus, but if we stick together, we can get more."

"An adult body, a child's body, or an infant's body," Neville murmured under his breath just loud enough for Priscilla to hear. When she nodded, he said to the resurrectionist, "That is sensible."

"Aye, but now 'e's come to stick 'is nose in where it don't belong."

"So 'oo is 'e?" asked Priscilla before she could halt herself. She used her fake accent because she recalled Neville's warning that there must be no sign she was used to a far gentler life.

Crouch looked at her and away.

"Ye don't know?" she persisted, watching closely. She did not push so hard that Crouch lost his temper. The man was already on edge, frustrated by this interference in what he considered his private bailiwick.

"Said I didn't know. 'Ow many times must I repeat myself?"

Neville stood and stepped over the bench. He seized Priscilla by the waist. Plucking her from the seat, he set her on the floor beside him. A pair of gold coins twirled on the table before Crouch snatched them and made them disappear among his rags.

"There will be twice that much if you learn the identity of this so-called ghost," Neville said as he reached for the door.

"And if ye find out—" The resurrectionist's voice had a weak, pleading sound.

"I will let you know, Crouch." He hooked his arm through Priscilla's and opened the door.

She remained silent until they had gone down the stairs, across the courtyard, through the maze of rooms, and out onto the street. Then she said, "He is scared."

"Very, and that warns me that we should be afraid too."

"I do not need that warning. I already am frightened."

He nodded grimly but said nothing more as they wove their way through the filthy streets and back toward Mayfair. She wondered if his thoughts were as convoluted as her own. Each chance they received to loosen a part of this jumble disclosed there were even more knots below it. One of those threads must be the one that they could pull and the whole bumble-bath would unravel to reveal the truth.

Priscilla heard the dismayed shouts as soon as they entered her kitchen. Exchanging a glance with Neville, she raised her skirts and ran toward the stairs. He grabbed her arm, halting her.

"Your aunt may still be up there," he said.

When she heard the thump of a body striking the floor overhead, she yanked her arm out of his grip and raced upstairs. She saw Gilbert leaning over a prone Mrs. Moore with a bottle of *sal volatile* in his hand. Around him, every face ashen with horror, stood the rest of the servants.

"What is it?" she cried. "What has happened?"

"There has been another body found," Mrs. Dunham said, wringing her apron.

For a moment, exultation leaped through her, then she realized the cook was not speaking of their search for Cecil Burtrum's corpse. She pressed a hand over her heart, which seemed to have become mired in molasses.

"Another death?" she choked. "Where?"

"At Lord Cagswell's house."

Before she could rush out the front door, Neville caught her arm again. "Pris, mind what you are wearing. If you are seen dressed like this—"

"What does it matter? Daphne and Leah are there."

"And the boy too," Gilbert said tightly. "I tried to halt him, my lady, but he would not be stopped when he realized *she* was here. *She* still is."

She knew he was speaking of her aunt. Aunt Cordelia would have to sit awhile longer. She threw open the door and jumped down the steps, hoping she would not be too late to protect her children.

Chapter Twelve

"What happened to you?" asked Lord Cagswell as Priscilla burst into his front hall. The man's face was as white as the plaster ivy climbing his walls.

"A charade," she said, not caring if he believed it was the truth or not. She panted, pressing her hand to her side. Behind her, she heard Neville entering. She wondered what had delayed him at her house, but that was not important now. "Where are my children? Are they unharmed?"

Lord Cagswell nodded. "The children are upstairs in Barbara's room with her governess overseeing them. I thought it best that they remain as far as possible from . . ." He swallowed roughly as his face became even more ashen.

Guiding the overwhelmed man to the stairs where he could sit, Neville said, "Take a deep breath, Cagswell."

She shuddered as his words brought back the scene of Cecil Burtrum's death. With the viscount sitting on the steps, she could not push past him to go upstairs to find his daughter's room.

"What happened to *you,* Hathaway?" Lord Cagswell asked.

"It is a long story, and we don't have time for it now. They are saying at Lady Priscilla's house that someone has been found dead. Is this true?"

The viscount nodded, pressing his hands over his stomach as if he could hold its contents in.

"Not one of your guests?" whispered Priscilla.

He shook his head.

"Then who?"

He became a very unhealthy shade of green. Standing, he rushed up the stairs in search of a chamber pot.

"Excuse me, Lady Priscilla," said his butler. "To answer your question, it is Mrs. Hartley who is dead."

"The housekeeper?"

He nodded, and tears rolled down his wrinkled face. He wiped them away. "Pardon me, my lady."

Seeing the box that her daughters had brought to the house, she ripped open the paper and withdrew a handkerchief. She handed it to the butler. "You should not be ashamed of honest tears. . . ."

"Saunders, my lady," he supplied when she paused. "Thank you."

"Will you take us to where Mrs. Hartley is?" Neville asked. "Unless you want to check on your children first, Pris."

"I do. I shall return as soon as I can." She squeezed his hand. "I must get them calmed down before they have to face Aunt Cordelia."

"Go ahead," he urged. "If you need help dealing with them, send for me. If you need help dealing with *her,* send for someone else."

She touched his cheek, hoping her fingers could say what words could not. When he put his hand over hers, holding her palm to his cheek, she gave him the best smile she could. It was very weak. Then she hurried up the stairs.

Behind her, Neville smiled sadly. Until she was sure her children were unharmed, she would not be able to focus on this newest murder, and he needed her insight into her neighbor's household in an effort to discover why this house and its housekeeper had been chosen as the murderer's latest target.

"Lead on, Saunders," he said when the butler did not move.

"Are you sure you want to *see* her?" His eyes widened, releasing a torrent down his face.

"Yes, I need to see her." He looked up the stairs. "Post someone here to bring Lady Priscilla to where we are going as soon as she returns."

Saunders nodded and ordered one of the gray-faced footmen to wait for Priscilla. "This way, Sir Neville."

The kitchen was half as big as the one at Priscilla's house, and the walls had been recently whitewashed. Even so, the area around the range that had been bricked into the hearth was black with soot. A half dozen servants stood around, silent. They stared at Neville as he passed with the butler through the main room and into what he guessed was a private room for the upper servants' use.

Mrs. Hartley looked as if she had fallen asleep at the table that was pushed against the wall opposite a sideboard. Her head was propped on her folded arm. When Neville tilted her head, he saw her face was drawn and tight. Just as Cecil Burtrum's had been. Her other hand was on her apron pocket, her fingers spread lifeless over a plain handkerchief on her lap. Beside her were a glass filled halfway with wine and a piece of cake with several bites missing.

The scene was a repetition of the one at Burtrum's house. No sign of an attack.

He picked up the glass and sniffed it. The strong scent of the wine could have concealed any poison in it. Asking Saunders to send to Bow Street for Thurmond, he sighed. No more clues than before, and now more questions he could not answer.

Priscilla slipped into the room, and he gave her a taut smile before saying, "I trust the children are fine."

"A bit distressed, but otherwise all right."

"I know the feeling well."

When Neville took her hand in his, Priscilla was grateful for the touch of living flesh. He glanced at the ceiling, and she knew what he was thinking as surely as if the thoughts were her own. As soon as they returned to her house, he was going to insist she move with the children to Berkeley Square. He might be right. Solving this puzzle was not worth her children's lives.

"This appears to be just like the others," she said. "Death suddenly and with no apparent cause."

He tapped the glass. "She was drinking wine too."

"Possibly."

"The glass is half empty."

"She may have taken only half a glass, for she would have been busy shortly overseeing her staff cleaning up from the party."

He laughed tersely. "You may be correct, Pris. She did have time, however, to enjoy some cake before she expired. No one else should sample a piece of it."

"Several have," Saunders said, coming back into the room. "None of them have shown any ill effects other than being terrified. Whatever it was that killed her must have done so quickly, because she was in here only a few minutes before she was discovered dead." He sniffed loudly on the last words and pulled out the handkerchief Priscilla had given him.

Although they talked to the other servants, nobody seemed able to add anything else to Saunders's facts. Mrs. Hartley had come into this room to relax while she waited for the birthday gathering to be over. She had showed no signs of illness or despair. Taking a piece of the cake, she had come into the small room to put up her feet while she could steal a few minutes of relaxation. When the cook had come to sit with her only moments later, she was dead.

Lord Cagswell wobbled down the stairs. One of the maids quickly found him a chair. Sitting, he said, "Lady Priscilla, do not think me rude, but I would prefer your children leave now. I do not want them to be attacked as well."

"I understand." She looked at Neville.

"I shall stay until Thurmond gets here." He laced his fingers through hers as she started for the stairs. She waited for him to say something, but he was silent while they went up to where the children were clumped together, looking haunted and frightened, by the front door.

Squatting, Neville said, "Isaac, now is the time when I need you to do something to help."

"You know I will!" He gave his sisters a superior smile. "Just tell me what to do."

"Go home with your mother and watch over her and your sisters. Your great-aunt is there, and you need to keep her busy while your mother changes. Your great-aunt must not see your mother dressed so."

Isaac whistled. "What are you wearing, Mama?"

"A costume," she replied as she had to Lord Cagswell. "Let's go so Neville can return to . . . so he can do what he needs to do."

Neville did not let Isaac follow his sisters and Priscilla

out the door. "Watch over your mother and sisters, Isaac. Don't let them leave the house or let any strangers in."

"But if Mama wants to go—"

"You are a clever lad. Devise some clever excuse why she cannot leave."

"I will try."

Standing, he smiled. "Good. I will be back as soon as I am done here."

Neville remained in the doorway, watching Priscilla leave with her children. In spite of her words earlier, she would not need his help—or anyone else's—in dealing with her children and her imperious aunt. He never had met anyone else, not man or woman, who was as capable of doing whatever was necessary. He wanted to make sure she did not have to.

"You want us to take her all the way up the stairs to the servants' quarters?" Cagswell turned even more gray. "I daresay that is a waste of time, isn't it? She will be going out the back door to the churchyard, so why not put her in the rear room?"

"A sensible notion," Neville agreed, hoping the man would not breathe his last right in front of him and Burtrum.

Having a very composed Burtrum arrive within minutes after Priscilla left had been a surprise. Unlike the sot who had been obnoxious at Parkman's house, Burtrum was compassionate and helpful today. Yet there was a lightness in his step that baffled Neville. Mayhap it was nothing more than Burtrum being glad this death had not taken place at his home.

Burtrum frowned. "Are you going to lay her out like she's one of the family? Giving servants the idea that any of them are equals to the *ton* is a bad precedent."

"No one said anything about that," Neville replied, wondering if he had been forgiving of Burtrum's past actions too quickly. Such a comment was what he would have expected from the man who was trying to get his daughter an even richer husband than the one he had promised her to. "Cagswell wants to move her out of the servants' gathering room."

"I will have no part of it." Burtrum went to the sideboard and opened a bottle there. Pouring himself a glassful of the wine, he drank it as he watched the footmen lift the housekeeper's corpse. "This is going to upset the servants on the square even more. She should be buried quickly and quietly like the others were."

A soft sound came from the stone floor, and Neville saw something roll into the shadows under the table. A snuffbox! It must have been in Mrs. Hartley's pocket. He snatched it from the floor before Burtrum finished refilling his glass. By the time the earl faced him again, the snuffbox was hidden beneath Neville's coat.

"Why are you poking around under the table?" Burtrum asked, his words already beginning to become garbled. He must have been drinking before he arrived to retrieve his daughter, who had been attending the gathering as well.

"Trying to see if there is anything that might point a finger at the murderer."

"Murder?" Burtrum choked on his wine. "Whatever makes you think that she was murdered?"

Neville frowned. "Do we need to go through the whole of this again, Burtrum? This is the fifth death on a single square in a month if we disregard the thief's death in Gowers Mews. Five people who were in apparently good health suddenly dying of no obvious cause. Don't you consider that unusual?"

"You cannot be suggesting that we link my son's death with those of these servants."

"Quite to the contrary. I can suggest it very readily, and I have." He smiled coolly at the earl. " 'Tis not just the servants who need to be worried here on Bedford Square. It is those abovestairs as well."

Neville left Burtrum to stew on his comments and gather strength from the wine. After helping Cagswell hold on to his fragile composure and sending for someone from St. Julian's to make the arrangements for the funeral, Neville was ready for a bath and clean clothes and a glass of something tasty in his hand.

Rain was falling fitfully as he crossed the square. No one stood in the center garden or walked along the streets. Draperies were closed at many of the windows, and he doubted he would get a response if he knocked on any door but Priscilla's. If terrorizing the residents of this square was part of the murderer's aim, it was succeeding.

"With Lady Cordelia," Gilbert said in answer to Neville's question of where Priscilla was.

"Still?"

"Lady Priscilla just went in to speak with her aunt."

Neville's lips straightened. He had to fight every instinct that urged him to stand by Priscilla's side as she faced her aunt's wrath at being kept cooling her heels so long. He appearing in these smelly clothes would only infuriate Lady Cordelia more.

Ordering a bath, he climbed the stairs to the guest room. It was a pleasant chamber with bright yellow walls and a comfortable bed surrounded by light blue curtains. He pulled off his boots and set them to one side as the bath and water were quickly brought. He suspected Mrs. Moore had kept the water warm in anticipation of his and Priscilla's wishing to bathe.

He chuckled under his breath. Now, there was an intriguing idea. He and Priscilla bathing together. An idea he must not speak of, for the connection between them—the connection that went beyond the friendship they had enjoyed—was tenuous and ethereal. For now he would have to keep such fantasies to himself.

He washed quickly and dressed with all speed. He needed to send for his valet, Riley, to join him here, because his waistcoat was almost as wrinkled as the one he had worn to meet with Crouch. Shrugging it on, he reached for his collar and cravat.

A knock sounded.

"Come in," he called.

"Are you decent?" came the reply through the door.

Recognizing Priscilla's voice, he opened the door and motioned for her to enter. "You should know that decent has never been an approbation added to my name."

"As long as you are properly dressed . . ." She entered and sat on the chest at the foot of the bed.

Neville was amazed. Priscilla usually was the definition of propriety within her house, so she must be even more distressed than he had guessed. "How much did the old tough scold you?"

"No more than usual." A smile warmed her pale features. "She gave me the choice of bringing the children to her house or returning to Stonehall-on-Sea. Neither alternative is acceptable to me, and staying here is not acceptable to her."

"You staying here or me?"

"Egad, Neville, she has no idea you are beneath this roof, or she would have lambasted me far more."

He tied his cravat around his collar and looked at her reflection in the glass. She was as tense as a race horse at the starting line. "There is another choice."

"If you are going to suggest moving my household to Berkeley Square, I accept."

"Then I am glad *I* made the offer." He sat next to her on the chest. Pushing aside his filthy clothes, he frowned when something clattered on the floor.

"What is that?" Priscilla asked as he picked up the small snuffbox.

He handed it to her. "This was the housekeeper's, I assume, for it fell out of her pocket when she was moved."

She ran her finger across the plain burnished top and reached for the latch to open it. He put his hand out to halt her.

"Don't, Pris. What is inside may have something to do with the murders."

"Snuff?"

"It may not be only snuff. I want to have it examined." He took the box from her and put it under his coat. "But that will have to wait. How long will it take you to close up the house and bring what you need to my house?"

"A few days, not much more." She sighed. "The poor staff has just finished unpacking for the second time."

"You don't need to bring much."

"I know. Neville, one more thing."

He folded her hands between his. "If you fear what your aunt and the other gossipmongers will say, I will sleep at my club."

"No, it is not that." She raised her eyes to meet his. "I want you to promise me that I will still be helping you find this murderer. Some of my neighbors do not have another place to hide. I must help them."

"I know." He stood and bent toward her. It took every ounce of his self-control to kiss her only on the forehead. "I promise you still will be helping me. I cannot turn aside any assistance when I do not know where to turn next."

"I think the answer is obvious."

"Then share it."

"We need to speak with Dr. Summerson, who has been very absent of late." She came to her feet. "I suspect he knows more than he has said. Far more."

Priscilla had doubted Neville would allow her to call on the curate alone the next day, but Neville had been asked to come to help Lord Cagswell when a pair of robin redbreasts from Bow Street arrived to speak with the viscount. Knowing he would rather help the Bow Street Runners than give Dr. Summerson a look-in, she wished him luck.

"Be careful, Pris," he had replied. "You are right. Summerson knows far more than he is letting on, but there is no telling what he would do to keep you from discovering it."

Neville's words echoed in her mind as she walked up the steps of Dr. Summerson's grand house. She tried to push them from her head as she waited for the door to open. Whatever the curate was hiding, it was not that he lived a luxurious life. This house was twice the size of hers and fancier than Neville's Berkeley Square home.

Priscilla tried to keep from staring as she was welcomed in and taken to a splendid chamber. The high ceiling was painted with the scene of mountains and a *palacio* with a fountain in its stone courtyard. Behind the numerous paintings of various sizes, the pale pink wallcovering appeared to be silk.

But what drew her eyes were the two candlesticks on the mantel. If they were copies from the Elizabethan period, they were the best pair she had ever seen. On the base of each, as proud as if still sailing around the world, was a miniature of *The Golden Hind,* Sir Francis Drake's ship.

Before she could examine them more closely, Dr. Summerson strode in. He had dispensed with his reversed collar and looked like any other gentleman who was swimming in lard. This wealth must have come from his family, because none of the other parsons at St. Julian's could aspire to a home like this.

"I am glad to see you, my lady." He bustled about the room like a harried wife trying to please her husband. "Do sit. Please. I hope all is well with you and the children."

"You would have heard otherwise, I am sure," she replied as she sat on the settee. A single brush of her fingertips against the fabric told her it was a choice satin.

"I have heard of the tragedy at Lord Cagswell's home, and I had heard that your children were there at the time."

"Every young person on the square was present." She did not let her sigh escape her lips. Tales of nightmares and children who were afraid to go to sleep or even to eat were circling the square, and she doubted if the rumors were exaggerated, as Daphne and Leah had come into the master bedroom last night to sleep with Priscilla. Isaac, who had snuck into Neville's room, had barely taken more than a score of bites at breakfast even when Mrs. Dunham brought out his favorite rose-petal jam for his toast. She had not thought anything short of the end of the world would keep Isaac from enjoying rose-petal jam.

Dr. Summerson finally sat. "My superiors are deeply concerned about the state of matters in this parish."

"That should not be a surprise, Dr. Summerson." She gave him her warmest smile. "After all, you need only tell them the truth."

"But I do not have answers to many of the questions they are posing."

"And which questions are those?"

She had not expected him to answer. When he did, she realized he was even more unsettled than she had believed.

"Lady Priscilla, I do not have anything I can tell them about why St. Julian's churchyard has been contaminated with resurrectionists. Nor can I explain this sudden series of deaths."

"Pardon me, Dr. Summerson, but those seem to be the only questions of interest at the moment."

"No, there is another." His shoulders rose and hunched again with his sigh. "The question of who might be the next to die."

She frowned. "Surely no one expects anyone at St. Julian's to know the answer to that. Only the murderer is privy to that information, unless we can find out before someone else dies."

"And how do you propose to do that?"

"Like you, I do not have an answer to that question. Sir Neville is assisting the fellows from Bow Street, and I understand more members of the Horse Patrol will be watching Bedford Square. I can only hope that will discourage the murderer. Dr. Summerson?"

"Yes?"

She tried to make her fingers unclasp from their tight grip. "I came to speak to you about the situation in St. Julian's churchyard. It bothers me deeply that Lazarus's last church has been blemished like this. What can you tell me about the memorial services and the burials?"

"Save for Lord Burtrum's son, the services were near the new crypt by the church's back wall. The graves were closer to the old crypt, as I recall." He shuddered. "One cannot be completely certain when bodies are coming and going from the churchyard with such speed."

"Was there anything else the funerals might have had in common? What about the mourners?"

He closed his eyes, and she assumed he was trying to recreate the scenes from his memory. "Each of the funerals was attended by Lord Burtrum and his future son-in-law and another man whose name I do not recall."

"Really?" she asked, astonished the earl had gone to pay his respects to those Neville had told her Burtrum labeled as *mere* servants. Mayhap he was not as heartless as she had deemed him.

"I do not make it a practice to lie to my parishioners, Lady Priscilla."

"Forgive me, Dr. Summerson." Berating herself for allowing her shock to cause her to say the wrong thing, she added, "What can you tell me of this third man?"

"As I said, I do not know his name."

"If you were to describe him . . ."

Again he shut his eyes. "A very tall man. I recall little of him other than he had a drooping right eyelid. I thought it might have come from a war injury, but, as I was never introduced to him, I cannot say for certain."

"If you were to see him again, would you send word to Sir Neville on Berkeley Square?"

"Not to you?"

She hoped she was not blushing. Even though taking the children to Neville's house seemed the most prudent course of action, she could not forget how the *ton* and the church would look upon such an arrangement. Quietly, she said, "Sir Neville is the one who would speak with the man, not I."

Dr. Summerson agreed and offered Priscilla some tea. When she declined his hospitality, saying she needed to get back to her house to keep a close watch on her children, he seemed relieved. She wondered how much work his superiors were piling on him in a demand for answers he could not give them.

Nor could she, but Dr. Summerson's comments had told her whom she should talk with next. She hoped Mr. Drake would be at home when she called. And she hoped he would have some answers for her.

Chapter Thirteen

Priscilla was astonished to discover two men talking amid the packing crates in her entry foyer when she reached Bedford Square. Neville and the red-haired man she recognized as Mr. Peel turned as soon as she entered, and she wondered what they had been talking about. Mr. Peel's face was as blank as Neville's, so she suspected they both were hiding something.

"Why, good afternoon, Mr. Peel," she said, holding out her hand. "This is indeed a pleasant surprise."

As he bowed over her hand, he said, "I begged a ride with Hathaway, and he wished to stop here on the way to the river."

"The river?" she asked, looking back at Neville. What was he planning now? And more important, why hadn't he told her?

As if she had not spoken, Neville said, "Your good friend Mr. Drake is awaiting you in the front parlor."

She swallowed her groan because she had not composed her questions for Mr. Drake; then, seeing Neville's smile, she let the groan slip out. "No doubt he is here to demand an update on what we have learned."

"He should be asking the watch instead of you," said Mr. Peel, frowning.

"But, as I was telling you, Peel, the watch has made itself scarce since Lord Cagswell's housekeeper's death," Neville replied. "I suspect those fellows are eager to keep as much distance between them and a murderer as possible."

"An intolerable situation all around."

Priscilla nodded. "And one that shows no sign of abating. The police in the City do not patrol here."

"Even if they did," Mr. Peel replied, his scowl growing fiercer, "they are so poorly prepared to investigate any sort of crime other than a broken window or a stolen pie, they do not deserve the title of policeman. We need a competent and trained policing force that would answer to a central authority. Bow Street has succeeded somewhat in that manner, but it has too few men to handle the work that needs to be done."

"Something for you to speak with the prime minister about," Neville said.

"I may do so when I take him the latest reports on the war that I have prepared for Palmerston. The secretary of war has already approved them, and I have an appointment with Prime Minister Perceval later in the month."

"With luck," Priscilla said, "this matter will be concluded long before then."

"There are always others."

Neville saw Priscilla flinch, but doubted if Peel noticed. When she excused herself, saying she had left Mr. Drake waiting overly long in her parlor, she gave Neville a steady glance. If she was trying to pass him a message, he did not know what it was.

"Go ahead and take my carriage, Peel," he said when she had disappeared around the top of the stairs, where more boxes were stacked, waiting to be taken to his house. "I think I shall prove that I know a gentleman's place by helping Lady Priscilla deal with Drake."

"The best proof that you are a gentleman, Hathaway, would be to keep Lady Priscilla from following her curiosity into trouble."

"I have found that is not easy."

Peel slapped him on the shoulder and chuckled before taking his leave.

Neville climbed the stairs, knowing Drake was most likely interrogating Priscilla at this very moment. The man had barely been able to contain himself when he discovered she was out and would not be returning for at least an hour. Even though Neville had offered to send word to the Burtrums' house when Priscilla returned, Drake insisted on waiting.

He paused as a blur rushed down the steps from the upper floor. Halting Isaac from flinging himself headlong down the steps, he set the boy on his feet in front of him.

"Where are you bound at such a pace, my boy?"

"Aunt Cordelia is looking for me to do my recitation for her."

"Again?"

Isaac grinned. "I have yet to do it for her."

"You could simply recite for her and be done with it."

"You don't understand, Uncle Neville. Once she gets me cornered, she will keep me reciting all day."

He laughed. "You're right. I failed to understand the enormity of the burden such polite behavior would put upon you."

"Are you going to make me go back upstairs?" He ruffled the carpet with his toe.

"I am going to offer you a suggestion. It would be wise of you to *offer* to recite for your great-aunt this evening after we dine."

"She will keep me reciting all night."

"You know your mother insists on your being in bed at the same time each night. I have heard you complaining about that fact on numerous occasions."

The lad's face brightened as he threw his arms around Neville. "Thank you, Uncle Neville. That is the perfect idea."

"Go on downstairs now." He gave Isaac a gentle shove toward the steps. "Before your great-aunt chances to see you and messes up your plans."

The boy scurried down the stairs as swiftly as he had the upper ones.

Neville chuckled but strode past the stairs. He had been able to avoid Lady Cordelia, since she had called shortly after Priscilla left, only because she wished to avoid him.

As he entered the parlor, Drake paused in mid-word to say, "Hathaway, I had no idea you were still here." He set his teacup back on the table beside him.

"I had finished up the errands I had to deal with this afternoon." He flashed Priscilla a smile that dared her to contradict him. When she returned his smile, hers was warm with gratitude. Very warm, he realized, for it swept over him like the first breeze of spring.

He took two steps toward her, not caring if Drake witnessed him pulling Priscilla into his arms, when he was halted by Drake's fist to his cheek. He reeled back, then instinct drove his own fist into Drake's chin. The man stumbled and collapsed with a moan. When Drake jumped to his feet and swung wildly at Neville, Priscilla stood with a cry.

Neville ignored it as he landed another facer to Drake. This time Drake fell and did not rise.

"What in perdition was that for?" Neville asked, wiping blood from his cracked lip.

Instead of answering, Priscilla went to tug on the bellpull. When June came to answer it, she gave the maid quick instructions, ending with "Do hurry." She closed the door after the maid.

She knelt beside Drake and asked, "Did you have to hit him so hard?"

"Your sympathy for me is hardly overmastering, Pris."

"He is not your match in fisticuffs."

"Would you have preferred pistols at ten paces?"

"Do not be absurd." She patted Mr. Drake's cheek sharply, and he moaned. "What did you say to him to rile him?"

"Me? Nothing. Place the blame where it belongs, with his future father-in-law."

Her eyes widened. "Lord Burtrum?"

"He was very clear that he had accepted Drake as his daughter's betrothed because he did not have a better choice."

Drake groaned and opened his eyes. Neville hauled him to his feet and, making sure he was not going to bleed on Priscilla's settee, sat him there. Drake pulled out a handkerchief and dabbed it across his cheek, seeming disappointed he had not suffered at least a bloody nose. He pushed himself to his feet, but his knees folded, dropping him back onto the settee.

"Stay where you are, Mr. Drake," Priscilla said as the door from the hall opened.

"But you are on your feet, Lady Priscilla."

Neville chuckled at Drake's misplaced gallantry, then wished he had not when his lip cracked anew. He grumbled a curse as the maid edged around him, her eyes so wide, he feared they would pop from her skull. As soon as she had left, he poured some brandy into Mr. Drake's tea and handed it to him. "This may help you compose yourself."

Mr. Drake's hands shook as he tried to steady the cup, but he said, "Quite so."

"Can you hear me well?"

"Excuse me?"

"I want to be sure your ears are not ringing when I tell you that I have no intentions toward your fiancée." Neville sat beside Priscilla. "If you will recall, any suggestion of my joining her for a ride in Hyde Park came from Burtrum."

Color flew up Drake's face, concealing the red outline of Neville's knuckles on his chin. "Forgive me, Hathaway, for letting my despair overcome my good sense. And forgive me, Lady Priscilla. I have waited for the opportunity to make my beloved Eleanor my wife, and I vowed to allow no man to prevent that from happening."

"Neville has made it very clear that he has no intentions toward your betrothed, in spite of Lord Burtrum's comments."

"You may rest assured I have no interest in marrying your betrothed," Neville added, "no matter how much her father suggests a match with me would be more desirable than one with you."

"Neville, refrain from baiting the poor man," whispered Priscilla.

He smiled when Mr. Drake did, but Neville's smile did not ease her concerns. Neville was enjoying taunting Mr. Drake, it was true; yet he must have another reason for saying what he did. If insulting Mr. Drake was Neville's only aim, he would have done so even more openly and then moved on to other matters.

"I am glad to hear that, Hathaway," Mr. Drake said,

sipping his tea. "My beloved Eleanor is very eager to please her father."

Neville leaned back in his chair. "So eager that she would agree to marry where her father bid her to whether she wished to or not?"

"Yes." Mr. Drake's smile wavered.

"A dutiful daughter is always to be commended," Priscilla said, frowning at Neville. He had a right to be furious with Mr. Drake for ambushing him, but he was preventing her from obtaining the information she needed. She must ask with care so as not to arouse Mr. Drake's suspicions. That would not be simple, for he had shown he saw a conspiracy in something as silly as Lord Burtrum's drunken ramblings. "Now, Mr. Drake, you were saying . . ."

He faltered, then replied, "I was about to ask you what you had discovered about—about—" He looked toward the door.

"Very little." She started to pour another cup of tea, then put brandy into the cup instead before she handed it to Neville.

"But this is downright irregular. Surely someone must have knowledge of what is happening in the churchyard. Our wedding is now planned for Saturday next! If my beloved Eleanor is not persuaded her brother is resting in peace, it will have to be postponed."

"You are asking for answers I don't have."

"But you said you would ask about!"

"I have, Mr. Drake." She glanced at Neville, then said, "I am just returned from speaking with Dr. Summerson. He told me something very interesting."

After gulping more of the brandy-laced tea, Mr. Drake asked, "Interesting? How?"

"He told me that each of the three funerals he presided over in the churchyard was attended by, along with a variety of mourners, Lord Burtrum, you, and another man. I found that most interesting."

"Not simply interesting." Neville chuckled. "That is downright—what word did you use, Drake? That is downright irregular."

Mr. Drake's face went from a bright red to an unhealthy white and then back to that crimson again. "It isn't as you are suggesting."

"Suggesting?" asked Priscilla. "I only said I found the fact interesting."

"There is a simple explanation. Lord Burtrum asked me to join him for the burials."

"For servants?" Neville shook his head. "I consider it unlikely, after his comments at Cagswell's house, that he would find it in his heart to attend the burial of anyone without a title."

Mr. Drake gnawed on his lower lip, then said, "I should not say this, for the earl will be my father-in-law, but he went because he did not wish any of them to be buried too close to where his family would rest at the end of their lives."

"Now, *that* sounds like Burtrum."

"But who is this other man?" Priscilla asked, wishing Neville would keep focused on the subject at hand.

"I believe Lord Burtrum said the man was his solicitor. Sylvester Andrews, if I remember correctly."

"His solicitor?" She bit back her astonishment. The image Dr. Summerson's words had created had not suggested the man was an attorney. "What was his solicitor doing there?"

"You would have to ask Lord Burtrum," Mr. Drake said. Coming to his feet, he swayed. Before Priscilla could reach out to steady him, he added, "I believe I shall be on my way. Please endeavor to find out whatever you can as quickly as you can, Lady Priscilla. I do not wish this wedding postponed.''

''I understand.'' She rose and heard Neville mutter something when he stood as well. ''Good afternoon, Mr. Drake.''

''Good afternoon, Lady Priscilla.'' His voice became chill. ''Hathaway.''

''Drake,'' Neville replied as lightly as if his lip had not been struck.

Mr. Drake regarded him with puzzlement, then left.

Putting her hand on Neville's sleeve, Priscilla asked, ''How do you fare?''

'' 'Tis about time you asked.''

She dipped one end of a napkin into the tea and patted it against his lip. When he yelped, she warned him to be quiet before one of the children came to investigate . . . with Aunt Cordelia in tow.

''You should take more care,'' she chided.

''I will do my best to keep my face out of the way of Drake's fist.''

She smiled and pressed the napkin into his hand. ''You are incorrigible.''

''That I am.'' He dropped the napkin back onto the tray. ''And, Pris, I am not badly damaged.'' His lips drew back in a savage smile. ''Not as damaged as Drake. The man is agog with the fear Burtrum the Younger's disappearance will halt this wedding long enough so Burtrum the Elder can find his daughter another suitor.''

''He has made it very clear that he will not stand by and allow that to happen.''

''He has made it *very* clear that nothing anyone might do will keep him from marrying his beloved Eleanor.'' Neville screwed up his face as he said the last two words.

''You may be assured that he has worked hard to make

this match possible. It is no wonder he has every intention of having this wedding held as soon as possible."

"I would agree he has intentions. Intentions of the gravest sort."

With a groan, she went to look out the window.

"Don't you appreciate my humor any longer?" he asked from behind her.

"Such uninspired puns I have never enjoyed." She faced him. "Until today. Thank you, Neville, for raising my spirits, which are always dreary after a conversation with Mr. Drake."

"What else did you discover during your conversation with Summerson?"

"Nothing more than I revealed to Mr. Drake. What did you learn from Mr. Peel?"

He smiled coldly. "I wondered how long you would wait to ask. He told me about another surgeon-anatomist not far from here. I intend to give Mr. Westwood a look-in after I leave this snuffbox with the apothecary."

"The apothecary on Tottenham Court Road? He's a gossip of the first order. Anything you say to him will not remain unrepeated for more than a few minutes."

Neville smiled coldly. "Do give me some credit for knowing better than to ask the help of that prattler. I was planning to leave it with a man I know who will be willing to examine the snuff without sharing his findings with anyone but me. He is located not far from Covent Garden."

"And Bow Street?"

"Now you get the idea, Pris."

Chapter Fourteen

"There may be something in here other than snuff." Stevenson poked a finger into the snuffbox Neville had brought to his shop. The man, who appeared to have one foot on the edge of the grave himself, for he was gaunt and colorless from his pale hair to his scuffed shoes, set the box back on the table. A tabby cat sitting on his shoulders watched with obvious disinterest.

"Can you tell what?" Neville asked.

"Possibly."

"Quickly?"

"The best way to tell if it is poisoned quickly is to try it on someone." He smiled, his thin lips almost disappearing. "You must have someone you would be glad to try it on."

"Not at the moment."

Stevenson picked up the box. Half of the snuff remained on the apothecary's table, but he closed the lid and handed it to Neville. "You could seek someone else's help. Someone who might have more time to help you find your answer."

"You know there is nobody in London better at these types of investigations than you, Stevenson."

"Not like you to give up so easily," the apothecary said.

"I have not given up. Test the snuff when you can and get an answer to me either at Berkeley Square or at Lady Priscilla Flanders's house on Bedford Square."

"I heard you had a new lady you were squiring about. She has opened her door to you swiftly, hasn't she?"

"She is the widow of the Reverend Dr. Flanders and a friend of many years. She is helping me find out the truth about these unexplained deaths."

Stevenson laughed. "Are you changing your ways, Hathaway?"

That question, Neville decided, did not merit an answer. He put the snuffbox under his coat. He did not want to allow it out of his sight on the chance young Isaac would be curious enough to test the snuff himself. "I am just being careful not to make any mistakes that would help this murderer kill again."

He picked up his hat and tapped it onto his head. "One more thing, Stevenson. You might want to make sure your cat doesn't get into that and prove it was poisoned."

Rain was spotting the walkway as Neville strode in the direction of Westwood's surgery school. The apothecary had been another dead end. He grimaced. No wonder Priscilla was vexed with his silly puns. That unintentional one only added to his own irritation with the clues that seemed to lead nowhere.

As he climbed the stairs in the run-down building that could have been a twin to the place where he had spoken with the bodysnatcher Crouch, Neville knew he should have been prepared after the visit to Lofts's workrooms, but he was not. The stench of rotting flesh and chemicals threatened to overwhelm him.

His knock got a quick response, and he was ushered inside without a single question being asked. He understood why when he saw a tall man in front of him holding a scalpel that was aimed right at his gut.

Holding up his hands, Neville said, "I am not here to close you down."

"Who are you?"

"Neville Hathaway." He hoped he was not about to say the wrong thing as he added, "Robert Peel told me to talk to you about the resurrectionists."

The dark-haired man lowered the blade. "What about them?"

"Are you Westwood?"

"Yes, but what do you want?"

"To know if you purchased any bodies from St. Julian's churchyard."

The man blanched, revealing a scattering of freckles across his face. "That is information I cannot share."

"No?" He watched the man, knowing he must be ready for any move Westwood made. He could not be unprepared, as he had been with Drake. "Would you rather I shared with a friend at Bow Street the information I have of how you provide instruction to your students here, Westwood?"

Fingering the handle of the scalpel, Westwood did not raise it. Neville was glad he had guessed correctly that a man who was determined to heal people would not kill.

"All right," Westwood said reluctantly. "I can tell you that I purchased some bodies recently from the St. Julian's churchyard. Three of them."

"Three?"

"The corpses of two men of advanced years and a young woman. I suspect she was not yet twenty."

Neville nodded. The older men would be Lampman's coachee and the butler from Sir Stephen's house across the square. Lord Traverson's tweener must have been of the age Westwood described. That left one corpse unaccounted for.

"What about a man of about my age?" he asked.

"I know you are asking about the earl's missing son." Westwood's smile was cool.

"You know of Burtrum's body's disappearance?"

"It may be a secret among the Polite World, but we know of such things here. I can assure you that no corpse of that age was brought from St. Julian's." He shook his head with what appeared to be regret.

"And that disappoints you?"

"It would be beneficial for my students to have the opportunity to study cadavers other than the very old or the very young. Ones that had not been half starved and crippled with disease and poverty."

"Mayhap you should send your resurrectionists farther afield."

Westwood frowned. "*I* do not tell them where to search for their wares. I want no part of that."

"So you have no idea why they have sought out St. Julian's churchyard?"

"I can only assume it is for the same reason they have moved from one churchyard to another in the past. Either the authorities refuse to look the other way any longer, or another gang forces them out." Pointing to the door, he said, "I have told you what you want to know. Now get out."

"One more thing I need to know. Who brought you the bodies?"

"Resurrectionists."

"They must have names."

"They would slit my throat for me if I revealed that." Westwood shivered.

"Give me the leader's name. I vow to you that he will never know you told me."

"I would be a fool to do that."

"I can assure you that the Bow Street chaps will not be so accepting of your lack of answers."

Again the doctor shuddered. "All right. I will tell you, but if you reveal that I did, I can promise you that you will end up on one of those study tables before the next month is over."

"You are threatening me, Westwood?"

"Not I, but Gowan and his fellows are always on the lookout for a corpse to sell."

"Even if they have to arrange for the deaths themselves?"

Westwood blanched and lowered himself to a chair near the wall. "What you are suggesting is . . . It is . . ."

"Ghastly? Ghoulish? Unthinkable?" When the doctor nodded, Neville motioned toward the doors along the hall. "Odd words for a man in your profession. Mayhap you should give some thought to where your cadavers come from."

"I have endeavored not to."

"Then I advise that you do, and consider as well the fact that with one powerful gang splintering the alliances and territories of the resurrectionists, some of them may be resorting to murder to provide you with your cadavers."

"Really, Neville, for Mr. Westwood to threaten you is outrageous," Priscilla said as Neville outlined his afternoon's visits. She watched him pace from one side of her study to the other. "So what else did Mr. Westwood tell you?"

"You are asking me to risk my future eternal rest with such a question."

She laughed shortly. "True, but you would not have told me this much if you did not intend to tell me the whole."

He slanted back against her desk and withdrew the purloined snuffbox. He examined it from every angle, but she knew there was nothing to identify it in any way. His mouth was rigid, showing his frustration with being able to get no answer from the apothecary. "He said the leader of the bodysnatchers working in St. Julian's churchyard is named Gowan."

"A not common name, but certainly there must be dozens of Gowans in London."

He reached under his coat, putting the snuffbox away and drawing out a slip of paper that was stained with something that looked too much like dried blood. "That is why, Pris, I got his address from Westwood. I intend to give him a look-in tomorrow."

"I am busy with the children in the morning, but I am free to go with you after midday."

"Go with me? It might be for the best for you to stay here."

"Do we need to go through that brangle again?"

"And if I disagree?"

"I will follow you." She stood and returned his scowl.

"You are a dashed obstinate woman, as I have said before." He chuckled, and she knew he was not truly distressed that she had insisted on accompanying him again. That he esteemed her opinions pleased her. "Do you still have the clothes you wore when we went to talk with Crouch?"

"I am afraid so."

"Then make sure you are wearing them when we pay

another call on a resurrectionist. This one may have the very answer we have been seeking."

Priscilla edged around some droppings in the street and stepped in something that squished beneath her high-lows. She shook her foot but kept on walking. To pause to discover what it might be would identify her as someone who was unaccustomed to the disgusting streets.

"We are nearly there," Neville said, and she knew his keen eyes had not missed her motion. "This is not as intolerable as the place we drank with our other friend."

"I have tried to wipe that from my memory." She walked around debris on the street and glanced at two children playing in the filth. "It bothers me far less to see those who choose to live in this squalor than it does to see innocent children here."

He nodded but hurried her along the street. His expression told her that he shared her disgust. Was he thinking, as she was, of how helpless she would feel if she had to raise her children in this terrible place?

She began, "I think I will ask Dr. Sum—"

"Watch what names you speak here, Pris."

"I am sorry. I shall ask our friend at our nearby church to raise more money to send to help these people."

"You cannot save them all."

"But I may be able to help some of them."

"If anyone can, I suspect it will be you." Climbing stone steps, he said, "Here we are. Watch how you talk."

"I talk right fine, m'chap," she replied in the lower-class accent she had used before.

"Aye, ye do." He winked and opened the door, ushering her in.

Before Priscilla could take as much as a look around, a

strident female voice asked, ''Yer bringin' yer own? Did ye ask 'Arry?''

''Who is Harry?'' Priscilla whispered as she followed Neville toward a staircase that might once have been painted. ''Another surgeon-anatomist?''

''This is an academy of a different sort, Pris,'' he said with a hushed chuckle that told her even more than the sight of the barely clothed woman who had come out into the hallway.

Priscilla grasped the banister and started up the stairs. Then she paused. Turning, she discovered Neville right behind her. His eyes were level with hers, and amusement crinkled their edges. She wanted to smooth out those lines before letting her fingers explore the rest of his mercurial face.

''Changing yer mind?'' he asked, and she pushed such thoughts from her head.

''I thought I would be wise to ask if there be anythin' up these stairs other than the rest of the brothel.''

He pressed his hand to his chest. ''Ye wound me.''

''Do I? 'Ow did I do that?''

''With yer assumin'. Why do ye believe I know the extent of this school of Venus?''

''Yer usually a good source of information on such matters.'' She laughed, then put her hand over her mouth. With his teasing, he was trying to ease her embarrassment at being in this brothel.

''Do ye think I'd allow ye to wander freely about a brothel when some man might suspect ye were one of the impures within it?'' He stepped up onto the riser where she stood and put one hand, then the other, on the banister behind her, penning her between his hard arms.

She gazed up at him, tilting her head back as he inched closer. Her fingers rose and settled on the thin fabric of his frayed shirt over his chest. Beneath them, his heart beat faster, as if trying to win a race against her pounding one. She whispered his name, needing to say something but unable to think of anything but him.

"Are ye takin' 'er?" asked a rough voice.

Priscilla turned her face away from the blast of a man's sour breath. He was standing a few steps below Neville. The man probably had not washed—either his clothes or himself—since those tattered garments were new. He was staring at her in the same way Daphne admired the gowns she longed to own.

Neville hooked his arm through hers and hurried her up the stairs to the landing. A rickety board under her feet threatened to send them careening back down the steps.

"I need to be careful which I words I choose, I see," he said.

"Let's hurry." She tightened her hold on his arm. "I don't want to stay here—*'ere*—any longer than necessary."

"A good idea." He curved his hand along her cheek again. "And, may'ap, next time I suggest ye stay 'ome and let me 'andle something, ye might accept 'tis a good idea."

"May'ap."

He smiled but grew serious when the crash of broken glass rang up the stairs. Shouts followed it, laced with curses Priscilla had never heard arranged in quite that order. This might not be a school, but she was going to be educated in matters she had never expected she would learn.

There was no lamp or window on the uppermost landing. As Priscilla waited for her eyes to adjust to the darkness, she heard Neville knocking on a door. He seemed to have gained the eyesight of a cat during his late-night sojourns before he received his title . . . and since.

"G'away," called a muted voice.

"At least, the chap is in." Neville knocked again.

"G'away," came the mumble through the door once more.

Neville pounded on the plank a third time. "Gowan, we need to talk t'ye. Westwood sent us."

No answer came. When Neville tried to lift the latch, the door refused to budge. He swore as vehemently and colorfully as the men on the floors below.

She put her hand on his arm. "He's not going to come out. He is too frightened. Just like Crouch."

"I know." He stared at the door, then led her down the unsteady stairs.

She wondered how many more blind alleys they were going to have to explore to get to the truth and how much time they had before the murderer struck again. She intended to discuss that with Neville when they returned home. If they spoke of it while she leaned her head upon his shoulder and he put his arm around hers, that would be even better. They could not go on pretending to be unaware of those moments when they were too aware of each other.

However, when Priscilla entered her house, Aunt Cordelia stood at the top of stairs to the first floor. No avenging goddess had ever worn a more fearsome expression.

Priscilla went up them and did not slow even when her aunt demanded, "Where have you been dressed like *that*? You smell."

"We have been calling on a man who was not able to receive us," she replied, continuing toward the stairs to the second floor. "Would you ask Gilbert to have supper served a half hour later than planned?"

"And that is it?" Aunt Cordelia asked, her eyes bright with astonishment. "You are not going to give me any other explanation?"

"There is no other explanation." She paused as a footman

came down the upper stairs. "Layden, have clean water brought upstairs for Sir Neville and for me."

"Yes, my lady." He made a wide arc around Lady Cordelia before going down the stairs.

"Priscilla, this is outrageous!" Aunt Cordelia sniffed. "I would expect it of *him*." She glared at Neville. "But I would expect better of you. If our family was to see the mother of the fifth Earl of Emberson dressed like a common beggar, I have no idea what they would say."

"Nor do I." She went up the stairs to leave her aunt blustering behind her.

She heard Neville add as he followed her, "A pleasant evening to you, Lady Cordelia."

Her aunt sniffed again and stamped away, warning the evening would be anything but pleasant.

"Lady Priscilla?" Her butler's voice from lower on the stairs was tremulous. With upset or amusement? It was difficult to tell because she had seldom seen Gilbert expressing either emotion.

As Neville paused beside her on the stairs, she said, "Yes, Gilbert. What is it?"

"Sir Neville has a caller."

"Me?" he asked. "Who is it?"

"He did not give me his card, sir. He said only that he had heard you were inquiring about him, and he decided to seek you out to discover what matter it was you wished to discuss with him."

"Tell him," Priscilla said, "we will be right down." As the butler went to do as she asked, she looked at Neville, who was several risers below her. It was an odd sensation to have her head so high above his. "Who is it?"

"As I have been asking about several people, I will know only when I greet him." He crooked his elbow. "Shall we?"

"Like this?"

"Some of the people I have asked about should not be left alone in your front parlor, Pris. You will find your finest things have disappeared."

She could not argue with that. Putting her hand gingerly on his soiled sleeve, she went with him to the front parlor. She wished she had insisted on changing before coming to the parlor when a gray-haired man with spectacles saddling his long nose stood and faced them.

"Good evening," Priscilla said, knowing it was too late to pretend nothing was amiss. "I am Lady Priscilla Flanders."

"*You* are Lady Priscilla Flanders?" he choked.

"And this is Sir Neville Hathaway." She forced a laugh. "I fear you have not encountered us at our best."

The man's nose wrinkled, and he withdrew a handkerchief doused liberally with perfume. As Priscilla tried not to sneeze, he said, "Apparently not. I understand you have been asking about me, Sir Neville."

"And you are?" Neville asked.

"Sylvester Andrews."

"*You* are Sylvester Andrews?" Priscilla asked in the same shocked tone he had used upon her introduction.

The short man nodded. "Is there a problem, my lady?"

"Sylvester Andrews, the solicitor?"

"Yes, my lady."

She stared at him. He did not match the description Dr. Summerson had given her of the man who had accompanied Lord Burtrum and Mr. Drake to the churchyard. As he asked her again if something was amiss, she shook her head.

No doubt Mr. Andrews considered her a widgeon, but she could not allow that to concern her. What she needed to think about now was a simple question.

Had Mr. Drake misunderstood her, or had he deliberately lied?

Chapter Fifteen

Malcolm Drake's house was more befitting a duke than a mister. It had columns across the front as grand as any in London. Connecting them was a pediment containing a life-size bas relief of several women in flowing robes, which Priscilla guessed to be either Greek or Roman. Set by itself amid a garden, the house could have been located somewhere in the countryside. Instead, it was just past the edge of London.

The carriage stopped beneath a porte-cochere, and Priscilla was relieved. The rain was driven on the wind on this dark afternoon, and she was glad for a chance to escape it. The conversation with Mr. Drake had been delayed because her aunt had dropped in each of the past four mornings and had remained until it was too late for Priscilla to call. Her aunt's less than subtle hints that Priscilla should spend less time worrying about other people's problems and more about her unmarried state were a litany that Priscilla believed she could now repeat by rote. Every attempt on Priscilla's part to persuade her aunt that she had no interest in the subject failed.

But this afternoon Priscilla had been able to slip out of the house when her son foolishly came into the front parlor and Aunt Cordelia insisted he review his lessons with her so she might be satisfied he was receiving a proper education. Priscilla felt guilty for abandoning Isaac to such recitation, even though she had asked Gilbert to interrupt with a reason for her son to escape shortly after she left the house.

A footman resplendent in gold livery opened the carriage door. He welcomed her to Drake House as he handed her out. Leading her to the door set above a quintet of marble steps, he backed away with a bow when the door swung open to invite her into the house. She wished she had brought Daphne with her, for her oldest would be delighted and awed by the grandeur.

But this was an errand she had to tend to by herself. While Neville conferred with his friends at Bow Street, she had come to find out if Mr. Drake had been false with her or if he had been betwattled too.

Priscilla gave her name to the butler, who stood at attention at one side of the round entry hall. A half dozen doors connected to it. Only two were open. Beyond one, she saw a fancily carved oak staircase rising out of sight. The butler led her through the other.

The reception hall was grand enough for the Prince Regent. She had never seen so much gilt, for it covered the furniture as well as the walls and the medallion in the center of the ceiling. The marble floors were the exact shade of the tops on the tables throughout the room, which was wider than her Bedford Square house. Sculptures and paintings were almost lost in the expanse and extravagant decorating.

"Please wait here, my lady." The butler's voice boomed against the ceiling.

"Thank you." She walked across the room and sat on a gold settee. She guessed many women among the *ton* would happily wear its silk and consider themselves elegant.

The butler returned almost immediately to announce, "Mr. Drake."

She wondered if Mr. Drake had been standing just outside the room, waiting for his butler to act as his herald. His chin was swollen and bruised, but she pretended not to notice. He bowed over Priscilla's hand, inquired as to her health and the health of her children and aunt, mentioned his concerns about the recent weather, and finally got to the question she had been waiting for him to ask so she could ask her own.

"No," she said, watching his strained face fall, "we have nothing more to share. We do know the name of the man who leads the resurrectionists who have raided St. Julian's churchyard, and Neville is trying to get Bow Street's help in flushing him out of his hole."

"That is something."

"Very little. Do not let your hopes rise too high, Mr. Drake. The man may have already vanished into the gutters of the City."

"True."

"I have to ask you something that is not easy."

"Please feel comfortable to ask what you must." He sighed. "If you are here to reprimand me for my odious behavior at your house, you should know that I deserve every word of it. I lost my head, I fear, when I saw Hathaway."

" 'Tis not that. Mr. Drake, you told me that the man with you and Lord Burtrum at the funerals was the earl's solicitor, Mr. Andrews."

"Yes." Bafflement lengthened his black-and-blue chin, and he winced.

"The description Dr. Summerson gave me of a man who had a drooping eyelid does not match Mr. Andrews, who called at my house yesterday evening."

"Are you sure we are speaking of the same Mr. Andrews?"

"Quite, for he owned to being Lord Burtrum's solicitor."

Mr. Drake set himself on his feet. "Are you suggesting that Lord Burtrum lied to me?"

"I am not suggesting it. Rather, I am saying that either he must have or you misunderstood him or—"

"Or I have lied to you." Entreaty deepened his voice. "Lady Priscilla, I would not have done that. Not only do you have my complete respect, but you are my dear Eleanor's and my sole hope of finding out what happened to Cecil's body."

"Then Lord Burtrum told you an out-and-outer."

"Why would he be false with me? He is eager for my dear Eleanor and me to marry."

She said nothing, and again he winced.

"You are thinking of how he tried to persuade Hathaway to call on my dear Eleanor, aren't you?" he asked, anger sharpening his voice. "I thought you were my friend, Lady Priscilla."

Her forehead rutted with bewilderment. "Forgive me, Mr. Drake, but I fail to understand why you are using that accusatory tone with me when I have been unfailingly honest with you."

"Good day, Lady Priscilla." He strode out of the room, his boots striking the floor as if the heels intended to drive right through the marble.

Priscilla came to her feet slowly. This conversation had not gone as she wished, although she believed Mr. Drake had been taken in by Lord Burtrum. Yet he was outraged at her for even broaching the subject of such subterfuge.

A footman appeared in the doorway, and she guessed he had been sent to escort her to the front door. As she turned to go with him, she halted and stared, unable to move even when the footman cleared his throat in an obvious request for her to take her leave.

The painting hanging on the right of the door was identical to the one in the room where Cecil Burtrum had drawn his last breath. She was sure she was not mistaken, because she had been awed, even in the midst of that horror, by the intricate brush strokes in the shepherdess's hair and skirt. And the candlesticks on the mantel below them . . . She had seen their twins at Dr. Summerson's house. She could understand why Mr. Drake would like copies of Sir Francis Drake's ship in his house to add prestige to his name, but why would such unusual—and identical—candlesticks be found in the curate's house? Were these made by the same master craftsman, or were these copies?

She almost laughed. If Mr. Drake's funds were at such a low ebb that he had to resort to filling his house with copies, then Lord Burtrum was in for an unhappy surprise.

All desire to laugh faded when she realized these could be originals brought here while the forgeries were in the other houses. A theft might never be noticed if the thief replaced the valuable piece with an inexpensive fake. The hullabaloo on Bedford Square would grant a thief the chance to enter a house unnoticed. She thought about the young thief who had been found dead in Gower Mews, then dismissed that thought. He had been found with only a few silver forks and a ladle.

Yet another puzzle that had no solution.

* * *

"Good evening, Mama." Daphne gave Priscilla an affectionate kiss on the cheek. "I cannot wait to show you the new gown Madame LaFontaine is finishing for me."

"She has given me regular reports, and it sounds lovely." Patting the end of the chaise longue in her sitting room, Priscilla said, "Sit here, please. I have something about which I must speak with you."

"About letting me participate in the Season now?" she asked eagerly.

"Daphne, you know that is an issue we have discussed too often already."

"Then do you intend to offer me another lesson in how one deports oneself amid the *ton*?" She rolled her eyes. "I have had so many lessons with you and Aunt Cordelia, I daresay I cannot fit another suggestion into my brain."

"It is not that either. Although you are deadly serious about your future Season, the matter we need to talk about is even more serious."

Daphne's smile disintegrated. "Mama, there hasn't been another murder, has there?"

"No, no." She squeezed her daughter's hand. "It is of a very different sort of crime I wish to speak to you."

"A crime of the heart?" Daphne giggled. "Has Uncle Neville finally persuaded you to let him steal your heart?"

"Daphne! I am trying to speak of something important."

"As I am, Mama."

Wagging a finger at her daughter, she said, "Leave the matchmaking to your great-aunt, who let me know on her last call that she will be finding me a husband so I do not go off on more *adventures*."

Daphne screwed up her face. "Mama, she has been talking

with that dreadful Mr. Wayland, who has called here several times when you have fortunately been out."

"Mr. Wayland has called here?" She stared at her daughter, so shocked she could barely speak. "Why wasn't I told I had a caller?"

"Because he came to make arrangements with Aunt Cordelia about formal calls on you." She lowered her voice and glanced toward the door as if she expected her great-aunt with suitor in hand to swoop through the door. "Even though Aunt Cordelia made me promise to say nothing, I would have warned you before he began calling on you. I know you consider him as odious as I do."

"Daphne, that is no way to speak of your elders."

"Even when it is true?" She giggled again. "I know you do not wish to marry him."

"You are right."

Daphne became abruptly serious. "But Aunt Cordelia would never approve of Uncle Neville."

Instead of agreeing to the obvious, Priscilla said, "Let us speak of what I need to ask you. You have called several times at Barbara Cagswell's house, haven't you?"

"Yes, she is very nice. Much nicer than that boring Lady Eleanor, who talks only of her upcoming wedding until one could believe no one else had ever been married."

"Has Miss Cagswell mentioned things are missing from her father's house?"

"Yes, Barbara spoke of things that had disappeared from the house after both funerals." Daphne sat straighter, her eyes wide with excitement. "She is sure that some thief slipped into the house along with the mourners and took the things, because there were no signs of someone forcing their way into the house, and the servants saw nothing out of the ordinary."

"What sort of things?"

"Little objects. A small gold statue of a cat and a miniature in a gold frame. Items like that."

She frowned. "Items that easily could go into a pocket or a reticule."

"Yes. Why are you asking, Mama?"

"Where is Neville? Do you know?" She looked toward the window, where rain splattered.

"He said he was going to visit St. Julian's."

Priscilla stood. "I thought he might be doing that." She counted the days in her head since Lord Cagswell's housekeeper's funeral. No doubt, Neville had done the same and guessed on a night like this, Gowan and his gang might be busy with their foul work in the churchyard. "Thank you, Daphne, for sharing what you know."

"You are wearing that expression, Mama."

"Which expression?"

"That adamant one. Uncle Neville says when anyone sees it, they should run in the opposite direction."

A soft rap at the sitting-room door brought Daphne to her feet with a soft cry of alarm. Patting her daughter's arm, Priscilla called, "Come in."

"My lady!" Mrs. Moore burst into the room, all aplomb gone. "Do you know where Sir Neville is?"

"Paying a call, from what Daphne tells me."

"Oh, my! Oh, my!" She wrung her hands.

After guiding the housekeeper to sit on the chaise longue before she crumpled, Priscilla motioned for Daphne to go. Her daughter gave a disappointed pout and flounced out of the sitting room. Later, Priscilla would apologize to her daughter, but the dreadful shade of Mrs. Moore's face warned that what the housekeeper had to say might not be fit for a young woman's ears.

"What is amiss?" Priscilla asked.

"A man just came with a message for Sir Neville. He said it could not wait, that I was to deliver it without delay."

"What is the message?"

Mrs. Moore held out a slip of paper. "He gave me this and said the funeral would be the day after tomorrow."

Priscilla snatched the page from the housekeeper's hand. Hating to read a message meant for someone else, she did not hesitate to unfold the page. She would owe Neville an apology, but she needed to know what was so urgent and involved a funeral.

Stevenson is dead. He tested the snuff you brought. He burned it and sickened. His final words were to warn you. Snuff was laced with minced poisonous leaves. Do not get it on your skin, for, if it is monkshood, even a single touch could be fatal.

She recognized the name of the apothecary Neville had taken Lord Cagswell's housekeeper's snuffbox to in order to find out if it had been adulterated in some way. But Neville had told her that the snuff was going to be tossed out. She shuddered as she realized the apothecary must have decided to test it.

Now he was dead.

Neville still had the snuffbox that had contained the deadly mixture. If he opened it to show it to someone and some of the remaining flakes fell out, he could die.

Priscilla went to the cupboard where her black cloak was stored. She pulled it out and threw it over her shoulders.

"You are going out, my lady?" gasped Mrs. Moore. "*Now?*"

"I must warn Neville."

"You should wait here. When he returns, you can tell him of this."

"This cannot wait." She tied a dark bonnet under her chin, glad she had not discarded it when she was done with first mourning. "With this information, we might be able to stop the murderer." Drawing the hood over her bonnet, she added, "Before his poison makes Neville its next victim."

Neville could not have picked a more disagreeable night for his sojourn, Priscilla decided as she pushed open the gate at St. Julian's churchyard. She wanted to call out his name, eager to avoid the minutes it would take to search the churchyard, but she could not forget—for a second—that others might be alive and hiding near the gravestones.

Her low boots slipped on the soaked grass, and she wished she could have brought along an umbrella. An umbrella would reveal that she was part of the *ton,* and she wanted nothing to categorize her. Her wool cloak stank and clung to her with dozens of drenched fingers. Each time she pushed it away so it did not adhere to her arms or skirt, it swept back to stick to her again.

The stones emerged from the storm like specters. Warning herself not to give in to such fanciful thoughts, she walked on the path that wound between the stones and the bushes that had grown up around them. If this had been the churchyard in Stonehall-on-Sea, she could have navigated the path without a pause. But Lazarus had been at St. Julian's for only two years before he died.

Something moved, something too short to be Neville. She clamped her hand over her mouth to keep from screaming. Then it moved again, and she steadied herself. It must be the watchman—either Mr. Johnson or his brother-in-law. With all the talk of grave robbers and other sorts of thieves, she was allowing herself to get as jumpy as if she believed in ghosts haunting the churchyard. That Mr. Johnson was abroad meant the resurrectionists were not. He would have hidden himself in the church porch if they were near.

She would ask him if he had seen Neville. She was tempted to ask him the questions she and Neville had not before. She smiled as she stepped around the crypt. She liked the sound of that. *She and Neville.*

As she crossed the shadowed churchyard, trying to follow Mr. Johnson's erratic path, she watched for the stones emerging from the rain. Her foot slid off the wet grass. Her arms windmilled as she fought not to fall into whatever was in front of her. Whatever? She knew what it was. An open grave. Grasping a nearby stone, she steadied herself. Quickly she backed away from a pair of steps.

Leaning on another stone, she took some calming breaths. Mayhap it would be more sensible to return to the street and go to Dr. Summerson's office. Then she could—

Pain exploded in her head. She fell, senseless, toward the open grave.

Chapter Sixteen

Priscilla heard a groan, then slowly realized it had come from her. She put her hand up to her throbbing head as she opened her eyes. Only darkness greeted her. Darkness and pain. Frantically, she stretched her hands above her head. She sighed with relief, for she had not been buried in the churchyard.

So where was she?

She took a deep breath, then gagged on the disgusting odor—which she recognized too readily now—of decaying flesh and damp. Sitting, she realized she had been stretched out on a stone. She groped through the darkness as far as her fingers could reach. Behind her was more stone. A wall, she guessed. Extending her legs, she used her toes to explore what she could not see.

When her foot thumped against wood, she pulled it back. She recognized that sound as easily as she did the reek. It was the side of a wooden coffin. Where was she?

She stood with care, holding her hands over her head to make sure she did not strike it again. Again? She had not hit it before. Someone had hit *her*! She wanted to know who and why, but first she had to find out where she was and get out of there and back to Bedford Square. She stretched out her hands and felt several wooden boxes in front of her. Were they all coffins?

The soft sound of one pebble bumping another flitted through the shadows to her right. She groped around and found a piece of wood atop one of the boxes. She grasped it and raised it over her head.

"Who is it?" Her voice did not echo, so this dark place was not big.

" 'Tis me, m'lady. Johnson." His fingers groped along her arm, then curled around her wrist, lowering her arm. "Ye be safe 'ere, m'lady."

"Where?"

"In the crypt. They don't come 'ere." His trembling voice told her what she needed to know.

The resurrectionists must be out in the churchyard. If Neville was there too, he could be killed.

As if she had spoken aloud, Mr. Johnson continued, "Ye don't want t'go out there, m'lady. They be a bad bunch."

"They must already know I am here." She touched the side of her head. A lump was already rising. "One of them struck me."

" 'Tweren't them, m'lady. 'Twas me."

"You?" She yanked her arm out of his grasp, stepping back and lifting the chunk of wood again.

He knocked it from her fingers. When she cried out as the concussion throbbed up to her shoulder, he urged her to be quiet before saying, "I'm not yer enemy, m'lady. I knobbed ye t'keep ye from meetin' up with the bodysnatcher's leader and 'is lads. If 'e 'ad found ye wanderin' about out there, 'e'd 'ave sent ye on to yer reward."

Priscilla picked her way through his thick accent and realized Mr. Johnson had knocked her senseless so he could bring her where she would not be seen by the resurrectionists. Mr. Johnson must have good reason to fear Gowan, and his men would have had no hesitation about killing her.

"Thank you," she whispered, although she could not ever have imagined thanking someone for striking her. "I appreciate your consideration for my well-being, but, Mr. Johnson, I need to warn my friend to take care."

"Yer friend? 'Athaway?"

She nodded. "He is facing more peril than the body-snatchers."

"Ain't nothin' worse."

"Yes, there is," she said grimly. Every moment that passed might be the one when Neville opened the snuffbox and put himself in danger.

"Stay 'ere, m'lady. I beg ye. If ye go out there, they'll slice yer throat and sell ye to some cutter."

"I cannot, Mr. Johnson. You stay here. Keep the door ajar in case I need to make a swift retreat."

"M'lady—"

"Please, Mr. Johnson. I do not want to be too late to save him."

She waited for the night watchman to argue further, but he said nothing. She tensed. Would he hit her again in misguided chivalry to prevent her from doing what he feared would lead to her death?

Then she saw a faint sliver of light—not light, but less dark—in front of her. A muted creak seemed as loud as a scream. The fragment widened, and she heard the door scrape back against the stone floor.

Slipping past Mr. Johnson, she put her hand on his arm

to say what she did not dare to speak aloud. She was astonished that he followed when she stepped out into the rain.

"You do not need to come," she said softly.

"Ye be Dr. Flanders's widow. 'E done plenty good for this parish, and I don't want him risin' out of the ground t'haunt me for the rest of m'nights 'cause I let you get served out and killed by these raffle-coffins."

Priscilla had not guessed he had this much courage. Motioning for him to follow her, she went toward the back of the churchyard, where the other bodies had been stolen. The faint sound of a shovel on stone told her she had guessed correctly where they would be disinterring the body of Lord Cagswell's housekeeper. Her stomach ached at the thought of the woman's rest being interrupted, but she had to concentrate on protecting the living.

Crouching behind a bush, she peered around it. Four men were gathered about the grave. Two were digging. When one spoke, she almost gasped aloud.

It was Neville! Somehow, he must have persuaded the resurrectionists that he was of their number. One of his allies from the dredges of the London streets could have been his liaison to Gowan's gang. She was safer with him nearby, but the danger to him had not lessened. Even though he wore clothes more decrepit than he had donned when they went to speak with the resurrectionists, he would not have left the snuffbox behind. He must still be carrying it among his rags.

She watched in silence as they continued to dig in the thin light from a low-burning lantern. Far more quickly than she had expected, the four men lifted the casket from the ground. She frowned. It must not have been buried very deeply. That suggested someone in the church was part of this conspiracy. Dr. Summerson? If it was not he, she suspected he knew well who might be involved.

"Come back with me, m'lady," moaned Mr. Johnson. "Ye are not safe 'ere."

"Not yet."

He muttered something, and she heard bushes rattle. He must be going back to his hiding place.

She hoped he would not alert the resurrectionists. She smiled coldly. Mr. Johnson was determined to evade them, and he would make every effort to keep them from noticing anything in the part of the churchyard where he hid.

"Open 'er up!" called one of the men by the grave, clearly not concerned about someone overhearing him.

She almost laughed at the thought. The resurrectionists had so terrorized St. Julian's parish that no one would come here after dark . . . save for her and Neville.

All yearning to laugh vanished when a crowbar was jammed beneath the top of the coffin, and the nails in the lid screeched as if they were being tortured. She put her hand over her mouth before her own shriek of disgust burst forth and betrayed her.

The lid was tossed aside, and two of the men reached into the coffin. Not Neville, for he and one other man had stepped back and now leaned on their shovels. When the corpse was lifted out and dropped with as little care as the lid, the men pawed around the coffin again. They stood, and their hands were filled with objects that glittered in the torchlight.

Priscilla could not mistake the glitter of gold. Not jewelry or coins, but what appeared to be small pieces of art. Stolen from the Cagswells' house? She sat back on her heels. Was *this* the reason for the deaths? A chance for someone to enter the house and, as a mourner, cache the stolen items in the casket, and let the treasure be buried until the resurrectionists assisted in retrieving it? It was so devilishly simple.

Neville leaned forward but shifted back when one of the

bodysnatchers glanced at him. He must have guessed the truth too. She wished she could guess what he might have planned so she could help him and protect him.

A man stepped out of the fog, and Priscilla stared. Not in disbelief, for she had suspected Dr. Summerson was involved.

"Thank you, lads," the curate said, taking the gold articles and hiding them beneath his dark cloak. She guessed it had pockets sewn into it because it sagged beneath the weight of what he had stuffed into them. "Take your prize away and get your money." Gold flashed again. "That will compensate you for your work here."

Priscilla tensed. Whatever Neville was going to do must be done soon. She must be ready to assist.

A hand clasped her arm.

"Go away, Mr. Johnson," she ordered in a whisper.

"Ain't Johnson."

She was jerked to her feet. The scream that had been battering her lips escaped, resounding through the rain-shrouded churchyard.

"Come 'ere," he snarled. "And stow yer jabber 'fore ye wish ye had."

She was shoved toward the open grave. All of Johnson's warnings exploded through her head. She did not dare to glance toward Neville, for she might betray him, too, when he had succeeded so far in keeping his identity hidden from Dr. Summerson.

As her captor stepped into the narrow circle of light, she drew back in dismay. She recognized him from Dr. Summerson's depiction of the third man who had attended the funerals. When she saw the curate's satisfied smile, she wondered how many other wrong paths Dr. Summerson had sent her and Neville down. He must have been greatly amused to describe this man knowing that neither she nor

Neville would suspect he had been describing a resurrectionist.

"What have you here, Gowan?" Dr. Summerson asked.

Gowan! No wonder the man had refused to open the door when she and Neville went to that horrible brothel. If they had seen him, they would have recognized him. She fought again not to look at Neville, but she needed some signal to know what he planned now that she had intruded on whatever he was doing here.

"Found 'er 'idin' in the bushes, Reverend."

"My lady," Dr. Summerson said, "it grieves me that you did not heed my advice not to involve yourself more. It was meant to insure your continued welfare."

"I heeded your lies. I fear I was foolish to do that," she retorted. Why was Neville doing nothing? She had to trust he knew the best moment to step in. But she needed to warn him not to let someone knock that snuffbox loose and scatter its remaining contents.

Dr. Summerson shook his head. "This is no business for a lady to be mixed up in."

"Or a churchman." She pointed to the corpse lying on the ground. "Hardly the resting in peace you speak of when you read the funeral service, Dr. Summerson. What are the exact words? Oh, yes. *'Thou hast set our misdeeds before thee and our secret sins in the light of thy countenance.'* "

He smiled coldly. "I said as well, *'Oh, grave, where is thy victory?'* You see my victory before you, my lady."

"Stealing from your parishioners and selling their corpses to the bodysnatchers?" She raised her chin. "How long, Dr. Summerson, do you believe this can continue without your part being discovered?"

"Say no more."

The dagger pressed up under her chin rather than his order silenced her. She risked a look to the right at Neville and saw he was balanced lightly on his feet. At the first chance, he would try to rescue her. In doing so, he could be killed by the poison he carried.

"D'ye want me t'kill 'er 'ere or somewhere else?" asked Gowan, anticipation in his voice. "We can bind 'er up so no one will 'ear 'er."

Dr. Summerson's smile faltered. "Kill her?" He rubbed his hands together. "Do you believe that is really necessary, Gowan?"

"If ye don't make 'er quiet, she'll be runnin' to the watch with the tale of wot we do 'ere. That'll be the end of yer work 'ere and inside the church."

"Yes, but she is not like the others."

Gowan growled, "D'ye think she be too fine for the taste of m'blade? Let me show ye 'ow well it cuts into a fine lady's throat just like it would into a poor lass."

The motion from her left was a blur, but something hit her, knocking her into the freshly turned dirt. Mud splashed in her face, but she saw Mr. Johnson strike Gowan again with his fists. Gowan released her as he tumbled beside her. Fearing he still had the knife, she picked up a rock and slammed it onto his right hand. He howled and grabbed for her cloak with his other hand as she tried to scramble to her feet. Two of the resurrectionists were racing toward the gate, their prize abandoned.

She was pulled away as Gowan was yanked to his feet. Neville struck him with the same blow he had used to send Mr. Drake crashing to the floor. Gowan stayed on his feet and hit Neville in the stomach.

"No!" she cried. "Stop!"

"Hathaway can handle him," said a man who was aiming a pistol at Dr. Summerson.

"You don't understand! The snuffbox he is carrying is filled with poison that could kill him if it is ruptured."

The gun was shoved into her hand, and the remaining bodysnatcher rushed toward where both Neville and Gowan were struggling on the ground. Were they trying to get the bodysnatcher's knife?

"Don't move," she ordered when Dr. Summerson edged to his left.

"You would not kill a churchman, my lady."

"Are you sure of that?" She pointed the gun at his middle.

She heard a thump of a body hitting the ground but did not dare to pull her gaze from Dr. Summerson's horrified face. She stayed motionless until a broad hand lifted the gun from hers.

"Thank you for watching him for me, Lady Priscilla."

She gasped as she recognized the voice of the Bow Street Runner. "Mr. Thurmond! Neville! Is he—?"

"Fine, Pris," she heard.

Whirling, she threw her arms around Neville. She was kissing him—and he was kissing her—before she had a chance to form a single thought. It was all she had imagined his kiss would be—fiery and tempting and strong yet gentle—just like the man himself. As his fingers sifted up through her hair, she realized she had lost her bonnet somewhere. She did not care. All she wanted was to be in his arms.

No, that was not all she wanted. Priscilla pulled away and ran her hands up his chest.

He laughed as he clamped her hands against him. "Pris, remember, a man can take only so much pleasure and remain a gentleman."

"Don't be silly!" She brushed her fingers down his sides. "Where is it?"

"What?" he asked, abruptly serious.

"The snuffbox. The snuff in it is poison, just as we suspected. Stevenson is dead."

"Dead?" He pushed her back and reached under his coat. Lifting out the box, he balanced it on his palm. "What do you know of this, Summerson?"

"Nothing!" he stated, the haughtiness returning to his voice. "You are asking the wrong man, Hathaway."

"Which suggests there is a right man to ask." He pointed toward the church. "Shall we take these two inside, Thurmond, and see what they have to say about this other man?"

His friend smiled. "Gladly." He took the snuffbox from Neville and motioned with the gun. "This way, if you please, Dr. Summerson."

"Pris?" Neville held out his hand.

"I will be with you in a minute. Just do not let anyone open that snuffbox."

"Thank you for the warning." He swore. "Stevenson was a good man. Someone has another innocent death to answer for."

He looked down at the body lying on the ground. "As soon as we are done with Summerson and Gowan, we will rebury her."

"It is not just that." She turned to where Mr. Johnson was struggling to his feet. "I need to thank someone first."

"All right, but don't be long. Gowan's boys are not the only resurrectionists who might be interested in this churchyard." He brushed his lips across hers. "And I don't want to wait too long to sample this again."

"I know." She touched his cheek.

He yelped. "Watch it, Pris. Gowan landed me a facer there."

When he went to wake the resurrectionist and get him onto his feet, she walked to where Mr. Johnson stood, rubbing his left knee.

"Be ye all right, m'lady?" he asked.

"Thanks to you. Twice." She smiled. "I don't know what reward you desire . . ."

"If ye could speak with Dr. 'Orwood, the pastor, and ask 'im t'give me and m'brother-in-law a job during the day, we both would be grateful."

"I promise I shall talk to him tomorrow. Thank you, Mr. Johnson."

"Ye be welcome, m'lady. Yer husband married me and the wife and baptized our first. I couldn't let the raffle-coffins kill ye." He limped away into the darkness.

Priscilla smiled. She was unsure what Dr. Horwood would be able to find for the two men to do, but if there was nothing for them at St. Julian's, she would contact St. George's and some of the other nearby churches.

The clip-clop of a horse's hooves struck the rocks on the path through the churchyard. Who was riding among the graves? She silenced her moan of dismay. Dr. Summerson had spoken of another man who was involved in this scheme. Was *that* man coming here now?

She grabbed the cloak Neville had dropped. Pulling it around her, she hunched over as the horse slowed near the disturbed grave.

"Where is everyone? Where is Summerson?" growled a far-too-familiar voice.

Lord Burtrum!

"You there, boy! Where are the gold statues I hid in her coffin?"

Out of her memory came the scenes of Lord Burtrum leaning over his son's coffin, reaching in, before he vanished from the room where the service was being held, only to come back and do the same. When she had followed him upstairs, she had noticed the clean places amid the dust where small items had been recently removed. Had he been robbing Cagswell even as the viscount did him the favor of holding the service in his house? Her eyes widened. Of course, Lord Burtrum could not have the funeral in his house or the church because that would have given him no chance to conceal the fruits of his robbery in Cecil's coffin.

She swallowed. Hard. A man who would kill his own son would have no hesitation about slaying her right here. She wanted to call for Neville, but he was inside the church and would not hear her even if she screamed.

"Where are my statues?" Lord Burtrum demanded. "Speak, boy, or you will wish you had." He raised his riding crop.

As she jumped back, Priscilla saw something glittering on the ground. She scooped it up. The small statue of a cat might have been from the pyramid of an ancient pharaoh or a replica. Either way, she knew it was valuable.

"Give it here, boy."

Making sure the cloak's hood would not fall back and reveal her face, she held up the statue. He crowed with delight, then cursed as he seized her wrist.

"Who are you? No bodysnatcher has hands with skin like this."

She tried to pull away. How want-witted could she have been? She should have run off as soon as she heard the horse. In the church, she would have found sanctuary.

Lord Burtrum dismounted, pulling her closer. She raised her hand to push him away, but he twisted her wrist. With a moan, she fell to her knees. He tore back her hood and swore in astonishment.

"Lady Priscilla, what are *you* doing here?"

She saw no reason to demur. "Stopping you and Dr. Summerson and your allies from killing someone else so you may steal from your neighbors." Recalling the candlesticks with Sir Francis Drake's ship, she added, "And from your future son-in-law."

"My daughter's fiancé has plenty of other things to show off his wealth. He has not missed what I have removed."

"Because you have replaced them with fakes?"

"Which cost me more highly than I had guessed, and Gowan started demanding more money."

"Did you bring him to the funerals so he knew where the bodies were buried?" She fought her way back to her feet but winced when he tightened his grip on her wrist. She feared he would break it if she tried to escape. "He could come here later in the dark to open the grave. He took the body and his fee while Dr. Summerson collected your plunder and kept a share of it for himself."

"You have guessed very well, Lady Priscilla." He pushed her back a step, and she gasped as her heel dropped over the edge of the open grave. He smiled, and she knew he was enjoying her terror. "Do you know why I had Drake join us?"

"No."

"Ah, for the simplest reason of all. He was there in case my gambit failed. Then he could be blamed for the robberies."

She fought to keep from falling backward as he pushed her away another inch. She tried to balance on her toes. "You killed innocent people to rob your neighbors!"

He shrugged. "There are many in London who seek employment, so finding replacements for them will not be difficult. And I did my neighbors a favor by ridding the square of a thief."

"You killed him too?"

"He killed himself by sneaking through my garden. He must have been dead by the time the carriage hit him." He arched a brow. "*You* should be pleased that I kept you from wandering through it."

Priscilla snarled, "Whether they were servants or a thief

or of the Polite World, they were alive and you killed them. Of course, why would you care? After all, you killed your own son with poisoned snuff!''

''No, that was a mistake.'' Sorrow sifted into his voice. ''I did not mean for Cecil to use the snuff mixed with monkshood.''

''From your garden?'' If she could keep him talking, she might find the opportunity to flee.

''It is not difficult to grow monkshood, and it mixes well with snuff. I meant that snuff for Cagswell's housekeeper, but Cecil, eager for some snuff, chanced to find it and died.'' His smile returned, and she knew that if he had been sane when he first devised the plan to rob his neighbors, he had been pushed into madness with his son's death.

''And you gave his body to the resurrectionists after you filled his coffin with what you had pilfered from Cagswell's house.''

''No! I made sure Gowan did not sell Cecil's corpse, although he disobeyed me and removed it from the churchyard after he retrieved the items within it.''

''Which sent your daughter to me asking for my help in finding it.''

He tossed the riding crop to the ground and withdrew a pistol from under his cloak. ''You shall fail her, Lady Priscilla. Your body will obtain Gowan a good fee when he sells it to be dissected.''

She screamed as he drew back on the hammer. A shot echoed off the thick walls of the church, and she dropped to the ground, not caring that her legs hung over the open grave. He had missed her. She clambered to her feet, determined to escape before he could reload.

In astonishment, she saw Lord Burtrum lying on the ground, clutching his shoulder. A form appeared out of the darkness, carrying a pistol that spewed smoke.

"Neville!" she shouted.

"Stay where you are, Pris!"

Lord Burtrum leaped up and ran. She heard a clunk and a thud as he fell headfirst to the ground. He did not move. Rushing to him even as Neville shouted to take care, she knelt by the earl. She pressed her hand over her mouth when she saw the black stream along his face. His foot was tangled in the handle of a shovel.

Neville touched the earl's neck and shook his head. "He died when his head hit one of the stones he was having torn up to get to the body buried beneath it."

Saying nothing, Priscilla looked up as a light bounced toward them. It was Johnson, curious about the shot, but waiting wisely until the gun stopped firing.

He stared at Lord Burtrum's corpse, then spat on it. " 'E got the justice 'e deserved."

"Do you know where his son's body is, Johnson?" Neville asked as he put his arm around Priscilla and drew her closer.

"This way."

Priscilla stayed close to Neville as the watchman led them to the crypt. In the back, among the open coffins, was one holding Cecil Burtrum's body.

"Dr. Summerson put it 'ere," Mr. Johnson said. "Once Lady Priscilla and ye came askin' questions 'bout this missin' corpse, 'e never figured a way t'put it back without someone bein' the wiser." He gave Priscilla a faint smile. "That's why I brought ye 'ere, m'lady. I knew 'e would not send the bodysnatchers into the crypt."

Neville drew out a handful of coins and pressed them into the watchman's hand. "That should buy you the help you need to rebury this body and Mrs. Hartley's out in the churchyard before dawn."

"Aye."

"Let's go, Pris." He held out his hand. As she took it, he said, "I have had enough of this churchyard tonight."

"Can you believe those two?" asked Priscilla as she watched Eleanor Burtrum and Malcolm Drake walk around the square on their way back to the house that now was Eleanor's. "They still are planning to be married just as they had before her brother's accidental murder and her father's death. Dr. Horwood will marry them while Dr. Summerson awaits his trial."

"Why are you surprised?" Neville leaned his elbow against the window frame. "They deserve each other."

"Yes, because she wants his money as much as her father did, and he wants that title for his son."

"And the fact she will be having that son in less than six months."

Priscilla looked up at him. "She is already in a delicate condition? Oh . . . that she was suffering from nausea may explain why she did not attend her brother's funeral."

"And wept so much." He chuckled. "I understand from Lazarus you were a regular wet-goose when you were awaiting Isaac's arrival."

"I was not!"

"He said you would cry for no reason at all."

"I did not." She raised one finger. "Do not try to betwattle me with your half-truths and—"

He pulled her up against him and slanted his mouth across hers. She curved her hand behind his nape, holding his lips close, because she did not want this to be as fleeting as the kiss in the churchyard. When his arm arced around her waist, she softened against his hard chest.

Too soon, he raised his head. She gazed at him, not sure what to say, for until quite recently, she had never imagined she would think of him as other than a friend. He *was* her friend, the very best one she had. What further he might become, she was unsure. She was eager to find out, and she guessed she would have the opportunity in the months to come.

"We need to do this more often, Pris," he said.

"This?" She looked back out the window at where Mr. Drake and Eleanor were standing in front of their door. "I think not."

"No, I meant *this*." He drew her back into his arms.

"Are you intending to kiss me again?" she asked as she slipped her arms up his back.

"I do have that intention."

"Good." She smiled as she tilted his mouth back over hers.

AUTHOR'S NOTE

Priscilla and Neville will return in June 2003 with their next adventure in *Faire Game.* Invited to a gathering to celebrate Lord Stenborough's birthday, they are at first amused by the troupe of actors who create a medieval world. Then people start dying . . . in very medieval ways. Who is stalking the guests and why? It might be easier for Priscilla to find an answer if Neville's kisses didn't keep distracting her. And Neville must be distracted as well because he is starting to talk about things she thought he never would. Things like love . . .

Readers can contact me at: P.O. Box 575, Rehoboth, MA 02769. Or visit my web site at: www.joannferguson.com.